JAMES Y. BARTLETT

An Open Case of Death

A Hacker Golf Mystery

Copyright © 2019 by James Y. Bartlett
Yeoman House Books Original Paperback
All rights reserved.

This Yeoman House edition of An Open Case of Death is an original publication. It is published by arrangement with the author.

This book is a work of fiction. All of the events, characters, names and places depicted in this novel are entirely fictitious or are used fictitiously. No representation that any statement made in this novel is true or that any incident depicted in this novel actually occurred is intended or should be inferred by the reader.

No part of this book may be used or reproduced in any manner whatsoever without written permission except in the case of brief quotations embodied in critical articles or reviews. For information, address Yeoman House Books, 10 Old Bulgarmarsh Road, Tiverton, RI 02878.

Cover Design: Todd Fitz, Fuel Media, Inc.
Printed in the USA.

ISBN 978-0-9852537-5-2

Library of Congress Control Number: 2019951790

To Susan

Sometimes if you want to see a change for the better, you have to take things into your own hands.

– Clint Eastwood

Prologue

THE VISITOR OPENED the door to the hospital room and was immediately struck by the dense, humid and fragrant air. The temperature in the room felt like it was set at about 80 degrees, and the fragrance came from the banks of cut flowers that competed for every square inch of counter space in the small private room.

There was just one bed in the room, occupied by an old man with a shock of long white hair. His face was loose and jowly, his skin was pale and patchy and he was connected, via a bewildering array of wires and tubes, to a bank of machines that were keeping track of every one of his bodily functions. Some of the machines emitted soft beeps and whirrs, while others just presented rows of colorful numbers and lines moving endlessly across the graphs and screens.

The old man's eyes had been closed, but now he opened them and, with a blink or two, focused them on his visitor.

"Geez," the visitor said, "You'd think someone died up here, what with all these flowers."

"Not yet, sonny boy," the old man said, his voice soft and wheezy, but still with some spirit. "Not goddam yet."

An Open Case of Death

The visitor pulled a chair over next to the hospital bed and sat down. He reached over and patted the old man's hand, which was resting on his chest atop the sheets and blankets that were drawn up almost to the old man's chin.

"How ya doing, J.J.?" the visitor asked. "Sounds like you've been through the wringer."

The old man struggled a bit, trying to sit upright. He was old and sick, but he still had pride, still wanted to sit up straight and talk business, man to man. He eventually gave up and let his head sink weakly back down on the pillow.

"I've been better," he said. "I think this is my fourth heart attack. None of them were any walk in the park, but I don't think this one was too bad. The docs tell me that I need a week or two to rest, and then I might be able to get the hell out of here and get back to work."

"Well, no sense rushing things," the visitor said. "The business is running itself. We made sure of that after your second incident a year ago. And you've got three partners ready and willing to pitch in if needed."

"Worthless pricks," the old man said. "The lot of 'em. Not worth a tinker's dam."

The visitor laughed. He'd heard this before, only about a thousand times. The four partners in the business were not overly fond of one another. Board meetings could be challenging, as alliances formed and broke. They were all willful. Proud. Used to being the alpha dog.

"All the more reason for you to rest up and get back in the saddle as soon as you can," the visitor said.

"Listen," the old man said, reaching for the visitor's hand, and gripping it tight. Surprisingly tight, for an eighty year old man who'd just had his fourth coronary in three years. "We have to do something about that real estate deal," he said, his eyes focused on the visitor. "There's exposure there. Too damn much."

The visitor nodded. "I know," he said. "I'm taking steps. Don't worry. It's under control."

A Hacker Golf Mystery

The old man's head sank back on the pillow and a look of relief washed over his features. "Good, good," he said, muttering almost to himself. He was obviously tired, weak. Not himself.

The visitor stood up and walked over to the banks of medical machines buzzing and wheezing by the bed.

"What the hell do all these things do?" he said, speaking to no one in particular.

The old man, who had fallen into a brief, sleepy reverie, started, eyes flying open.

"Whaa?" he said. "Oh, those things? I have no idea. I guess one machine pumps shit in to keep me alive, the others keep track of what's going on inside." He paused, thinking. "You once thought of becoming a doctor, didn't you? Back when you were in college?"

The visitor kept looking at the machines, the intravenous tubes, the clear bags of liquid something hanging from the metal poles. He was reading labels and trying to figure out what was going on.

"Hmm?" the visitor said. "Oh, yes, that's right. I was in pre-med, then I joined the Navy and served two tours on an aircraft carrier. Medical corps. Taking blood samples. Shooting sailors full of antibiotics after shore leave. They'd come back from the whore houses happy but infected with every STD known to man."

He glanced over at the bed. The old man had slipped away to sleep again. He was weak, very weak. No wonder, given what he had been through.

"But then the old man called and I had to go back into the family business," the visitor said. "But that's life. Doesn't always work out the way you think."

He turned away from the machines, returned to the bed, patted the old man's hand again. "See you down the road, old friend," he said softly, and left the hot, humid room filled with the scent of a thousand flowers.

An Open Case of Death

The old man continued to sleep. His lips moved a few times, like he was trying to say something, but was too tired to make the words come out. His chest rose and fell ... once ... twice. And then it stopped. And he died.

CHAPTER 1

IF THERE'S ONE part of the human condition that we all share and none of us can control, it is change. And yet, we are always unprepared when change happens. Which it does with infallible regularity.

I had not been home long from my last trip to Scotland to cover the Open, a trip from whence I returned a married man. (See? Change, right there.) There were a couple of fraught weekends after we returned during which Mary Jane, the new bride, was trying to decide which of our two apartments in Boston's North End neighborhood to give up. One would think it not a huge decision, since we lived in the same building, just one floor apart. But one would be very wrong. I was fine either way, and my cat, Mister Shit, who already was used to living in two places, I believe could also care less whatever we two-leggers came up with for a solution. It was Mary Jane who fretted about it for a couple of weeks, even started making lists of pros and cons, before Victoria, her ... well, now *our* precocious eleven-year-old (change!) ... finally brought the drama to its close.

"This apartment has a room for you guys, and a room for me, and other than that, they are exactly the same," she said, looking at us like we were idiots. "So why should two of us have to move, when if Hacker comes up here, only he has to move? And, no offense, Hacker, but your furniture is kinda ugly."

So I moved, one floor up. *See?* I told myself, *change isn't that hard.*

Then Mary Jane had to fill out some form or other, and that meant she had to decide what her name was. Now, because I'm a member in good standing of the patriarchy, I never have had to worry about things like that. And I do understand how unfair it is that women are expected to just abandon their lifelong last names and assume the one of the moron they just married. I mean, who came up with these rules? Now again, if she wanted to remain Mary Jane Cappalletti –two p's, two l's, two t's—or if she wanted to henceforth be known as Mrs. Hacker … either way was okay by me. I am just thrilled to death she agrees to let me sleep in the same bed, washes my clothes and occasionally feeds me. But this decision was good for another month or so of agonized contemplation, lengthy advice sessions with her posse of girlfriends, and even a teary late-night call to her ex-father-in-law, Carmine Spoleto, the *capo di tutti* of the New England mob in these parts. You know it's serious if Carmine is involved. She never told me what he said, but I'll bet he said he didn't give a *ratto's* ass what name she chose. Carmine, who absolutely dotes on his granddaughter, had never been particularly fond of his son, Angelo, born out of wedlock, but still of the capo's blood. Angelo's career path in the Spoleto organization hit a dead end not long after Victoria was born, in a dingy Charlestown tenement hallway and a hail of bullets. *Riposare in pace.*

Maybe she wanted me to make the decision, but my rather logical thoughts on the subject ("Hacker has six letters, Cappalletti eleven," I said. "You'll save lots of time and effort writing out your name if you go with Hacker. And with all that free time on your hands, we can spend more time doing other things. Like a little afternoon delight, maybe.") did not seem to impress her. "You are such a pig," she said.

Anyway, after the weeks of agony over the name were finished (she chose to become Mary Jane Hacker, but left Victoria as a Cappalletti) I went into work one autumn morning at the Boston *Journal,* where I write about golf on the PGA Tour and a few other sports, and was unceremoniously laid off. Got the boot. Hit the road, toad. Buh-bye!

Change. Ain't it grand?

"Sorry, Hacker," said my obese and mentally challenged executive editor, Frank Donatello, "The paper lost another two million dollars last year, and the new owners are cracking the whip." To his credit, which is not something I generally am willing to admit, Frank did look upset at having to can me. I found out that the new owners, an investment group from Baton Rouge which was going around the country buying up failing second and third-tier newspapers on the cheap, had issued the call for another round of layoffs. I don't know if their business plan was to amass all these properties in hopes that one day Americans by the millions would once again begin their day with a home-delivered newspaper and a cup of joe; but until that much anticipated and highly delusionary day arrived, the front-office boys were slashing payrolls and combining newsroom operations at a furious pace. Frank told me that this round of layoffs would eliminate about 30 percent of the *Journal* staff. Most of it came out of the newsroom while others being deep-sixed included the production side: our Boston paper would henceforth be copy edited and laid out by some people in an office park in Denver, and printed at a company-owned plant near Springfield, Mass., instead of the massive printing complex across the back alley from our building. Oh, yeah: most of the print jobbers had been laid off as well.

Ch-ch-ch-changes!

An emotional pall hung over the building like a noxious fog as I started to clean out my desk. But I couldn't do it. I couldn't stay there, sifting through twenty-something years of employment detritus. I couldn't stand to watch one old friend after another come up with tears in their eyes for a last hug and a husky whispered invitation to get together soon for a couple of cold ones at the Inkstain Tavern across the street from our venerable brick building in the Back Bay. I grabbed an old golf shoe bag that had been part of some tournament swag package at some unremembered event of the past, filled it with as many sleeves of golf balls as I could find hiding among the dusty piles of papers, magazines, newspapers and books on my desk and shelves, and just walked out. Didn't look back, because what the hell good would that do?

I stopped and bought a bottle of Jack Black on my way home, and was not quite halfway through it when Mary Jane and Victoria got home that afternoon from school. Mary Jane had found a part-time job as a teacher's assistant and was scheduled to be promoted to full-time fourth grade teacher next semester. MJ took one look at me and herded Vickie into her room. She came back and plopped down next to me.

"Talk," she said.

I told her. She took my hand and gently stroked the back of it.

"Well, that sucks," she said.

"Yes," I said, "It does."

"Why don't you make me a drink, too?" she said. "No sense in getting drunk alone."

"I'm not getting drunk," I said as I got up to go bring her a glass with some ice. "I'm meditating on my life."

I handed her the glass and she poured some bourbon into it.

"Well," she said, after taking a delicate little sip—Mary Jane, like most women, is not a gulper; she can nurse a cocktail for hours on end if she wants to— "You get one day to meditate, and then we'll have to come up with a new plan."

"I've been meditating on that, too," I said. "Which tends to lead back to a need for more meditation." I slopped some more Jack into my glass. "Plan B is pretty bleak. Given my advanced age and the crapulous state of the newspaper industry today, there probably isn't going to be a quick renewal in some other place. The *Globe* and the *Herald* are both thinly staffed and in danger of bankruptcy, and neither one needs a new golf writer. All the other papers in New England are either shutting down or being snapped up by the same ownership group from Baton Rouge, or one like it. Not much opportunity there. I could look for work in Texas, or Florida, or some other Sunbelty place; but that would mean moving, and I really don't want to upset Victoria's life. Or yours, for that matter. You're just getting started with your new career here."

"Oh, don't worry about that," she said, rubbing my shoulders. "We'll adjust if we have to. How about freelancing? Can you pick up some magazine work?"

"Oh, yeah, probably," I said, nodding. "But I don't know if I can find enough to support us. Magazines are a dying breed, too." I took a deep pull from my glass of bourbon. Unlike most women, I am not a sipper; I tend to meditate in larger doses. "Need some more meditating."

"Well," Mary Jane said, flashing me one of her brightest smiles, even though I could tell her heart wasn't totally in it. "You know what they say ..."

"Oh, Christ," I said. "Is this where you tell me that when God closes a door he always leaves a window open? Please don't go there. It would require me to go out and buy some more meditation."

She laughed. I always loved to hear her laugh. It usually made me laugh, too. Today, I just managed a weak smile.

"Nope," she said. She picked up her glass and clinked it against mine. "They say go ahead and get totally smashed. You earned it. But tomorrow, after the hangover wears off, something good will happen."

"Really?"

"I swear," she said, and she kissed me, then went into the kitchen to start making dinner.

I almost believed her.

CHAPTER 2

As it turned out, Mary Jane was wrong. But not by much.

I did have a five-alarm hangover the next morning, but nothing good happened. Mary Jane and Victoria had gone off to school, so I got dressed and went out for a walk. I threaded my way through the North End's warren of narrow streets and lanes, most of them originally laid out by the sheep and cattle of pre-Colonial settlers, stopped for a large coffee and a couple of donuts and took my feast over to Langone Park on the waterfront, where I parked it on one of the long stone benches near the bocce courts, overlooking the harbor. It was a chilly late-October morning with just a rumor of sunshine, but there were still a group of eight players, dressed in drab jackets, saggy corduroy pants and most with woolen caps, tossing their heavy wooden balls up and down the court, gesticulating madly at each other and debating the finer points of bocce strategy in high-speed Italian.

I covered my chest and lap in donut sugar and drank about half the coffee. I actually started to feel better, although I wasn't quite ready for total redemption yet. I watched a big natural gas tanker making its way slowly through the harbor, working its way carefully towards the fuel farms in Everett, followed closely by a little red tug with a flashing light. I realized that neither the captain of the tanker nor its crew of a dozen or so Indonesian sailors gave much of a crap about Hacker's sorry life and prospects. Nor, for that matter, did the bocce-playing Italians, nor the two young mothers wheeling their toddlers toward the playground off to my left. In fact, I decided after some thought and another deep draught of Mr. Dunkin's finest, that nobody in the world, except possibly for Mary Jane and Victoria, was wasting a lot of time worrying about Hacker on this fine, if slightly chilled, morning. So why should I?

Change is what life throws at us, I thought to myself. *Happens to everyone. Might as well pick yourself up and figure out what to do next, because sitting around and moping sure as hell ain't gonna get you anywhere.*

So I finished my coffee while the bocce game came to an exciting conclusion. (The last ball of the blue team knocked into the second-closest red ball and then ricocheted into the closest red ball, knocking it away and giving the walk-off blue win to Guido and Enrico. They cheered; their opponents cursed.) I mentally composed a fascinating lede for a nonexistent story on the bocce match for a nonexistent job on some nonexistent newspaper, then I got up, broomed the sugar off my sweatshirt, tossed my trash in the bin and walked home.

I spent the rest of the day, and the one after that, and those that followed for most of the next month, making calls and sending emails to all of the people I knew in the golf publications business. Told them all I had been laid off and was open for any freelance assignments. Everyone I spoke with was sympathetic—it's not like this kind of thing wasn't happening on an almost daily basis, all around the country—but the amount of new work I generated was pretty depressing. I told myself it was autumn, the golf season was mostly over, there were no major tournaments on the horizon, everyone was into football and looking forward to the start of hockey and basketball seasons. Mary Jane kept telling me not to panic, that the universe would soon intervene. I managed to resist quipping in return that maybe what the universe had in mind was a close personal meeting with a moving city bus just outside the marked crosswalk. Then I made a mental note to update my life insurance policy to make sure Victoria was listed as a beneficiary.

It was close to Thanksgiving when the universe finally piped up. I threw myself into working on the three or four freelance pieces I managed to pick up: a round-up of the best public courses one could play in Las Vegas; a quick telephone interview and 500-word piece on Freddy Couples, the ageless wonder; and 50-word captions on five new golf shoe models to be unveiled at January's PGA Show in Orlando. When the checks for all this fine work finally rolled in, six weeks later, I would be about $400 on my way to earning my first million. Which I thought was such a funny idea that I actually spent a couple of hours with a calculator and my bad math skills trying to figure out how long it would actually take me to earn a million bucks at this rate. The answer made me long for another long and deep meditation session with Mr. Jack Daniels, Esq. Except I couldn't afford it.

That's when the phone rang.

"Mister Hacker?" said a cheerful female voice, "Please hold for Mister Strauss."

She clicked me onto hold before I could ask "Who?" But then Strauss himself came on the line.

"Hacker? Jake Strauss here. How are you?" He spoke rapidly, in staccato, one sentence following the next as if they were Siamese words, connected at the breastbone. That rapid-fire delivery was one of the hallmarks of Jacob

An Open Case of Death

Strauss, executive director of the U.S. Golf Association. He had been running the USGA for about five years now.

"I'm fine, Mr. Strauss," I said. "What can I do for you?"

"Actually, I'm calling because I might be able to do something for you," he said. "A little birdie told me that you've been laid off by the Journal."

"Yes," I said noncommittally. "Couple of weeks ago."

"Looking for a job?"

"Maybe," I said. "Like what?"

"Like working for the USGA," he said. "For me, actually."

"Doing what, exactly?" I asked. "I'm a newspaper reporter. Never looked good in a blue blazer."

He laughed. Two short connected bursts. HaHa.

"And you're a wise-ass," he said. "They told me."

"Who is 'they?'"

"Never mind that," he said. "Can you meet me in New York for lunch. Say, next Tuesday? I think we should talk."

I didn't say anything. To be perfectly honest, I was thinking that my bank account might not have enough lying around to afford a train ticket down to the Big Apple. He took my silence as a sign I was thinking hard about his offer.

"Look," he said, "Come have lunch, listen to my offer. If you decide not to take it, no hard feelings at all."

"If there were hard feelings, does that mean you'd dick around with my official USGA handicap?" I said.

I got two more short bursts of laughter.

"I'll have my girl call you and make the arrangements," he said. "Tell her if you want to fly down on the shuttle, or take the Acela. I've always preferred the train, but it's your choice."

"Okay," I said. "I'll see you next week."

"Beautiful," he said and hung up.

A Hacker Golf Mystery

A FEW DAYS later, I made my way over to South Station and climbed aboard the south-bound Acela. It was a chilly November day, gray-black clouds blocking out the sun and a frigid northerly wind slicing down from Quebec. If it wasn't winter, it was surely the announcement that winter was on the way and right around the corner.

I made my way to a comfortable leather seat in the so-called quiet car—where one is not supposed to talk except in subdued whispers. Of course, no one from New York has ever spoken in a subdued whisper in their entire life, so the car is usually as noisy as any other. I had bought a New York *Times* so I could catch up on the political hysteria of the day and then tackle the crossword puzzle. At least it was a weekday, which gave me a fighting chance.

But as the "high-speed" train made its pokey way down the Eastern seaboard, stopping in the gray and grim concrete station at Providence before angling down through Connecticut, I put the paper down after skimming the front page, and began to think about what I knew about Jacob Strauss, executive director of the blue-blood institution that ruled over the game of golf on those portions of the globe that had not been colonized by the Royal & Ancient in St. Andrews.

Strauss' appointment as executive director had been somewhat controversial, but only partially because he broke the Jewish ceiling at the USGA: he was the first executive director who was a practicing member of the Hebrew faith. And that was newsworthy only because the USGA has since its founding been one of the last remaining bastions of WASPishness in the country. Only in the last twenty years has the USGA ventured a hesitant toe into the cold waters of diversity, naming Judy Bell and one other woman as President of the organization. But even the women had both been as WASPy as Theodore Havemeyer (1894-96) and the sixty-something presidents who had followed. The

An Open Case of Death

position of executive director, basically the chief operating officer, had also been reserved for rich, white, Protestant country club men until Jake Strauss had been appointed.

But Strauss had been anything but a bomb-thrower for social justice during his term at the USGA. And as a retired director for one of Wall Street's biggest investment banks, no one had ever expected he would be. Instead, he was genial, competent, well-liked by most, raised a ton of money for the organization, and showed up at all the various championships run by the USGA, from the US Open down to the Girls' Junior, to hand out the trophy to the winning golfer. He had been the ultimate no muss-no fuss kind of executive director.

He had joined with other golf industry officials to fight a rear-guard action against the general drift away from golf participation in the country, a drift that the banking crisis and economic malaise that followed had not helped. Just a few decades ago, it seemed like golf would overtake football as the country's favorite sport, but that was proved to be a myth. The truth is there have always been around 20 million golfers in the USA. In some decades that number rose a bit; in others it declined. And of that 20 million, perhaps half were frequent or avid players of the game—most people played once, twice or three times a year and that was that.

The USGA, of course, was an organization that catered to the top one percent. Those who belonged to private clubs. Who played almost every weekend. Who jealously obtained and guarded their official handicaps. Mostly male. Mostly white. Mostly rich. And despite the pretty pictures in the advertising spots the USGA produced to show during its major championships during the year, ads which showed happy and diverse crowds of the young, the female, and persons of color all golfing happily together in the pleasant afternoon sun, most of the old white males who ran and who controlled the USGA were quite happy with the way things were.

And why not? The USGA had tons of money, and as long as the rich white segment of the population continued to exist, it likely would always have tons of money. There might be lean decades until a new Tiger or a new Nicklaus came along to capture the public's fancy and generate the sale of more tee times; but the game would endure as it always had. Sometimes money speaks loudly and with great authority, and sometimes it just keeps its mouth shut, compounds its interest quarterly and just grows and grows and grows. The USGA belonged to the latter group.

The train let me off in Penn Station, which in its current iteration is easily the most dreary and uninspiring train station in the free world, and I decided to stretch my legs and walk the ten blocks north up Sixth Avenue. Even on this cloudy and chilly day, the streets were full of people buzzing about as if all the Starbucks in town (at least one per half block as far as I could tell) were adding a nice rounded teaspoon of cocaine to each coffee sold. I love New York, really I do, but it's a city that takes some getting used to. Most of the people one encounters in the city are completely encapsulated in their own little world: they live in New York; New York is the most important place in the world; therefore whatever each resident there is engaged in is the most important thing in the world. And if some poor unemployed schlub from Beantown happens to get in their way…well, there's a look for that. And I got a couple thousand of those looks before I reached West 44th Street and turned right towards Fifth Avenue.

The Harvard Club of New York City had been built out of a row of horse stables in the 1890s, turned into an elegant red brick building whose entrance was designed—by the high-powered architectural firm of McKim, Mead & White—to look just like the gateway entrance to Harvard

An Open Case of Death

Square. It's just down the street from the nautically inspired façade of the New York Yacht Club, the famed Algonquin Hotel of the 'Round Table' fame and within a seven-iron shot of the New York alumni clubs of most of the rest of the Ivies.

I walked into the entrance beneath the crimson "Ve-Ri-Tas" banner and was shown up a flight of stairs into the impressive Harvard Hall. Old Charlie McKim outdid himself with this room: 45-foot ceilings, dark paneling and marble wainscoting, two humongous fireplaces and elaborately framed portraits of impressive aristocrats, er, Harvard grads hanging everywhere. I felt like I should either be carrying my squash racquet or looking for an oar and a polished shell, or memorizing the lyrics of the Cambridge version of the *Whiffenpoof* song. Instead, I parked my non-Ivy butt in one of the butter-soft crimson leather chairs and waited, soaking in the essence of upper-crust WASPishness. I sat there and watched people coming and going, greeting one another and heading off to lunch and tried to imagine the size of their personal investment accounts. It was a fun game, and I managed to mostly not spend the time hating everyone I looked at.

It wasn't long before Jacob Strauss came strolling in, looking like he owned the place. Maybe he did. He was in his late 60s, long graying hair framing his well-tanned face. He had prominent brows, a large but not stereotypical Jewish nose, and was folding a pair of reading glasses to tuck away in his blue blazer. He wore gray wool slacks, black slip-ons and the requisite maroon and white striped tie. There was a woman with him, middle-aged, well-dressed and wealthy looking, like everyone else. Strauss leaned close to her and said something. She nodded, smiled at him and headed back towards the lobby stairs. He saw me as I rose from my chair and, with a wide and welcoming smile, came striding across the oriental carpet with his hand extended.

"Hacker, my man," he said. "Glad to see you. Have a good trip down?"

"The train didn't hit any cows," I said, "So I guess it was a success."

HaHa. The brevity of his laughter burst told me I'd have to work harder. Strauss escorted me into the main dining room, another three-story high-ceilinged room dark with carved paneling and bright with chandeliers. There were rows of round tables for six and eight in the center of the room and a smattering of booths and tables for two set against the far wall. All of the tables were decked in spotless white linen tablecloths, and many of them had pools of light from small brass lamps set in the center of the tables.

Strauss decided we should sit in one of the smaller tables, and led me over to one of the booths along the far wall. The woodwork was elaborately carved at the edges and along the top, and once inside, it felt like we were in our own private room, cut off from the hubbub of all the deal making going on outside.

"Ever eaten here?" he asked me as we settled in. I shook my head. "Pretty good food," he said, handing me the leather-bound menu. "Don't miss the popovers. They're famous for the popovers."

A waiter sidled up silently and wondered if we'd care to have anything to drink. Strauss ordered a wine spritzer while I asked for some iced tea. For some reason, I wanted to keep all my wits about me, and the two fingers of good bourbon that I really wanted seemed like a bad idea.

"You probably want to know why I asked you down here," Strauss said. "But it's the tradition in the Harvard Club that we don't discuss business over a meal. So we'll wait until the coffee."

I laughed. "I'm nothing if not a traditionalist," I said.

AN OPEN CASE OF DEATH

He ordered the garlic shrimp over rice and I went for the baked scrod. It came with three small boiled potatoes and some easily ignored vegetables. Our silent waiter did bring us a basket of freshly baked popovers, and I ate two of them. Strauss was correct: they were excellent. We chatted about golf in general, the Tour in particular, and a few people we knew in common in the business until our lunch was done. Silent Sam cleared away the plates and brought us each a demitasse of fine Harvard coffee. Pinkies up, boys.

I dabbed my lips with my crimson napkin and sat back. "Okay," I said. "What's up?"

"I'm worried about the Open," Strauss said, leveling his gray eyes at me across the booth, his face rearranged into that investment banker's look: serious, stern and no-nonsense.

"Really?" I said. "The U.S. Open that's in the middle of a billion-dollar contract with Fox Sports that has another ten years to run? Or the Open that sells out all its tickets in about an hour and a half? I have no idea how you manage to sleep at night."

HaHa. I was rewarded with one of his shotgun bursts. "No," he said, "You're right. We're making tons of money from the Open. To be more specific, I'm worried about next year's Open."

"Pebble Beach," I said. "The greatest meeting place between heaven and earth as William Shakespeare once said."

He smiled, but kept his gunfire laugh to himself. "Actually, it was Robert Louis Stevenson, and he called it 'the greatest meeting of land and sea.'"

I laughed. "Actually, it was an Australian painter named Francis McComas who said it," I said "And he was talking about Point Lobos and Big Sur. Don't tell Jim Nantz. His head might explode."

Strauss waved his hand as if to brush away my finely spun cobwebs of irrelevancy.

"So what are you worried about?" I asked. "The golf course hasn't changed since the last Open. You guys ought to be able to shrink the fairways, grow the rough ankle-high and speed up the greens so no one can make a birdie. You've done it before. And I don't think the Lodge is going anywhere."

Strauss twitched, sitting across from me in the private little booth. It was just a small twitch, mostly in the shoulders, but I saw it.

"Ah," I said. "It *is* the Lodge. Something's up? They can't be going out of business. How can you charge $550 for a round of golf and go broke?"

"The Pebble Beach Company is *not* going broke," Strauss said, frowning at the very thought. "But there have been some recent changes there that have been of concern. You might have heard that J.J. Udall died a few weeks ago."

"He was one of the Four Amigos, right?" I said. "Are they all still the principal owners of that joint?"

"J.J. was one of the four controlling directors in the company, yes," Strauss said. He apparently didn't like the Four Amigos terminology. Investment bankers and USGA executive directors can be such humorless snobs.

But it had been about twenty years since the Four Amigos, er, controlling directors, had purchased the Pebble Beach Company, which owned the famous Lodge at Pebble Beach, the famed Pebble Beach Golf Links, the big modern convention hotel at Spanish Bay, the so-so golf course there, and the course at Spyglass Hill, along with assorted other parcels of acreage dotted here and there on the Monterey Peninsula, which was one of the most pricey pieces of real estate anywhere on the California coastline. Where pricey real estate was invented.

An Open Case of Death

The golf course at Pebble, which was celebrating its 100th anniversary, was world famous. Partly because the PGA Tour had played there every year since 1947, first in the Bing Crosby Clambake which later morphed into the AT&T National Pro-Am. Partly because the U.S. Golf Association had staged several of its national championships there, beginning with the 1929 U.S. Amateur, famously lost by the great Bobby Jones. (Jones won the medal qualifying, as expected, then lost most unexpectedly in the first round of match play to a young kid named Johnny Goodman.) And now the U.S. Open was scheduled to return to Carmel-by-the-Sea for another go-round.

But twenty-some years ago, there had been concerns that Pebble Beach was in financial stress. That's when the Four Amigos, all very rich men with local Northern California ties, had stepped in to buy the place. There had been a series of corporate owners before them, both foreign and domestic, all of whom seemed more interested in trying to pull as much cash out of the place as possible than in running a good business. So the Amigos bought the place at a near-bankruptcy bargain, raised a bunch of cash and began fixing the place up, trying to keep its reality in line with its reputation.

They'd done such a good job that people eventually forgot who the owners were. Because that had been news when they bought the place. All four of the Amigos was famous for something.

J.J. Udall had been a well-known figure in sports for decades. He'd been part owner of an NFL team, then took over the commissioner's job for a short time after Pete Rozelle died. He'd been part of a group of bigwigs who put up the cash to bail out the Los Angeles Olympics and turned it into a money maker. He'd owned a big share of an international sports television network, which raked in profits. Anything J.J. Udall got involved in made money by the truckloads. And in his earlier years, with matinee idol good looks, he had run through a stream of starlets and heiresses, making headlines with every affair and divorce along the way.

The other financial power among the Amigos was Harold Meyer, a gnome-like San Francisco-based businessman who was much less public-facing than Udall, but equally as wealthy. If not more so. Meyer had purchased a big international airline for peanuts, ran it for fifteen years and sold it for billions just before a market crash killed it off. He took his profits and bought a company that made the kind of private jet which every wealthy mogul, foreign dictator, CEO, politician and PGA Tour star had to have. He was said to own pieces and parts of dozens more international companies involved in mining and military and manufacturing all over the world; some had called Harold Meyer a walking, talking military industrial complex.

For the public face of Pebble Beach, they had brought in two more locals. One was Jack Harwood, the movie star, whose career started with a bunch of spaghetti westerns shot in Italy and then, thanks to a bit of lucky casting in an obscure movie that suddenly captured the world's attention, he was transformed into a romantic matinee idol. Women swooned over him and men wanted to be him. After becoming a surefire box office smash who could and did command untold millions per film, he switched sides of the camera and began directing. Three Oscars later, he was at the top of that game, too. Fabulously wealthy and notoriously cheap, he still lived in a smallish mansion above Carmel by-the-Sea and had even done a turn as mayor of that determinedly iconoclastic little village.

The last of the Amigos was Will Becker, one of the PGA Tour's top stars in the late 1960s and early '70s. Becker had played in the era of Nicklaus and Palmer and Watson, made tons of cash on Tour and won a small handful of majors, enough to solidify his reputation as one of the near-greats. The other three Amigos had brought Becker into their little ownership group because he was universally beloved by golf fans, had been born and raised in nearby Gilroy, the garlic-growing capitol of the free world, and, when wheeled out in front of the cameras next to Jack Harwood, was automatic good copy for the media.

"OK," I said, "Pebble Beach is experiencing some changes. Happens to everyone, right? Udall has joined the Choir Invisible. So what? He was, what, eighty years old? Didn't he have a couple of heart attacks recently? His death can not have been a big surprise to anyone."

"No, of course not," Strauss said. "But there's a problem."

"There is?" I tried not to sound like a wise-ass, but failed miserably. Like I usually do. "You mean you trained me all the way down here to West 44th and fed me popovers because the Four Amigos are fighting over who gets to hold the biggest share of Pebble Beach? No wait, I mean the surviving Three Amigos."

"Do you mind if I explain?" Strauss looked unhappy. "The partnership agreement between and among the four principal partners was of course well structured and thought out and prepared with succession issues in mind."

"Of course," I said. I sounded peevish, but was actually a little interested to hear where this thing was going.

"J.J. Udall, despite all of his many famous relationships and four marriages, had never had any children," Strauss said. "At least, none that anyone knew anything about."

"Hoo, boy," I said. "Here it comes."

"And then, two weeks after his death, I received this …" Strauss reached into his coat pocket and extracted a folded paper, which he handed across the table to me.

I opened it and read it. It was hand written on a blank white sheet of paper in blue ink. It was dated about a month earlier, or shortly after Udall's death. It basically said the writer was the one and only offspring of the great James Jackson Udall and he wanted whatever portion of the Udall estate was due and pending, including all ownership shares of the Pebble Beach Company, a California corporation. It was signed "Michael Newell, Eureka, California."

"Nice," I said. "Is it real?"

"We don't know," Strauss said. "We're trying to find out."

"I assume the appearance of this heir throws a monkey wrench into the plan to reorganize the company among the remaining three Amigos?"

"It does indeed," Strauss said. "The trust plan calls for a one-time distribution of Udall's investment share to his estate and the redivision of the balance of assets into three equal shares to be controlled by the surviving shareholders. But the agreement says that any heirs to Udall's estate would also receive a beneficial distribution equal to his original investment."

"How much did Udall put into the company at the beginning?"

"Two hundred and fifty million," Strauss said.

I whistled. "So if this letter is true, this Newell guy stands to walk away with a quarter of a billion bucks. Does the Pebble Beach Company have that much money lying around?"

"No," Strauss said, shaking his head sadly. "It can probably raise that amount, since it is one of the premiere golf resorts in the world. But it will take some doing."

"How come you're involved in all this?" I asked. "What does any of this this have to do with the U.S. Golf Association?"

"Good question," he said, nodding to himself. "First, I handled the Pebble Beach Company account at Baruch Brothers. I helped put this deal together for them twenty-odd years ago. Yes, I am retired from that firm, but working for Baruch is not unlike working for the CIA...when they call, you answer."

Silent Sam the waiter stopped by to see if we wanted anything else. We didn't.

"And as far as the USGA is concerned, we're staging our national championship at Pebble next June," he continued. "It would not be in our best interests if a nasty ownership battle blew up before or during the tournament. We'd rather the focus be on the golf, not the squabbling between parties."

"And there would be public squabbling because...?"

"Because the remaining shareholders would have to contribute more equity, according to the terms of the trust. You see..."

I cut him off. "It's like a margin call," I said. "When everything is going swell, they just cash their quarterly dividend checks. But if the doo-doo hits the fan, they have to make a withdrawal from Hip Pocket National Bank."

Strauss smiled at me across the table. "Your terminology is rather amusing," he said, "But you've got the general idea."

"So if this Newell person is really J.J.'s long-lost kid, it will take a lot of money out of the pockets of Jack Harwood, Will Becker and Harold Meyer," I said. "A movie star, an old golf pro and a big industrialist, any one of whom is likely to file a big lawsuit. Maybe all three."

"Which would create a public relations mess and a headache for the U.S. Golf Association and its national championship," Strauss said.

"And what is it you think I can do about any of this?" I said. I was half dreading and half fascinated by what he might say.

"You seem to have been blessed with the ability to sort out problems like this," he said.

"Some would say cursed," I said.

He waved his hand. "Whatever. I've heard about your special talents and thought you might be of use in this one."

I kept silent.

"I'd like to hire you to find this Michael Newell person," he said. "Find out if he is indeed the legitimate offspring of the late J.J. Udall."

"They have private investigators for things like that," I said. "Call your friend down at Augusta National and ask if you can borrow his Pinkerton men for a month or so. They'd be better at it than me. I'm just a golf writer. Unemployed, at that."

"I need this done quickly and quietly," he said. "I'd much rather it didn't get into the newspapers."

"And you think a former newspaper guy would know how to poke around on the Q.T."

"Yes," he said.

So there it was. The thing the universe had belched up for me. Lying there in all its fragrant rottenness on the nicely starched linen tablecloth of the Harvard Club in Manhattan.

"I'll do it," I said. The words escaped my mouth before my brain got out of first gear. "But I need a cover story. Some unemployed bum asking a lot of personal questions in Pebble Beach is going to trip the alarms with someone."

"I can help there," Strauss said, looking relieved. "Do you know Dickie Steinmetz?"

"Yeah, sure," I said. Dickie was a longtime PR guy at the USGA. He used to edit the association's magazine, *Golf Journal*, before they closed it down after everything in the world of print went digital.

"Dickie had been working on a book, called 'The Courses of the U.S. Open,'" Strauss said. "Coffee table thing, lots of old black and white photos, all about the courses we've used for the Open. You know, Shinnecock, Winged Foot, Baltusrol, Oak Hill, the Country Club…venues like that. Pebble Beach, too."

"Sounds like a best seller," I said. I was being sarcastic.

"Oh, I doubt that," he said with a small smile. "But each of those clubs would purchase a few hundred copies to give to their members, so it would have a pretty good base of sales. And we can use it as a premium to give away if you sign up for a $100 annual membership in the U.S.G.A. So I had no trouble arranging for someone to agree to publish the book."

"Good for you," I said, waiting for the other shoe to drop.

"Unfortunately, Dickie is not well," Strauss continued. "He can't finish the book. A small part of it is done. But I can appoint you to finish the last few chapters and that will give you cover, as you said, to work on this little project."

I thought about it. It sounded reasonable. I hoped.

"And how much money are we talking about for this little project?"

He smiled. We were now back on his kind of terra firma. He mentioned a number, which was almost enough to support my family for the next year. I tried to keep my face neutral while I nodded sagely. *Oh, sure…I get offers like this every day. No biggie.*

"Can I think about it?" I asked. "Talk to Mary Jane? Let you know by the end of the week?"

"Of course," he said. He reached into his jacket pocket and pulled out a billfold. He rooted around and found a business card which he handed across the table. "This is my private number. Call me any time."

We stood up and shook hands.

CHAPTER 3

MARY JANE WAS over the moon when I reported back.

"Hoo-yah!" she exclaimed, giving me a high-five. "I knew you could do it! My man, the author. We'll get you some tweedy sports coats with leather patches at the elbows and maybe a cardigan or two for winter. What do you want for Christmas: the Oxford English Dictionary or a new Roget's?"

I held up my hand in a stop signal. "Thanks for the enthusiasm, but calm yourself," I said. "I don't even know if the book thing is really real, or just a ruse to get my toes inside the door out at Pebble. I'm really more of a private eye than an author. Maybe you should get me a deerslayer hat, a cape and a magnifying glass."

"Oh," she said, sounding a little deflated. But just for a couple of beats. "I think you should do the book anyway. It's a good idea and you would kill it. I don't know anybody who knows as much about golf as you do."

"Who else do you know who knows *anything* about golf?" I asked.

"Shut up," she said. "I mean, this Strauss guy wants you to finish the book, right? The snoopy stuff is just on the side, right?"

An Open Case of Death

Even though I'd officially been a married man for less than six months, I knew better than to disagree with my bride.

"Yeah, sure," I said.

Mary Jane was back on cloud nine. She went off to search the Internet for a catalog that sold clothes for authors and I sat back and thought for a while. I still had a lot of questions…questions about why I had agreed to stick my nose into the middle of someone else's problem. Yeah, the money was helpful. And finishing off the book manuscript seemed easy enough. But there had to be a down side to this deal. I just hadn't found it yet. But I did wonder why Jake Strauss just didn't call in an army of Wall Street lawyers and have them crawl over every aspect of this case. *They* could find this Newell person. *They* could put him under the bright lights and hammer his kidneys with a leather-bound sap until he fessed up. *They* could then write codicils and postscripts and supplemental riders until the cows came home and make sure every dollar of profit at Pebble Beach was preserved and protected and delivered to their rightful owners.

But he wanted me. One part of me was grateful and proud and agreed with his obviously brilliant decision to hire me. But another part, deep down in my lizard brain, I could hear the little *ping ping* of a warning signal going off.

Mary Jane was sitting at our dining room table, engrossed in her laptop.

"Hey," she said. "Have you ever smoked a pipe? I just found a great sale on Meerschaums. You get a free bag of Borkum Riff with every pipe. Every author ought to smoke a pipe."

"You trying to give me throat cancer?" I asked.

"That reminds me," she said. "How are you fixed for life insurance?"

"I had a policy at the *Journal*," I said. "But I think it only covered me if I died while committing journalism."

"Well, don't look now, but you've come close to collecting more than a few times," she said. "Victoria and I would miss you a bunch if you were gone, of course, but we'd think more highly of you if we had a couple million in the bank after you croaked. Help get us over our sadness."

"Ouch," I said, chuckling a little. "Okay Mrs. Black Widow, I'll look into it."

She closed the lid on her laptop. "And I won't insist on the pipe," she said. "Probably stink up the place anyway."

My cell phone beeped at me. I picked it up and answered.

"Hacker?" It was a male, raspy voice. I couldn't immediately place it. I glanced at my screen and saw the number had a 415 area code.

"Yeah?"

"Andre Citrone," he said. "San Francisco *Chronicle*."

"Drey? Geez, man, how are ya?" I said. "I haven't seen you since …" I actually couldn't remember when I last saw the well-known sports columnist for the Chron. I couldn't remember seeing him at the PGA at Hazeltine in August or the Open in St. Andrews last July. But then, we were not actually BFFs; we'd say hello to each other at the big golf events and I recall we'd played a round or two together at one or another media happenings over the years. He was a nice fellow, covered all the sports in San Francisco, and appeared on TV occasionally on one of ESPN's sports pundit shows. They liked him because he often dressed oddly—he favored things like flowing capes, tie-dyed shirts and sometimes one of those Muslim skull caps or *taqiyahs*—and had all the right political views. Or left, since he was from San Fran. He liked to pose as a mysterious man of the world, although I knew he had been born and raised in Hannibal, Missouri, in a rather commonplace middle class family. A child of the Sixties, he had headed for the Left Coast as soon as he could, managed to snag a position as a runner in the Chron's sports department and worked his way up the ranks to become one of their marquee sportswriting stars. It's the American way.

"I know," he said now, with a chuckle. "I didn't make it to any of the majors this year. That's the first time in I don't know how many years for me. The paper had me doing other things, for some reason. I think golf is dead."

"Or dying. Well, it's good to hear from you," I said. "What can I do for you?"

"First of all," he said, "I was sorry to hear that you got laid off. That's tough. How ya holding up?"

"Oh, thanks, Drey," I said. "Yeah, that's never easy, especially after all these years. But I hear it's going around."

"That's the damn truth," he said. "There may not be a newspaper business in ten years. We're all dinosaurs walking."

"Good book title," I said. "American Journalism: Dinosaurs Walking."

He laughed.

"Speaking of books, I hear you're writing one," he said.

That took me by surprise. *How in the hell did he know that?* I wondered.

"I am?" I said. "Where'd you hear that?"

He laughed again. "Oh, I have my sources," he said. "They told me you're coming out this way to do some research. I just wanted to call and offer any help I could for the project."

"Oh," I said. "Well, actually, I haven't signed any contracts with anyone yet. Haven't even decided if I'm going to do it. So, thanks for the offer…I really appreciate it…but there's no project to speak of, yet."

He was silent for a few beats. "That's not what I was told," he said. "I'd heard it was a done deal."

"Yeah, well, you heard wrong," I said. "Who'd you hear all this from?"

"I can't tell you that," he said. He paused again in what I hoped was an embarrassed silence. "Well, listen…I think the Warriors are playing the Celtics in January at the Garden. I'll probably come east with them. Maybe we can get together, have a drink or two, catch up."

"Sure, sure," I said. "Sounds good. Gimme a call."

"Will do," he said. "And if that deal does go through, just remember: I know a lot of people out here. Be glad to help you navigate your way through the rocky shoals at Pebble Beach."

I laughed, forcing out some ha-has. "Ten four on that," I said. "Thanks again."

I put the phone down, stood up and went to look out the window at the North End street scene below. There was nobody down there. There usually isn't. It's a quiet street.

"Who was that?" Mary Jane asked from the kitchen.

"Andre Citrone from San Francisco," I said. "Calling to offer help with my research on the book on Pebble Beach's history."

"That's nice," she said.

"That's weird," I said. "Somebody told him I was doing this book. He wouldn't tell me who."

"Is it a big secret or something?"

"It hasn't happened yet," I said. "I haven't signed anything. I haven't agreed to do the book. Only me and Jake Strauss know about it, as far as I know. So who told Drey?"

"I guess Strauss did," she said.

"Good guess, but I don't think so," I said. "Jake wants me to find this missing heir. The book is incidental to that. Why would he call the sports columnist for the newspaper in San Francisco and tell him anything about our arrangement? Makes no sense."

"So who else might know?" she asked.

An Open Case of Death

"No idea," I said. "Maybe someone has bugged Jake's office."

"Or maybe someone has bugged this place," she said. She poured us both a bourbon on the rocks and put the drinks on a tray with some nuts, crackers and cheese and brought it into the living room. That right there is the difference between men and women. Or, one of thousands. Alone, by myself, I would have just poured a drink and grabbed the jar of nuts from the cupboard. Mary Jane did the whole presentation thing. With dishes. Yin and yang, right there. I liked yin. Or was she yang? Can never remember.

"Or maybe I'm walking into a shit storm of Biblical proportions," I said.

She shrugged. We clinked glasses.

"Wouldn't be the first time," she said.

CHAPTER 4

THANKSGIVING REARED ITS ugly head a week or two after my trip to New York. It has never been one of my Top Ten favorite holidays, along with Christmas. My parents had died in a car crash when I was just an infant, and the aunt and uncle who raised me were not into big family holiday dos. Or small ones, for that matter.

Mary Jane, on the other hand, was big into the family thing, and so I found myself at an Italian Thanksgiving presided over by the patriarch of all patriarchs, my kinda-sorta father-in-law, Carmine Spoleto, the local Mob boss. About forty of us assembled on a cold, dreary afternoon at a magnificent mansion in Milton, perched atop a bluff overlooking an endless brown salt marsh that seemed to reach all the way to Boston Harbor. I tried to ignore the *paisans* all in black who took up positions at every entrance, no doubt heavily armed and ready to shoot holes into anyone bold enough to try and break in and steal our sweet potato casserole. And I tried to circulate, since Mary Jane told me, in the car driving out to the 'burbs, to do just that. "They're ordinary, nice people," she said. Except for the crime and the violence and the propensity for gunplay. Like that which had brought an early end to Mary Jane's former husband, shot to death when Victoria was just an infant.

I shook hands with Carmine when we arrived, grabbed a glass of grappa and tried to find a way to fit in with the rest of the family, who seemed to be moving around the three large rooms on the ground floor like meteors in space: seeing an old cousin or nephew or niece, they'd move together as if gravity bound, come together in a smacking loud embrace and begin to pound each other on the back as if they had not seen one another since Rutherford B. Hayes was President. Not being the world's greatest hugger, except where my wife is involved, and not wanting to spill a drop of my grappa, because it was quite good and I wanted to utilize every drop of it to get through this afternoon, I found myself standing, back to wall, just watching the fun unfold before me.

Mary Jane, who is one of the world's great huggers, was having a high ole time greeting her cousins and step-relatives, catching up on gossip and news, and just doing the things that any large Italian-American family does. Victoria had run off with a posse of cousins and kids her age, and they were probably upstairs watching TV, smoking reefer and planning future hits and heists. Or not.

Carmine snuck up on me, tapped me on the shoulder and motioned for me to follow him into his private den, well away from the crowds. He closed the door behind us and led me over to the bay windows and motioned for me to sit in one of the two upholstered tub chairs there. He sank slowly into the other.

"Noisy bunch," he said. I took it as an observation more than an apology.

"They all seem nice," I said. "Good family. I'm just not a crowd person."

He shrugged. *Que sera* and all that. "How's Victoria doing in school?" he asked.

"She's smart as a whip," I said. "Knows more math than I've forgotten, which is almost everything. Pretty good writer, and I had absolutely nothing to do with that. She likes to read books, which I understand is rare these days. Teachers all seem to like her. No reason why she shouldn't get into a good college one day."

He nodded, pleased. "What about high school?" he asked. "I've been looking into prep schools. Boston Latin is okay, but it's still a public school. No good. I'm thinking Andover, St. Paul, Choate, one of those fancy pants schools. Would make it easier to get into Harvard or Yale, am I right?"

"No doubt," I said, nodding. "But you have to get past Mary Jane first. Not sure she's ready to let Vickie go quite yet."

He thought about that for a bit, his lips pursed, his brow furrowed. It was not a problem he could have solved by putting it in concrete overshoes and tossing it into the Charles River.

"Yeah, well…we'll cross that bridge when we get to it, I guess," he said. He bridged his fingers and peered over the top at me. "What about you?" he asked. "Find some place to work yet?"

Ah, I thought. *The father-in-law interview.* I smiled at him. "Yeah, actually," I said. I told him about the meeting with Jake Strauss, the offer to do a book on the history of the U.S. Open, and my decision to accept the assignment, which I had done the previous week. I left out the part about tracking down a mystery heir. None of his business.

"A book?" he said, frowning a bit. "Can you make any money doing that?"

I explained that a publisher had agreed to pay me an advance upfront, betting that the book would sell enough copies for them to make their money back and then some.

An Open Case of Death

Jake had promised to make up the difference privately. We had signed a Contract for Services.

"Will they?" he asked. I look confused. "Will they make enough money on sales to recoup what they pay you?"

I chuckled. "Probably not," I said. "It's a stupid business. Book publishers make all their money on a handful of best-sellers—you know, Stephen King, Tom Clancy, Nora Roberts, people like that. Then they use those profits to toss a few bucks at people like me, hoping to at least break even. Most of the time, they don't. So they just wait for Stephen King to write another novel and let the money roll in. Crazy, huh?"

He shook his head. "Imagine that! Like if I was making tons of cash from one neighborhood's numbers racket, that mean I'm gonna let two other neighborhoods ride? Don't think so."

"Yeah, the rules of the book business don't translate well to other enterprises," I said.

"If it was me and your book don't sell? I'd hafta break someone's legs. Probably yours."

I nodded sagely and felt a wave of thanksgiving that my leg bones were, as yet, unbroken. On the other hand, I wondered how many unsuccessful authors would be staggering around Manhattan on crutches if Don Carmine's business model was in effect.

"So I have to go out to California to do some research on the book," I said. "I'm planning to make my first visit next week. You know anyone out there?"

"Cali?" He sat up a bit and smiled. "Talk about the wild, wild West. When I first came into the business, Jackie Dragna was the man out in L.A. The fellas in New York tried to send Bugsy Siegel out to take over, but he got shot. His guy, Mickey Cohen, took over and ran a pretty solid organization against the Dragna people for years."

He fell silent, stroking his chin. "But there was a lot of competition out there, both in L.A. and Frisco," he continued. "The chinks and the gooks each had strong organizations in those cities." My semi-father-in-law was never one for political correctness.

"They had to be dealt with, either by alliance or war," he continued. "Made for interesting times. But of course, I had my hands full here at home, so I never got really involved. Just met some of the guys, knew who they were, that kind of thing. To answer your question, yeah, I know some people out West. Why? You need help to write a goddam book?"

I laughed. "No, I think I can handle the writing part," I said. "But some of the people I'm supposed to be talking to appear to have some connections, especially in San Francisco. I just wanted to know if things got tight, I could give you a call."

He nodded. "I see," he said. "Be better if you don't let things get tight."

"I know," I said. "But sometimes those things are out of my control."

There was a soft knock on the door to the study. "Papa?" came a woman's voice, "Dinner's on the table. Come, *mangia!*"

We stood up. Carmine rested a hand on my shoulder. "You're a good man, Hacker," he said. "I appreciate that you're taking care of Mary Jane and Victoria. If you get in a box, let me know. I'll do what I can to help."

The dining room had been rearranged and additional tables brought in to form a large U-shape. It was bedecked with candles, linens, sprays of fresh flowers and plates, bowls and platters of food. There was a roasted turkey at one end and a huge leg of lamb at the other, and in the middle were antipasti, stuffed mushrooms, and bowls of olives. Side dishes included tortellini, risotto with baked squash, rosemary roasted potatoes and red and yellow roasted beets.

Mary Jane had saved me a seat next to her, while Victoria was off in another room with all the other kids. I sat down and we spent the next hour stuffing ourselves silly, drinking vats of wine and listening to this big happy family celebrate being together on a cold November day.

CHAPTER 5

Two weeks later, I found myself on an airplane chugging my way across the fruited plain en route to San Francisco. It had been a busy fortnight.

First, Jake Strauss made an unannounced visit to Boston and we met for lunch at Parker's in the Parker House Hotel downtown on School Street. I walked over in a drizzly late November rain. He was waiting for me in a booth in the large dining room with its honey-colored paneling and beams, complex chandeliers shedding a golden light in the space. He had ordered a cocktail and was busy buttering up one of the eponymous rolls.

"Good to see you again, Hacker," he said as we shook hands. "Park it at the Parker House, as they say." I settled in and a waiter appeared almost instantaneously. I ordered a Sam Adams. "I miss Locke-Ober," Strauss said. "Great old place. You just knew, sitting down there, that some great business deals had been made at those tables, over those dishes of lobster bisque and baked scrod. Too bad its gone."

"No deals being made here?" I asked, sipping my bottle of beer and motioning at the space around us. It seemed grand enough for deal-making to me. And I, a New England native and longtime city resident, had never eaten here.

Strauss laughed. He pointed to a table against the far wall. "That booth over there?" he said, "Was where JFK proposed to Jackie. That was a pretty good deal, eh? And Ted Williams used to eat in here all the time, they said. Always had the pie."

"The pie?"

"Boston cream," Jake said, picking out a second roll, tearing it in half and applying an oversized slab of soft butter to it. "Supposed to have been invented here."

"Did I ever tell you I was a descendant of Paul Revere?" I asked.

He shook his head. "No," he mumbled, his mouth full of Parker House roll. "I don't think you did."

I shrugged. "Oh," I said. "Maybe that's because I'm not."

I got one of his patented laugh barks –*haha*– and he began rooting around in his leather briefcase at his side, pulling out a folder of deep green and passing it across the table at me. I let it sit there, unopened.

He motioned his butter knife at the folder. "That's all the poop we got on Michael Newell," he said.

"The missing heir?"

He nodded. "Some generalized stuff and the Baruch report," he said.

"Baruch report?"

He slathered butter on the second half of his roll and popped it into his mouth. His eyes closed in pleasure as he chewed. I envisioned his cholesterol level increasing by about ten points, and hoped he didn't stroke out before I got my first check.

"At Baruch Brothers, we've got our own internal intelligence systems," he said when he was done. I noticed he was talking as if he was still employed at the investment bank, not the USGA. "As you can imagine, we do a lot of deals in a year. Always good to know who you're dealing with and what's in their background. So we have our own investigators who can do a deep dive on virtually anyone in the world."

"Got one on me?" I asked.

He didn't answer, but looked across the table at me with an amused expression on his face.

"I don't know whether I'm honored or appalled," I said.

The waiter reappeared and took our orders. Jake had the scrod, probably in memory of Locke-Ober, while I went for the fried clams. When the waiter left, I reached over, picked up the green folder and opened it up.

It was pretty thin. But I expected it would be. The Baruch investigators had run down and printed out data on four Michael Newells they had found in Eureka and the rest of Humboldt County in northern California. None of the four appeared to be connected to J.J. Udall in any shape, manner or form. There was another three-page spreadsheet which listed every Michael Newell in California. There were two hundred and twenty-seven of them.

"Are your gumshoes going to track down the Michael Newells in the rest of the state, or is that part of my job?"

"We'll do some more poking," he said, "But we don't think that's his real name."

"How come?"

He shrugged. "We've had plenty of cases like this, when someone tries to pose as an heir to scoop up a big payday," he said. "They usually use a fake name, to throw investigators like you and the boys at Baruch off the scent. About sixty percent of the time, the first name turns out to be real; the last name is usually fake, but just over fifty-five percent of the time, the last initial matches the perp's real last name."

"So I'm looking for somebody named Michael N?" I said.

"Possibly," he said. "And with a probability of just over half."

"What about Eureka?" I asked. "Real or fake?"

"Don't know," he said. "Probably fake. Eureka is infamous for its missing persons."

"How come?"

"Humboldt County is in the Golden Triangle," he said. "It's one of the prime marijuana growing places in North America. Thousands of people go up there hoping to strike it rich in the pot business. Or maybe they go hoping they can get a job with free weed as a side benefit. I don't know. Even though weed is mostly legal now, it's still a rough place and a rough business. Several hundred persons a year are reported missing in Humboldt. Most are never seen again."

"So if you're tracking a missing person in Eureka, there's a long line of cases ahead of you," I said. "Smart place for a missing person to hide, or pretend to hide."

Our lunches arrived, so I kept quiet and we ate. My clams were great—tender and sweet. I'm sure they're not the healthiest food in the world, all battered and deep fried, but I only allow myself the pleasure once or twice a year. They came with French fries, cole slaw and lots of tartar sauce, and I needed another Sam Adams to wash it all down.

"Do you have any idea how you're going to look for this guy?" Jake asked when we finished.

"Not a clue," I said. "California is a pretty big haystack, and I'm looking for a needle with no name."

The waiter came by with coffee and asked if we'd like to try a piece of the Boston Creme Pie, invented in the hotel's very kitchen by a French pastry chef named Sanzian in the year of our Lord 1856. Strauss passed, but I asked for a nice big piece. Happy, the waiter wiped the table and danced away.

"Do you know Andre Citrone?" I asked.

Strauss thought about that for a minute, then shook his head. "Don't think so," he said.

"The sports columnist for the San Fran *Chronicle*?"

"Oh, yeah," he said, sitting forward. "Yes, I have met him once or twice. Can't say I know him that well, though."

"So you didn't tell him that I was going to be working on a book project about Pebble Beach for the USGA?" I pressed. "Or that I might be going out west soon?"

"No," he said, shaking his head firmly. "Of course not. Why would I do that?"

"I don't know," I said. "But somebody told him all about it. He called me right after we met down in New York and offered his help with the book."

"How did …?"

"Yeah, that was my question," I said. "Still is."

Strauss couldn't shed any further light on the mystery, so after I ate my piece of pie and drank my coffee, we shook hands and parted.

A couple days later, I got a call from Dottie van Dyke, the public relations person for the Lodge at Pebble Beach.

"Hacker?" she said. "I hear you're coming out to see us. How wonderful."

"Yes," I said. "And I hope you've reserved the Point Lobos Suite for me. It's always been my fave."

I had once done a freelance piece for one of the golf magazines on the costliest hotel rooms at America's top golf resorts. The Point Lobos Suite, in a free-standing cottage tucked away behind the 18th green at Pebble Beach, goes for around four grand a night. The views themselves—back down the 18th, with the blue ocean to the right, the beach at Carmel in the distance—are worth the tab, but so is the private balcony, the wood-burning fireplace, plush furniture and the beck-and-call service. I was, of course, just pulling Dottie's leg, which she understood.

"Ha, ha," she said. "You're always such a kidder. Jake Strauss said to take care of you. Do you want to stay at the Lodge, or in one of the Casa Palmero suites? The Casa units are spectacular and you can walk to the spa."

"Ooo, the spa," I said. "Do they still have the massage with the two naked Swedes and the soap suds? Put me down for that one."

"Must have been some other place," she said. "We don't do soap suds. But I can make sure Ingmar and Hans are free when you visit. Of course, what arrangement you make with those guys is completely up to you."

That made me laugh.

"Touché," I said. "I don't care where you put me, as long as it has a bed and a bathroom. I'm coming out to work."

"Jake told me," Dottie said. "I'll have some material ready when you get here, and I have a list of some people around here who would probably be willing to talk with you about the history of the place. What an interesting idea!"

I could tell from the tone of her voice she thought it was anything but. But I knew she would come through with lots of reading material. She might be hard to take sometimes, but Dottie van Dyke was a good PR flack.

"Sounds great," I said. "Say, you didn't happen to mention to Andre Citrone that I was coming out, did you?"

"Drey?" She sounded surprised. "No, I don't think I've spoken to him in a couple of months. Why do you ask?"

"No reason," I lied. "Thanks for calling. Look forward to seeing you next week."

I rang off. I wondered for a moment if she was surprised I had mentioned Andre Citrone, or if she was surprised that I knew someone had spilled the beans on me. But I decided to just file that away for now.

Soon, the plane dropped down onto the runway at San Francisco. I collected my bags, picked up the keys to my rental car and set off south towards the Monterey Peninsula. California, here I come!

An Open Case of Death

Chapter 6

DOTTIE HAD FIXED me up with one of the suites in the Sloat Cottage at The Lodge: not as large as the Point Lobos suite, but just as luxurious. There was a king-sized canopy bed framed with heavy mahogany timbers, a nice sitting area in front of the huge windows looking down on the 18th green at Pebble and the crashing ocean beyond the seawall occasionally throwing up sprays of water, and a bathroom filled with enough smelly unguents to keep a hairdressers' convention busy for a couple of weeks.

I tossed my bag down on the bed, looked around and decided to go wander around. Partly because I had been sitting on my keister for six hours encapsulated in that shiny tube of steel; partly because I am a contrarian and that room was practically begging me to kick my shoes off, lie down and sleep for half a day. So I just said no and went out.

I wandered through the lobby, which, as always, seemed to be abuzz with activity, even more so now it was decorated for the Christmas season, and passed through the front entrance and across the drive, where the huge central putting green anchored The Lodge with the golf clubhouse and the row of fancy high-priced shops extending down the way. The huge, wrought-iron Rolex clock told me it was three in the afternoon. That explained the dearth of golfers: there was only a few hours of daylight left, and certainly not enough for anyone to even get in a quick nine. Not at Pebble Beach, home of the six-hour round of golf.

I decided to skip a drop-in at the pro shop: the one at Pebble Beach has all the warmth and welcoming spirit of the city morgue. Oh, it's not that they're totally cold there…flash your American Express card and they'll at least smile in your direction. But you can tell that the golf staff at Pebble is interested only in separating you from as much of your money as possible: how you feel, how excited you are to be crossing something off your bucket list, how much you want to create a lasting experience—none of that is important to them. What is important is which card you wish to use and will it pass the authorization procedure. And nothing else.

I thought about making my way over to the Tap Room and start pounding down some of their finest $12 beers, but that idea was more than a little offensive. So I pulled out my phone, looked up a number I hadn't used in a year or two and pushed the call button. It rang about six times before someone answered.

"Yowsa," said a deep, gruff voice. "Speak."

"Sharky?" I said. "It's Hacker. I'm over at the Lodge and feel a need to reconnect with the common man. You free?"

"Hack-Man!" He sounded glad to hear from me, always a good thing. "What the hell are you doing in town this time of year? And, yes, for God's sake, get your ass out of that hellhole, stat! I was just thinking of heading over to Steinie's."

"I'll be there in thirty minutes," I said and rang off.

As I drove down 17-Mile Drive heading toward Pacific Grove and Monterey, I recalled the first time I had met

An Open Case of Death

Sharky Duvall. I had been covering the National Pro-Am one February many years ago, on one of those dreary, cold, rainy February days when being outside was hellish, and being outside watching amateur golfers rake their shots all over the place was like being chained in one of Dante's lowest circles of Perdition, with birds pecking at your liver or something. I had followed one of the Tour's rules guys into one of the food tents set up to provide hot food to volunteers, caddies and other worker bees at the tournament. They had burgers, chicken and hot dogs on the grill, fries, salads and other sides and urns full of hot coffee, which was much in demand.

So we had gone in, loaded up our trays and taken a seat at one of the long wooden tables covered in cheap paper tablecloths. And across from us, Sharky Duvall was holding court.

As I learned that day, and later on experienced for myself, Sharky was one of those institutional figures at Pebble Beach. He was then, and still is, of that indeterminate age roughly known as "over 50." He was a large man, big beer belly, with a bushy head of graying hair and a neatly trimmed goatee. His knees and hips were pretty much shot, because he had worked as a caddie at Pebble Beach off and on for more than twenty years, beginning when he was just a teenager. But although he couldn't loop himself anymore, he had kept a hand in, spending some years as the caddiemaster for the resort, and later as a union boss when the caddies, for a short while, tried to organize themselves against The Man. That effort was quietly crushed by the Four Amigos when they took over the place and Sharky had officially retired. Unofficially, of course, he was still the man to see if you wanted to find work at Pebble, whether out on the golf course, or in an inside job cleaning rooms, vacuuming hallways or bussing in one of the restaurants.

Sharky knew everyone who worked at Pebble Beach, and was considered a close personal friend by most of them.

For me, Sharky quickly became one of my best sources about all things Pebble Beach. Whenever I came to town, I made it a point to touch base, and I was almost always rewarded with a nugget or two of good information that I could use in a story. He knew everybody, from the big shots in the C-suite to the newest Mexican immigrant hired to rake leaves. He knew all their stories, all their secrets, and he knew when it was the right time to pass along some of those things to a nosy reporter like me.

He lived in a rickety old shack on the outskirts of Monterey; a rickety old shack that was probably worth something north of a half million bucks, given the insanity of California's real estate values. He had grown up in the old fishing town, gotten his nickname when, as a youthful hand on a fishing boat, he had wrestled a large mako into submission when it had been hauled by mistake into the boat and began thrashing around. He had played baseball and football for his local high school, becoming something of a legend, and then took up a job at Pebble, joining the caddie corps. He was a pretty steady employee, save for a few interruptions for brief stays in the local penitentiary for some drug deals and a couple of visits to a detox facility. But he was older and wiser now, and saved most of his substance abuse for his favorite bar stool at Steinbeck's, a semi-scary biker's bar where the beer was cold and the music was loud. I loved the place, and I especially loved the knowledge that being a friend of Sharky's meant no one would attempt to bother me inside Steinie's dark depths.

When I walked in, he was sitting in his favorite spot at the far end of the polished cypress-wood bar, where he had quick and easy access to the men's room and from which he could keep an eye on who came into the place. He saw me, smiled and waved.

An Open Case of Death

"Hey, Sharks," I said as I pulled up a stool next to him. "Gettin' any?"

"Oh, hell," he said, shaking my hand and patting my back. "I'm way too old for chasing the ladies. Although a couple of them are still chasing me, for reasons known only to God."

The bartender brought me a cold one and a big bowl of peanuts and we spent a happy hour or so catching up with life. The music was loud, as always, and ran heavily into songs by Garth Brooks, Keith Urban and Carrie Underwood. Just before the crush of happy hour, the bar was half empty, but the large, bearded and heavily tattooed clientele present were no less serious about drinking. There were three pool tables off on the side, but only one was in use. I had been in Steinbeck's on a weekend night and recalled the place being wall-to-wall bikers, a scene that had come complete with cue-swinging fights that carried from the pool room all the way out to the parking lot. I counted it one of the miracles of all time that I had never shed a drop of blood in the place. Many others had.

"What's this I hear about you writing a book about Pebble?" Sharkie said after we had discussed almost everyone else both of us know. "You trying to go legit or something?"

I laughed. "I'm as legit as I'm gonna get," I said. "And how did you hear about that?" It seemed everyone in northern California knew more about my business than I did.

He chuckled, his big beer belly jiggling with the pleasure. "Oh, hell, Hacker," he said, "There's not much that goes on over there that I don't hear about, sooner or later. So what is this book about?"

"It's about the history of the place," I said. "And the history of the Opens they've had here. The book is sponsored by the U.S. Golf Association. I'm going to write about some of the other courses that have hosted Opens…you know, the Shinnecocks, Winged Foots, Olympic Club, maybe Pinehurst, few others. It's gonna be a coffee table type book, with lots of big pictures so I don't have to write too many words."

"Yeah," he said with a twinkle in his eye. "Words suck."

"So, Mister Inside Man, what have you heard about the ownership situation? I guess with Udall gone, they're gonna do some rejiggering?"

He tipped his glass up and drained the last of about two inches of beer, slammed it down on the bar and nodded at the barkeep for another.

"There's nothing like a death in the family to concentrate the mind," he said, nodding at the bartender when a fresh glass was placed in front of him. "Little factions start forming, everywhere from the pro shop to the laundry. People start placing bets on who they think is going to survive the coming shakeout, hoping that their job or department is safe."

"Safe from what?" I asked. "It's not like the death of J.J. Udall means they're going to start selling off chunks of the company."

"That may be so," he said, "But nobody believes it until they see it in writing. Everybody thinks that big changes at the top mean big changes where they are. And that makes everybody nervous. And I can tell you, everybody is especially nervous about the guy who sent you out here."

"Jacob Strauss?" I said, amazed. "What are they afraid of him for?"

"Oh, I don't know," he said with a chuckle. "Big New York banker feller, rich as hell, has his hands on every lever of power there is. Yeah, he makes people nervous. I'd be wary myself."

"But he's the head of the U.S. Golf Association, not Baruch Brothers," I said.

Sharky looked at me, eyebrows raised, head cocked.

"Yeah, you're right," I said. "He's involved. He put together the deal when the Four Amigos took over. He thinks he's going to have to land the plane again now."

"Exactly," Sharky said, nodding. "That's why most of the employees are nervous. And why more than a couple of them have asked me about you."

"Me? What have I done?"

"Nothing, yet," he said, laughing. "But the timing of your arrival is, umm, *interesting*."

"I've got an assignment to write a book," I said. "Actually, to finish up a manuscript that someone else started."

He looked at me. "Right," he said.

"Strauss wants the book to launch at the Open next June."

"Okay," Sharky said.

"It's legit."

"If you say so," he said.

"You ever hear of anyone named Michael Newell?" I decided to quit beating around the bush. It was obvious that no one in Pebble Beach was buying the story that I was there to write a book. Least of all, my old friend Sharky.

He thought for a minute, running that name through his mental data base.

"Don't think so," he said finally. "Who is he?"

"Somebody I need to find," I said. "And talk to."

"And you can say no more," Sharky said. I nodded.

He shrugged. "Whatever," he said. "I'll see if I can find out anything."

"Discretely," I said.

He nodded. "Of course."

I sipped my beer.

"Andre Citrone," I said.

"Asshole. Bad writer. Friend of Harold Meyer. Who is also an asshole."

I had to laugh. Sharky's summation was succinct and pretty damn accurate.

"Drey knew about me coming out here before I did," I said. "I wondered how he knew."

"Strauss tell him?"

"He says not," I said.

"Interesting." He drank some beer and thought for a bit. "Meyer is quite the piece of work," he said. "Some say he's connected."

"Connected to what?"

"The bent-nose guys," Sharky said. "He's always managed to lay his hands on the capital he needs to do his deals. Always has, from way back. Except no one has ever really been able to determine where that capital comes from. It's assumed he just made or inherited lots of money somewhere and saved his shekels up nicely. But that explanation has never stretched far enough to explain some deals he's made. So people think he might have some silent backing along the way."

"From the Mob?"

He shrugged. "That's what some people say. But as a trained professional journalist, I know you need two independent sources who can verify that on the record."

I laughed. "One, I'm no longer a trained professional journalist," I said. "Two, that two independent verified sources standard went out the window a long time ago. All you need these days is one anonymous source who you can say is familiar with the matter but not authorized to discuss it publicly, and you can go to town with whatever bullshit you want."

His eyes twinkled. "But you're not bitter."

"Me?" I held my arms out wide. "Why should I be bitter because journalism standards of objectivity have been tossed over the side? I'm an author now. We have a higher calling."

An Open Case of Death

"You know about the condo project, right?" he asked.

"Condo project?"

Sharky laughed. "Yeah, I didn't think so," he said. "They've done a great job keeping that thing under wraps."

"Tell me," I ordered.

He sat back on his stool. Stroked his goatee. Organizing his thoughts.

"Okay," he said, "The last time Pebble Beach and the CCC went at it was about ten years ago."

"CCC?"

"California Coastal Commission," Sharky said. "The environmental Nazis. Any kind of development that takes place anywhere on the California coast has to get approved by the CCC. You want to pick up a rock on the beach and put it over there, you gotta get it OK'd by the CCC, right? And they usually tell you no. The CCC would be happy if all fifty million residents of California would move inland a hundred miles and leave the coastline to the fish and the birds."

"Which doesn't make the Pebble Beach Company happy," I said.

"Oh, hell, they've gone toe to toe with each other for years," he said. "Anyway, about ten years ago, they signed an agreement, Pebble Beach and the CCC, on what could be developed in the Monterey Forest and what couldn't. It was part of the deal that allowed Pebble to build its fake rock walls along the 18th fairway, which was in danger of being washed out to sea by any given winter storm."

"I vaguely remember that," I said. "I remember they dug up the golf course for about a year to install the new footings. Sprayed gunnite into the forms and then painted it all to look natural. Fucking with Mother Nature."

"Right," he nodded. "Well, as part of that deal, the Company agreed to set aside some land up in the hills permanently. No development, ever. Save the Monterey pines. Freedom for the birds and spiders."

"All for the seawall?"

He smiled at me. "You've got to be kidding. Pebble agreed to set aside building rights in Saw Mill Gulch and some other tracts, and even agreed to abandon plans for another golf course, but in return got agreements to allow new construction here at the Lodge, permission to sell some house lots around Poppy Hills, and received preliminary approval for a fancy condo complex up in Huckleberry Hills."

"Huckleberry Hills?" I said. "Sounds like a Looney Tunes cartoon."

"Ain't no joke," Sharky said. "The land and the proposed condos would be a three- to five-hundred million payday once finished."

"Zowie," I said. "Have they started building that yet?"

"Nah," Sharky said. "Like anything else that comes before the CCC, it takes five to ten years to get through the permitting process. They're about halfway done getting it through the process. While fending off the anti-development crowd."

"Which I would imagine is quite energetic," I said. "California being the land of fruits and nuts."

"Oh, yeah. Protest marches, sit-ins, people getting arrested at meetings…the whole nine yards."

"So Huckleberry Hills is still pending?"

"Very quietly," Sharky said. "Under the radar. But yes, it's still pending."

"Real estate," I said. He looked at me questioningly. "You always think about Pebble Beach as a golf development, or a fancy hotel development. But it's not. It's a real estate development. Worth a few billion."

Sharky was about to say something snarky, but just then two biker chicks walked past us on the way to the ladies' room. Lithe, tanned, tall, blond and oh-so-California, they were whispering and giggling together as they passed us, giving us one of those over-the-shoulder, come-hither looks, with tossed hair, wry smiles and, once past us, exaggerated fanny wiggles that showed off the very tight, very low-cut jeans they each wore, jeans that showed just a portion of the tramp stamps on each of their lower backs before descending downwards and disappearing from view.

"How's your higher calling now, Hack?" he said.

CHAPTER 7

I GOT BACK to my luxurious room at The Lodge at about eight. The message light on my room phone was flashing. I punched a few buttons, saw that the call had come in from "Ms. Van Dyke" and hit callback.

"Hacker," Dottie said when she answered. I guess saying "hello" is passé out on the Left Coast. "Where the hell have you been?"

"Out doing research," I said. "I came out here to work, y'know."

"Ha ha," she said, not sounding happy. "Such a card. Did you even look at the itinerary I left for you?"

I looked around the room and saw the large envelop resting in front of a bottle of wine, next to a large fruit basket wrapped in colorful cellophane, that had been set on the cocktail table in front of my comfy sofa.

"Oh," I said. "No. Sorry. I'll open it right away."

"No you won't," she said with a sigh. "So you already missed the pleasure of having dinner with me tonight. Do you want to play golf in the morning, or shall I cancel the tee time?"

"What time in the morning?" I asked.

"I got you an early tee time at Pebble," she said. "Tried to get you out before the crowds, and leaving your afternoon free. Do you want to play, or not?"

"Sure," I said. "I'll make the ultimate sacrifice. Will I be done in time for you to buy me lunch?"

"God, I hope so," she said. "How about I meet you at one in the Tap Room?"

"Sounds marvy," I said. "See you th—"

She had already hung up.

Shrugging, I called home.

"Hi, honey," Mary Jane said. "How was your day? Anybody shoot at you?"

"No, I don't think so," I said.

"So, you had a good day!" she giggled.

"How's the Vickster?"

"Fine," Mary Jane said. "She's asleep. She got a hundred on her spelling test. I had to pay off with some ice cream."

I had a moment, a little internal shiver, when every part of me was wishing I was sitting there in my North End apartment, holding Mary Jane's hand, sipping on a cocktail, looking in on the sleeping girl who could spell to beat the band. There were probably millions of people who wished they could be where I was right now, sitting in a fancy hotel room on the Monterey Peninsula, scheduled to play the Pebble Beach golf course in the morning. And I wanted nothing more than to be home, with the ones I loved. I sighed.

"What's the matter?" Mary Jane asked. She didn't miss much.

"Oh, I was just missing you guys," I said. "You seem to be a long way away."

"No," she said, "*You're* the one who is a long way away. We're right here where we belong."

"I suppose you're right," I said. "I'll be home as soon as I can."

"Or sooner," she said.

MY TEE TIME was at 7:30 in the morning, and I had no trouble making it with time to spare, as I woke up in the dark at about 4:30, still on East Coast time, which gave me plenty of time to figure out how to work the coffee machine and to call in an order for some room-service breakfast.

At the golf shop, I was informed that I would be joined by Charlie Sykes, one of the young assistant professionals. And did I wish to ride or walk?

"I'll ride," I said. "I have a lunch date at one. Will that be a problem?"

"Not at all, sir," said the young man standing at the check-in register. "It is our policy to maintain a pace of play that adheres to our standard time of four hours and fifteen minutes for an eighteen-hole round."

It was pretty early in the morning, but I could recognize bullshit when I heard it. But the kitchen had done a great job sending me five slices of bacon, some hot biscuits and cheese, and my stomach was too happy for me to call him on it.

I went out to hit a few putts. It was a pleasant morning, a few scattered clouds drifting across the sky and little to no wind. The temperature was a balmy 60 degrees, not bad for an early December morning. The putting green was empty except for one other guy, so I lost myself in the pleasure of rolling my ball across the pristine surface of the green.

"Mister Hacker?" The man's voice interrupted my meditation. He was holding out his hand, a large grin showing his teeth. He was tall, in his mid twenties, with a shock of bright red hair, dressed in slacks, golf shirt and a sweater with a Pebble Beach logo. "Charlie Sykes," he said. "We're next on the tee."

"Morning," I said. "Let's do it."

There was a foursome ahead of us, and although they had already teed off, they hadn't gotten very far. Two of them appeared to be searching for balls in the shrubbery down the right side of the first hole, next to the privacy fences that had been erected to shield the expensive rooms of the Casa Palmero wing. Beyond that, the new cottages of the Fairway One section rose near the fairway. Lucky for us, the group ahead had hired a forecaddie, and when he looked back and saw one of the assistant pros and I ready to go, he waved us to play through.

"Shall we play for a little something?" I asked.

Charlie looked at me with a wry smile. "You used to play on the Tour, right?" he asked. I nodded approvingly. He had done his homework.

"Yeah," I said. "About thirty years ago, for parts of three seasons. I play to a five these days. And I haven't swung a club since September. Meanwhile, you played your college golf where, again?"

"Stanford," he said. The wry smile never left his face. "How 'bout I give you two a side?"

"Done," I said. I gestured to the tee. "Play away, please."

He stepped up, planted his tee and knocked his drive down the fairway. I followed suit. The first at Pebble is one of several pedestrian holes on the course, a simple par four of under 400 yards that bends slightly to the right. You don't need to mash a driver here, so I just corked a three-wood out to the left, keeping my ball short of the fairway bunkers out there.

Taking a cart at Pebble Beach is not a great time saver. There is a hard-and-fast paths-only rule, so walking the course with a caddie is usually faster and more efficient. But then nothing about playing at Pebble is fast: when you pay the kind of money they charge for a round of golf, you are going to play every last shot. You want to get your money's worth, especially when you're laying out half a thousand bucks.

In any case, we sped past the ball-searching foursome, hit our approach shots up onto the narrow green and both of us putted out for par. Standing on the second tee, I couldn't see any other groups in front of us. We had clear sailing. The second hole is a par five, which the USGA usually converts into a long par four for the Open. Again, nothing very spectacular: long straight fairway, a sand-filled barranca across the fairway about sixty yards short of the green, so you can't bounce a second shot all the way onto the green.

Charlie's long drive drifted right and found one of the fairway bunkers waiting down there. I overcompensated by pulling mine into the left rough. It wasn't as deep as it would be next June, but I still had to lay up short of the barranca. Charlie did the same, and we, again, both made pars. All even, so far.

He drew the first blood on the third, a short par four that doglegs almost 90 degrees to the left and heads down toward the sea. Charlie cranked a monster drive up and over the trees guarding the corner and his ball disappeared heading toward the green. I hit my hybrid club and was glad to see the ball didn't carry all the way to the row on bunkers on the far edge of the fairway. Still, I had a full seven-iron to hit the green, while he had a flip wedge, which he stuck to about three feet and sank for the birdie. One up for the home team.

Four is another *meh* hole: from the tee next to the Beach and Tennis Club along Stillwater Cove, it's a short par four up the hill. Both of us hit irons, trying to find some green amid the puddles of bunkers scattered all over the fairway. We did, and then wedged up onto the green. This time, I sank a nice fifteen footer for my bird, while his lipped out. All square!

An Open Case of Death

Next came the Nicklaus hole, the par-three Jack designed and built to replace the old sixth hole, a project which had to wait several decades until the little old lady, whose husband had built a house where the tee box now sits, had passed away. The new hole crosses the barranca from the back tees, rises up a gentle hill and the green is tucked away behind several bunkers. The hole calls for a high fade into the green, which should surprise no one, since that high fade was Nicklaus' go-to shot all his life. Were I an architectural critic, which I am not, I would point out that an architect ought not to design holes that favor his own game quite so much, but that's just picking nits.

We parred out and carried on to the sixth. Here, the course finally begins to grow some teeth. This par five shows the ocean for the first time, as the rocky cliff down the right side falls away into Stillwater Cove, where there are usually some sea otters floating around or diving for abalone. You don't want to lose a tee shot right, but to mess your mind up, they installed a nest of bunkers down the left, which is where you want your ball wants to go.

Both of us left the drivers in the bag and found the fairway. Now we had a long carry up to the green, which we couldn't see: there's a tall, rough-covered hill and the rocky cliff over the water blocking the view, while the fairway up on top moves slightly to the right. I tried to put a little extra mustard on my hybrid iron and pulled it a bit left, which, I recalled, I seemed to do every time I played here. Charlie hit a beauty, which looked like it was going right towards the hole.

I found my ball short of the greenside bunker and chipped it on. Charlie's approach had stopped just a foot or two off the front of the green, and, showing a nice short game, he chipped it up to kick-in range. I didn't make him kick it. One up again.

Next was the iconic seventh—the short par three runs sharply downhill from tee to the green, which looks like it's surrounded on three sides by the crashing Pacific surf. Actually, there's bunkers and grass between the green and the ocean, but it looks scary, even if the hole is just 100 yards. We both made it onto the surface, but neither of us could coax our putt to go in.

Finally, on the eighth tee, we entered the heart of Pebble Beach. For the next three holes, every shot had to be precise, starting with the tee shot. On eight, it's a mostly blind shot uphill, and the landing zone, while it looks large, is actually segmented. For the best approach, you need to be as close to the cliff's edge as possible. If playing to the plateau on the right, you only need a three-wood. If you want to crush a driver, keep it left of center, or kiss it goodbye.

Charlie crushed a three wood dead straight, and ended up ten yards from the cliff. I pulled my driver again and found the ball in the left rough, but in a not-impossible lie.

Now came the best shot at Pebble. It's a long way to the green, but it's also steeply downhill. You launch the ball from atop the cliff, over the rocks and surf below, down towards the narrow little circle of green, framed by bunkers, with a little green run-up space below the hole, and nothing but penalty strokes for anything that goes right into the gunch that clings to the hillside above the beach. The winds were calm in the early morning, so that didn't factor in as much as it usually does.

I had 190 yards left, downhill, so I took a five-iron and stepped on it hard. A little too hard, as my shot hit on the back part of the green, bounced high and dribbled off the back. I was left with a tough chip to a green running away sharply.

Sykes was able to loft a seven-iron onto the front of the green, where it stopped nicely, leaving him an uphill twenty-five footer for birdie. There wasn't much I could do to stop my chip, so I ended up with about fifteen feet for par, which I missed. But I got a shot on this hole, so Charlie had to make a run at his birdie, which slid by the left and kept going for another four feet. But he calmly sank his par putt to remain one-up.

We stopped and looked back at the craggy rocks and the fairway which stopped abruptly some 50 feet above the beach and sea. "When was the last time someone went over the side?" I asked.

"Last I remember was about thirteen months ago," he said with a soft laugh. "They drove out onto the plateau, which you're not supposed to do, forgot to set the brake, went to play their shots and the cart went over the side. Happens maybe once every year or two. We charge the idiots 2,500 bucks to recover the cart, and the entire pro shop goes out to dinner."

So I was one down going into the ninth. Nine and ten are almost carbon copies: long, narrow par fours that run downhill, with the beach all down the right side. It's a lovely beach to look at: the folks who live in Carmel-by-the-Sea come out to walk with their dogs and children, toss Frisbees, have picnics and do assorted other casually California things on the beach. But any golf shot that drifts right is as gone as a California teenager's innocence. And protecting from going right at any cost usually means overcompensating to the left, which is full of thick rough and deep bunkers. Every shot has to be precise.

I played what I thought were two excellent shots, but my approach was perhaps a shade heavy—that downhill lie will get you every time—and my ball caught the top of the front bunker and fell in. Charlie was on in two, but a good forty feet away.

Climbing down into the sand, I tried to remember the last bunker shot I had hit, but couldn't think of one. That's not a good mental picture before hitting a tough shot, but maybe it worked, because I managed to thump my ball out just right, saw it fly towards the hole, hit, bite and jump to the right before stopping on a dime. Three feet.

"Nice shot, Hacker," called Sykes. I waved my thanks and raked the sand smooth.

He missed, I made, and we finished the front side all even. It was a good match. The morning had developed nicely, with the warming sun bathing the course and, without any breeze, keeping the temperatures nice.

My attention wandered a bit and I made more than a few squirrelly shots over the next few holes, including my approach on ten that went all the way down to the beach, where an Irish setter ran over and sniffed at it and looked disappointed when the ball didn't take off and run. Suffice it to say that when we putted out on the par-three twelfth hole, I was three-down and searching for an answer.

Luckily, Pebble Beach provides a nice little snack shack between the twelfth green and the thirteenth tee, and Charlie stopped the cart there.

"Want anything?" he asked.

"How about a new golf swing," I said.

They didn't have that on the menu, alas, but I settled for a cold beer and a hot dog. Not my usual mid-morning fare, but then my breakfast had been before the sun came up and my stomach was growling. Charlie went for a coffee and a sweet roll. I signed the chit without looking at the ridiculous amount of money they charged, since the USGA was picking up the tab. Maybe next time the rules mavens get together, they should consider adding a Rule against overcharging for beer and dogs.

We were not being pressed by anybody—that foursome we had blown through back at the beginning was probably putting out on five—so we sat in our cart to eat and stared out at the achingly beautiful ocean and the rocks over at

An Open Case of Death

Point Lobos. A sailboat went by, sails down, motor running, the bow rising up and down as it struggled through the waves rolling in from Japan.

"Not a bad place to work, is it?" I asked.

"I'm sure there are worse," he said.

"How long have you been here?"

"Coming up on three years," he said. "I was lucky—my Dad knew one of the owners, and after I graduated from Stanford, he put in a word. I knew I was never going to play on the Tour, so this was my Plan B. After working here as an assistant, I should be able to find a good head professional job somewhere."

"I would think so," I said. "Working here is like going to Harvard."

"Or Stanford," he said, and gave me a wry grin.

"Touché," I said, chuckling. "Either way, it's less about what they teach you and more about the people you get to know who can come in handy some day."

"True that," he said, draining the last of his coffee. "Holds true for this job, too. You never know who you might meet on a given day that can be helpful to you some day. I try to keep my eyes and ears open. You meet as many people as you can and try to treat everyone nicely. You never know."

"Say," I said, "You ever meet a guy name of Newell? Mike Newell?"

He jumped out of the cart like someone had goosed him, walked over to the bin and dunked his trash in like he was Stephen Curry of the Warriors. With some violence. When he came back, his face had gone white. He didn't look at me, but climbed in behind the wheel and slammed his foot down on the pedal. The cart jerked forward, snapping our heads back, as he drove down the curving path towards the thirteenth tee.

"I take it that's a 'no,'" I said.

"W-w-what?" he said, his voice a little thin and shaky. "What did you say?"

"Newell," I said. "First name Michael. I wondered if you knew him."

"No," he said. "Why should I?"

That was a bit of a weird non-answer, I thought, but I let it lie. He had the honor, so he stepped up on the tee of the par-four that ran up a gentle hill all the way to the green, with the ocean off to the left, across the fairway of the ninth hole. He teed his ball, took a hurried practice swing, then stepped up and belted it. The ball started down the right side and then began curving even more to the right. Eventually, it disappeared into the back yard of one of the marble and concrete mansions that sat regally along the fairway. O.B. Gonzo.

"Shitfuck," he said, and pounded his driver in anger on the tee. "Shit, shit, shit."

I got out of the cart, stretched, and took my time getting out my driver, rooting around for a new ball, trying to delay as long as possible to let Charlie get his composure back. He stood on the back of the tee, waiting, his hands clenched tightly at the top of his driver, staring down the fairway. At nothing.

I played my drive, which fetched up safely down the left just past a fairway bunker, snatched up my tee and stood back. He re-teed, took another nervous practice swing, then made another pass. This one went even farther right than the first. I clenched my shoulders together, waiting to hear the tinkling crash of a Titleist plowing through window glass. But we heard nothing.

"Goddamit to hell!" Charley shouted and reared back and tossed his driver down the fairway. Almost immediately, however, he got control of his anger. He took a couple of steps down the fairway after his helicoptering driver, then stopped and turned to me.

An Open Case of Death

"I'm very sorry, Mister Hacker," he said, his face beginning to redden with embarrassment. "I apologize for my behavior. Those were two of the worst swings I think I've made since I've been working here. But that's no excuse for losing my composure like that. I'm terribly sorry."

"Forget about it, kid," I said, and I meant it. "Happens to all of us, one time or another. This game can sneak up and kick you in the shorts when you least expect it. I'd say I won this hole. Let's just play on."

"Thanks," he said, and went after his driver.

We finished the round without any other incident. But something had definitely changed. Charley was quieter, withdrawn into himself. His golf game didn't change—he played steady golf the rest of the way and easily held me off to win our little match. But he wasn't the same person. I tried talking about different things, trying to jolly him out of his funk, but he responded mostly in monosyllables, didn't laugh much at my jokes or stories, and just seemed preoccupied. I tried not to read too much into it. Maybe he had been shooting his best score ever, and the two out-of-bounds shots had ruined what he thought was going to be a great card. Maybe he had screwed up that hole before, and was berating himself for falling victim to the mental heebie-geebies that lurked there.

Or maybe, I thought, my question about Michael Newell had come at him out of left field, completely unexpectedly, and had smashed his mental equilibrium into a zillion pieces, right there on the thirteenth tee at Pebble Beach. *That would be interesting*, I thought.

I stopped hitting shots sideways, which was good, but lost all touch on the greens, and three-putted three times coming in. At the end of the round, I gave Charlie forty bucks and thanked him for the game.

"Any time, Mr. Hacker," he said. He managed a half smile, but couldn't look me in the eyes. We shook hands.

A Hacker Golf Mystery

The big Rolex clock on the putting green said it was half-past noon, so I headed for the Tap Room.

An Open Case of Death

Chapter 26

THE WEEKEND BEFORE the U.S. Open, Mary Jane, Victoria and I flew out to San Francisco, rented a car and drove south. When we hit Carmel-by-the-Sea, we kept going for another half hour or so until we arrived at Big Sur. Turning up the mountainside that dropped down towards the Pacific for the last thousand feet or so, we found the laid-back hotel and spa I had booked, tucked away in the trees.

Mary Jane signed up for yoga classes, an all-organic full body cleanse, and a daily reiki massage. Of course, she was still awash in maternal hormones, so I just smiled and told her that sounded great. Victoria oohed and aahed about everything, but was especially taken with the free bike rentals and the horizon pool that seemed to be perched at the edge of the cliff cascading down to the rocky shore. Wouldn't we all love to be eleven again?

And me? Our room had a nice patio with two comfortable chaises and the swimming pool, about fifty yards away, had a bunch more. With waiters hovering and asking if they could bring you another cool and refreshing drink. I had brought four new books I wanted to read, and had about another twenty on my laptop, so I was pretty much in hog heaven as well.

I tried not to think too much about Mike Nelson, who was not in hog heaven at the moment. Although he might have been in real heaven if I had not intervened.

My father-in-law, asterisk division, heard me out when I had called him a few weeks earlier. And then he quickly arranged for a safe house for Mike Nelson. Well, *I* called it a safe house. I imagine Mike Nelson called it involuntary servitude or something worse. In any case, Carmine found him a place to stay, a back bedroom in a third-floor tenement walk-up in the wilds of Dorchester. His host was a bachelor who owned a liquor store and was one of Carmine's trusted foot soldiers.

Carmine had sent a car and when it arrived at Gennaro's, I patted Mike on the back and told him to go with the flow for the time being. I said I'd try and straighten it all out. I had no idea how, but he didn't need to know that.

I went down to Dorchester to check on him about a week later. He seemed fine: he had been well-fed with Italian food and had drunk a lot of cheap red wine. And his host, Arturo Scavini, had put him to work in the liquor store, Big Al's Spirits, sweeping, restocking shelves and taking a turn at the counter to ring up sales.

"He's a good boy," Artie told me. "Hard worker. Doesn't say much."

Mike had looked at me with his puppy dog eyes and asked when he could go home. He missed Cassie and wondered if he'd ever get his job back.

I told him that we'd gotten word to Cassie that he was still alive and missed her. I had called Sharky, and he had volunteered Aggie to drive out to the vineyard and speak directly to Cassie, making sure no one else was listening. Cassie had burst into tears at the news, but quickly recovered and was now OK.

I had nothing I could tell him yet about coming back home. Sharky was working some angles at his end, and I was scheduled to return to Pebble for the U.S. Open, which was now scheduled for the following week.

And here I was. We had five nights in Big Sur before we had to move over to the Inn at Spanish Bay, the Pebble Beach property that the U.S. Golf Association had booked for us for Open week. My book signing was scheduled for Tuesday night at a bookstore in Carmel.

The days passed blissfully. We all had breakfast together staring out the window at the banks of fog that socked the coastline in … it's an official secret, closely guarded by the Chamber of Commerce and tourism board types, that summertime on the Monterey Peninsula is fog season. The temperature inversions between the ice cold Pacific and the hot, semi-arid mountains usually result in thick, soupy, sunless mornings all along the coast. If there's any kind of a breeze, the clouds will usually blow away by noon.

But we dealt with it. Victoria and I would set off on a long bike ride through the dripping forests and open vistas, stopping to gaze at one of the private mansions that dotted the hillsides, and pulling into our favorite little cafe for a fruit smoothie. Mary Jane usually disappeared into the spa after breakfast for one of her treatments, not to be seen again until dinner.

One morning, I drove the Vickster down Route 1 to San Simeon to look at the Hearst Castle. There wasn't much to see from the parking lots at the bottom of a hill—looking up we could see the bell tower and the tall palms in the gardens. Vickie took one look at the busloads of visitors lining up for the tours and decided she wasn't all that interested.

"Seen one castle, seen 'em all," she said with that unarguable logic of children. We went back to Big Sur.

In the afternoons, Vickie would splash in the pool with some of the friends she had met, and I would lie on a shaded chaise and read. And sleep. And worry a little bit about what I was going to do next, now that the book was finished and the advance money almost spent. And about the case at hand and how I could figure that one out.

Mary Jane noticed that last bit. She would reach over at dinner, frown, and rub her thumb against my forehead.

"Worry wrinkles," she would say. "They have this lovely hot stone massage where they put them on all of your chakras. Just melts all your stress away."

"Are you sure I have chakras?" I said. "I don't think they were allowed in the Sunday school I used to go to."

"You went to Sunday school?" Victoria piped in. "What was that like?"

"Very religious," I said. "And not much fun. Except for sixth grade. That's when I met Connie Stone. She was gorgeous, at least for a sixth grader, and if you overlooked her braces. I was certain I would marry Connie Stone and live happily ever after."

"Did you?" Vic asked.

"Nah," I said. "She dumped me for some nerd with a Game Boy."

"What are you worried about?" Mary Jane pressed. "We're in Big Sur. Living with Nature. Getting in touch with our inner selves."

"My inner self is worried about making next month's rent," I told her. "So's my outer self."

She blew out her breath. Then stopped and took another deep one in. I think it was something she had just learned.

"The universe will provide, Hacker," she said. She sounded a little sing-songy, like Baba Ram Dass.

I let it drop, because this was bliss time. I wanted Victoria to have a good time, and I wanted MJ to relax and let little Junior soak in nothing but good vibrations down there in her womb. But I knew I'd have to come up with some kind of plan for the future. Little Junior was going to

An Open Case of Death

need diapers. And amoxicillin. And four years of tuition at Harvard. Nothing but the best for my kid!

I looked around for a helpful waiter and told him to bring me a Scotch on the rocks. On second thought, I said, make it a double.

Sunday afternoon, blissed to the max, we drove back up to the Peninsula and took 17 Mile Drive out to the Inn at Spanish Bay, where the Pebble Beach Company had constructed a big modern hotel overlooking the ocean, and added a golf course next door.

The golf course, designed by Robert Trent Jones Jr., the son of the man who designed Spyglass Hill, had great ocean views, but is just an OK track. Part of the problem was that the environmental crowd had gotten involved in the project early, and had designated all kinds of places around the course as "environmentally sensitive," which meant places no humans were allowed to tread. Now, I'm as sensitive about the size of my carbon footprint as the next guy, but if I tug a little on my sand wedge approach to a green and my ball rolls off into a sandy area next to the green, an area fenced off and larded up with big neon signs telling me this is an environmentally sensitive area and to KEEP OUT!, and I can see my brand-new Titleist Pro-V1 sitting there doing nothing but polluting the environmentally sensitive area…well, I'm going to walk in there and pick it up, and if you don't like that, I suggest you call Ansel Adams and complain.

But I wasn't playing golf on this visit. The hotel, while comfortable and nicely appointed, is just a big old convention hotel, with wings full of meeting rooms, lots of restaurants of various cuisines and a couple of big ballrooms for that corporate event. And on the Sunday before the U.S. Open, the lobby was full of conventioneers: the officials and people of the world of golf. I saw some of the same contingent of golfing officialdom that I had seen at Augusta for the Masters, and in St. Andrews for the Open Championship. It's one of the perks of the job, whether you're chairperson of the Wyoming Golf Association or the grand poohbah of the Indonesian Golf Federation: You get to go to all the major tournaments, stay in the official hotels and party like it's Woodstock.

Jake Strauss had kindly offered to put us all up for the week, courtesy of the US Golf Association. The girls planned to visit the Monterey Aquarium, shop Cannery Row and probably spend a day or two up in San Francisco. After my book signing on Tuesday, I'd pretty much be free to watch the tournament. It felt more than a little odd not to have any deadlines or worries about stories to write, but I figured I'd get over that pretty fast.

We checked into our junior suite. Mary Jane decided to lay down for a brief nap and Victoria and I looked at the room service menu to see if we were hungry for anything yet. We decided to wait a bit. The golf tournament on TV was Memphis, where three nobodies were vying for the title. Victoria was engrossed in her telephone screen, I was half asleep and Mary Jane was softly snoring on the bed when a horrible grinding noise made all three of us sit up, wide-eyed and stunned. I first thought it was a trash compactor that had gotten stuck mid-crush, but the sound kept going on and on and eventually turned into what sounded like musical notes.

I opened the sliding glass doors and went out on the balcony to look. We were on the third floor, and down on the grassy terrace overlooking the Pacific, some guy dressed in a kilt, knee socks, tam o shanter and sporran was blowing air into a set of bagpipes. Once inflated, he began playing some descant or other while pacing back and forth.

Mary Jane came out and stood next to me, watching. She put her arm around me.

An Open Case of Death

"You looked better in that kit than he does," she said.

"You're slightly biased, I think," I said. "And you've had a peek at what's under the hood, too."

"A peek?" she said with a chuckle. "Son, you threw open the hood and let the whole neighborhood stare at the engine."

"TMI! Too much information!" Victoria called from inside.

CHAPTER 8

THE TAP ROOM is one of the great clubhouse bars in all the world. Dark, wood-paneled, bedecked with black-and-white photos of Hollywood stars and PGA Tour pros enjoying the hell out of the once-enjoyable pro-am weekend known as the Crosby Clambake, the place feels like it should be smoke-filled, except if you dared light one up today, alarms would sound, lights would flash and seven kinds of law enforcement would descend on the place to haul you off to the hoosegow. Other than that, the place reeks of atmosphere. Of course, a glass of beer will set you back around twelve bucks, and a cheeseburger starts at around twenty-five, but the surviving Amigos have to make a profit somewhere, and that somewhere is The Tap Room.

Dottie van Dyke was waiting for me at a table towards the back of the room. She had her laptop open and humming, and had made the server leave an entire pot of coffee on the table so she could do her own refills. She saw me come in and waved me over.

Everything about Dorothy van Dyke shouted "career woman." She was tall and stocky in her build, impeccably dressed as always, today in a maroon business suit. Her hair, cut in a slightly mannish style, was that shade of grey-blonde that gave away her age. She had spangly bracelets around both wrists, eyeglasses hanging from a chain around her neck, and just enough makeup to set off her high cheekbones. She looked businesslike, her aura was corporate and, as a man, my initial impression was that what she most wanted was to relieve me of all my money. There was absolutely no sexual electricity. None. With Dottie, there was no "me woman, you man," but simply "let's make a deal."

She held out her hand for me to shake as I came to the table. "Hacker," she said coolly. "Good to see you again."

"Hi, Dottie," I said. "Been waiting long?"

"Ten minutes," she said. "I had someone call me when you reached the 18th tee."

"How efficient," I said.

She leveled her eyes at me, in a neutral look that said *of course I'm efficient. This is what I do.* For the record, her eyes were pale blue. They were also cold, calculating and a bit scary.

I ordered a cup of artichoke soup—they are grown all around Monterey, and mine were said to come from Castroville—and the only cheeseburger I could find on the menu. Made with Kobe beef and some warm melted brie, it was priced at a cool $31. Dottie ordered a salad. When my beer arrived, price unknown, I lifted it in silent thanks to Jacob Strauss, who was paying for it.

"In addition to the stuff I left in your room, I brought along a few more historic records," Dottie said, pushing some leather-bound books and an inch or two of files across the table towards me.

"Gee, thanks," I said. "I guess I know what I'm doing this afternoon."

"Unless you want me to book you a massage at Casa Palmero," she said.

"Thanks, but no," I said, as my soup arrived. "I do need to start digging in."

"Is there anyone you'd like to talk to while you're here?" she asked. "I can make a call, help set it up."

"How about Harold Meyer, Jack Harwood and Will Becker?" I said. "That would work. For a start."

Her eyes widened. "Geez Louise," she said. "Why don't you ask me to get you an appointment with the governor? Why do you want to speak with the ownership team?"

"I just thought it might be interesting to talk with them about what it was like buying this famous property, how the experience has been over the years, and what they intend to do now, without J.J. Udall." I was making this up on the fly, as usual, but someone once advised me, when doing an interview, to ask for the moon first, and then whittle down the request to something more manageable.

Dottie was shaking her head. "I dunno, Hacker," she said. "I can ask, but I can't guarantee what they might say. Meyer's up in San Francisco, hardly ever comes down here. Jack might be off shooting a movie in Indonesia, for all I know. Becker's usually around—he lives just over the hills from here—but I'd have to see what his schedule is like."

"Well, do the best you can," I said. "I'll study up with this stuff in the meantime." I waved a hand at the books and files she had brought with her.

"I hear you're married now," she said with a smile.

"Yeah, sorry," I said. "I realize I've broken the hearts of many thousands of women."

She snorted. "Not hardly," she said. "It was kind of surprising to hear, though. We all had you pegged as a lifelong bachelor."

"We?"

"The many thousands of female Hacker fans," she said.

I laughed. I told her a little about Mary Jane. I did not bring out my wallet and show her pictures. Which reminded me that I ought to put some pictures of my family in my wallet, so I could bring them out and show people.

Our lunches arrived and we ate in silence for a while. Even though I'd had a hot dog and a beer just a couple of hours earlier, I was hungry. Must have been all the hacking on the back nine and the sunny day.

"When is this book going to be published?" she asked, after we'd done some damage to our plates.

"Jacob hopes to launch it at the Open in June," I said. "He's thinking a captive audience will jump start sales."

"Well, let us know if there's anything we can do," she said. "We'll certainly carry it in the pro shop."

"Thanks," I said. There was another coffee cup next to Dottie's pot of coffee, so I poured myself some.

"I'll let you know," I said. "Listen, what's the current status of this condo project up in Huckleberry Hill? I just heard about that."

She dumped some sugar and a dollop of milk into her coffee and slowly stirred it with her spoon. As an experienced reporter, I could tell she was delaying her answer, probably until she could come up with something other than the truth.

"To tell you the truth, Hacker, I have no idea," she said finally. It sounded like she was being honest. "I mean, I know about the project, but I haven't heard anything about it for more than a year. The application has been before the CCC for about five years now, and they tend to move pretty damn slowly."

"So it's still on the to-do list," I said.

She squirmed a little. "Well, yes and no, I guess," she said. "I mean, yes, it's still a project that we want to do at some point in the future, but that depends on getting all the approvals from the Coastal Commission, and we know how hard that can be. Believe me, we know. We've danced with that group before, many times."

"So you don't have the bulldozers all gassed up and ready to go," I said.

She smiled. "Oh, hell no," she said. "My guess is at least five years out. More like ten. Why do you ask? That project doesn't have much to do with the history of Pebble Beach and the Open, does it?"

She looked at me, challenging me to defend sticking my nose into something she obviously didn't want to talk about."

"Oh, just from my research," I said. "I saw a reference to Huckleberry Hill and asked someone about it."

"That someone wasn't Jake Strauss, was it?" she asked, frowning. "He should know better."

I laughed. "You know we writers never divulge our sources, Dottie," I said. "But no, it wasn't Jake."

She sipped some coffee and ate a bite or two or her salad.

"Of course, you would protect him if he was the source," she said. "You reporters are all alike. Sneaky."

"Only because corporate bastards like you are secretive," I said.

"'Corporate bastard'?" she said with a sniff. "Well that's a new one. Been called just about everything else in the book."

I laughed. I knew she wouldn't take it seriously. Dottie van Dyke has been around the block a few times.

"What else can I help with?" she said.

"What's going on with the corporate leadership?" I asked. "I understand that with Udall dead and buried, there may be some changes coming."

She nodded, as if she had been expecting this line of questioning.

"Yes, I suppose that is to be expected," she said. "But we've all been told that the management structure will remain the same. The remaining three principal owners will continue in their roles. I believe the next annual meeting of the corporation is scheduled for July, a few weeks after the Open, so any announcements of any tweaks to the corporate structure will happen then."

"What is the difference between a tweak and a change?"

She paused, looked at me with what appeared to be a stern expression.

"Are you being an asshole?" she said.

"I don't think so," I said, smiling my best winning smile at her.

"Then let me try again," she said. "I've been told that nothing is going to change. But if something does change, then it will be announced at the annual meeting of the corporation in July. OK?"

"Got it," I said. "Nice bit of tap dancing."

"Bite me," she said.

"Last question," I said. "Do you know someone named Michael Newell?"

She paused, thinking. "I don't think so," she said. "Am I supposed to? Who is he?"

"I don't know," I said. "But I'm supposed to find him."

She got up, closed her laptop and pushed her chair back in.

"Well, Hacker, there are only about 40 million of us living here in the Golden State," she said. "Good luck to you."

"And the Red Sox," I said softly. But she had already left.

CHAPTER 9

I WENT BACK to my room and added the pile of new stuff Dottie had brought to the pile of old stuff she had delivered yesterday. My fruit basket was still there, untouched and beginning to smell like well-ripened fruit. I ate a strawberry, just so no one could accuse me of being ungrateful.

My reading and research pile now contained three books and at least two inches of paper. I looked at all that, then looked at my comfortable king-sized bed, draped with fine linens of Egyptian cotton with a thread count even a Pharaoh could love. I had been up since 4:30, played eighteen holes, and had consumed a couple of beers and a rich hamburger. And artichoke soup. My eyes suddenly felt heavy and I knew that trying to read anything right now would last for exactly one paragraph before I fell asleep. So I skipped the part of opening a file folder or a book cover and just stretched out on the bed, turned on the TV and dialed up the cable news channel for background noise and fell fast and deeply asleep.

When I woke up a few hours later, the December twilight was coming up fast and the ocean out my window was colored a deep shade of gold by the setting sun. The idiots

An Open Case of Death

on the box were telling me the same news they had been telling me a couple hours earlier, trying hard to make me believe it was still "breaking news." I shut it off, got up and stretched, looked at the pile of reading and thought about taking a long hot shower and ordering some coffee. The phone rang.

"Mister Hacker," said a deep and somewhat familiar voice when I answered. "This is Jack Harwood. Am I interrupting you?"

When he told me his name, I put that voice with the famous face it belonged to. Deep, intelligent but with a menacing undertone, that voice had been entertaining people for decades. Starting with those early spaghetti Westerns, where the dirt-streaked, sweaty Jack Harwood had survived attacks from both the Indian savages and the white double-dealers in the dusty desolate towns to win the love of the girl at the end of Act 3; through the popular police dramas of the '80s and '90's, when his recurring cop character, Bad Barry, had patrolled the dark and dangerous Big City streets, getting shot at by bad guys and undermined by corrupt bosses; and on into his later years, when he directed and acted in all kinds of dramas and romances and comedies … through all of that, the voice of Jack Harwood had remained indelibly the same. And now, improbably, it was talking to me.

"Not at all, Mr. Harwood," I said.

"Call me Jack," he said. "I wonder if you are free to join me for a little dinner tonight? Maybe around seven? I was going to grill a couple of steaks. I know you're staying in the finest resort in the world, but I'd appreciate it if you could make your way over here to my place. I don't like to go out after dark any more. My eyes aren't quite what they used to be."

"Not a problem," I said. "I'd be glad to come over."

"Wonderful," he said. He gave me the address and some directions. "We'll look for you around seven. Ta-ta."

I called Mary Jane. It was a little after eight back on the Right Coast.

"Hi, honey," she said when she answered. "We're just finishing dinner. We had fish sticks."

"Yum," I said. "I just got invited to dinner at Jack's."

"Jack who? Nicklaus??"

"Jack Harwood," I said. As nonchalantly as I could.

"Get out of town!" she exclaimed. I heard Victoria in the background say "What, Mommy?"

"It's true," I said. "He just called and invited me over. Around seven."

"Oh my God," she said. "What are you going to wear?"

I laughed. "Clothes, I think," I said. "I'll wait until I get there for the nightly movie star orgy to get started before I strip down."

"Shut up," she ordered. "That is so exciting. Why does he want you to come over? Did he say?"

"No, actually, he didn't," I said. "But I suspect it has something to do with the book. I asked Dottie van Dyke at lunch today to get me interviews with all the ownership. Hell, he knows more about the history of this place than anybody. He used to play in the Crosby."

"What's a Crosby?" she asked.

`I sighed. "I'll explain it later," I said.

"Well, mind your manners and try not to piss him off," she said. "Having someone like Jack Harwood in your corner could prove helpful down the road. Maybe you two could collaborate on a golf movie or something."

"What if he pisses *me* off?" I asked. "Pissing off can be a two-way street."

"That's the Hacker I know and love," she said and rang off.

An Open Case of Death

SHOWERED, SHAVED AND wearing a fresh coat of deodorant, I jumped in my car just before seven and followed the directions Jack had given me: across 17-Mile Drive from The Lodge and up the hill above the resort. This was a neighborhood of *mansions summa est*—each one looked bigger and more elaborate than the next: huge gated entrances, flowing formal gardens, outbuildings for the servants. As I passed all this opulence, most decorated gaily for Christmas, I began to wonder if my ten-year-old blue blazer, purchased for a hundred bucks from Land's End, and still a little wrinkled from the plane ride west, would pass muster.

I pulled into the address Harwood had given me, and found myself on a large square parking lot covered in crushed seashells outside a rather plain looking one-story brick hacienda. After driving past all the mega-mansions, I was a bit disappointed: Jack's place didn't look like that much, at least from the outside.

A guy dressed in a long-sleeved black polo, chinos and black sneakers appeared from somewhere and waved me into a parking space near an open archway.

"Right this way, Mister Hacker," the guy said when I got out of my car. "Mister Harwood is waiting for you on the terrace."

"Lovely," I said. "Lead on, MacDuff."

MacDuff led me through the wooden arch and into an expansive open courtyard, tiled in herringbone ceramics with a central fountain gushing water upwards, the spray caught in the bright floods. There were large liveoak trees at the corners of the courtyard, and the walls of the surrounding building—which I could now see was an impressive rectangle of a hacienda—were all old yellow adobe brick with windows and doors framed in heavy oak timbers.

We walked in through a pair of towering oak doors, five inches thick and dotted with squares of black wrought iron, and entered a massive, forty-foot long living room, criss-crossed above in heavy wooden beams. At one end, a floor-to-ceiling fireplace, covered in intricate Spanish-style tiles, contained a crackling fire which threw out the scent of resinous wood that infused the entire room.

MacDuff motioned for me to continue to follow, and he led me out to the broad terrace which looked down to Carmel Bay and across to Point Lobos. The sun had set an hour ago, but the Western sky still glowed faintly with the last light of the day. The twinkling lights of the houses across the Bay, and the floods the mansion owners around us had thrown on to show off their trees and lawns, were quite pretty. Another arm of the hill we were on and the tall trees growing there blocked any view of the village of Carmel at the eastern end of the bay, but a soft glowing aura in the night sky told us it was still there.

There was another fire going in a round rocky pit built into the terrace, and a jumble of cushioned chairs and chaises were scattered across the space. Jack Harwood was standing next to his fire pit, poking at the logs burning there with a metal tool, sending red sparks rising up into the night air.

"Mister Hacker, I presume," Harwood said as I approached, nodding my thanks to MacDuff who turned and disappeared back into the house. "C'mon in."

We shook hands. "Too bad your view sucks," I said, motioning out towards the beauty of Carmel Bay. "Otherwise, this place might be worth some bucks."

He chuckled, which I took as a good sign, and waved me into a chair near the firepit. The heat it was throwing off felt good as the chill of the night set in. MacDuff came back out carrying a small silver tray with two cocktails on it.

"Bourbon Old Fashioned," Jack said, picking one glass off the tray and motioning for me to take the other. "For some reason, I always drink them here and nowhere else. They seem to taste better here with my crappy view than down in L.A. or out in Wyoming."

I took a sample sip: the rich bourbon contrasted with the sweetness of ginger ale, but allowed the tartness of the Angostura bitters to fill in at the bottom. And my glass had three nice round maraschino cherries and a slice of orange stuck on a wooden toothpick, floating in the drink. I love maraschino cherries.

"Nice," I said. "But I'd have to try one in L.A. before I arrived at a final judgment."

He laughed. "Well, we'll have to see if that can be arranged," he said.

Jack Harwood was, I knew, in his early-eighties, but only the lines I could see etched around his eyes and on his neck gave away any sign of advanced age. He was a small man—most movie actors are short in stature—but looked quite fit. His body was lean and chiseled, and he gave off an aura of energy and masculine fitness. He had a full head of wispy white hair, matched by his famous errantly bushy eyebrows. When he smiled, his teeth were bright white, almost glistening in the firelight. He was dressed casually in corduroy slacks and a designer sweatshirt of some kind: it looked plain and simple, but, likely made from the wool of endangered yaks, probably cost $500 in some Rodeo Drive men's shop. He looked at me with that famous Jack Harwood scowl: a squinty, eyes narrowed glare that almost dared me to make my move. But I had seen enough Jack Harwood movies to know what happened to the poor sap who made that first move: it was never good and often fatal.

He came and sat down next to me, put his feet up on a wooden stool. He raised his glass. "Welcome to the House of Harwood," he said. We clinked glasses and drank. Me and Jack Harwood, having cocktails in Pebble Beach, on the terrace of a mansion likely worthy seven or eight times what I would make in my entire lifetime. Pretty damn cool.

"House of Harwood," I said. "Don't you have some appropriately Spanish name for this place? Cortez's Revenge or the Hacienda de Heaven or something?"

He chuckled. "I always thought naming houses was pretentious," he said. "It's my goddam house, and has been for about twenty-five years now. So I call it the House of Harwood, because that's what it is."

"Why did you settle down here?" I asked. "I mean, I know Los Angeles is a rat's nest of a city, but that's where your industry is based. Why do you live up here?"

He sat back and took a sip from his drink. "I was in the Army, stationed over at Fort Ord north of Monterey," he said. "This was years and years ago, late fifties, early sixties. I'd come over to Carmel with some of the guys from the base, looking for some cold beer and hot chicks, of course, and kinda fell in love with the place. So when I finally started to make some money in the movie business, I came up here to look around. This is about the fourth or fifth place I bought up here, each one a little better than the last. Hit the jackpot with this baby, though."

He took another sip and looked around, with a sigh. "Hate the idea of selling it, although I suppose all things must end. My manager wants me to deep-six it, but I guess I'm kinda attached to it by now."

"Well," I said, "If you can't find anyone to leave it to, the name's Hacker. H-A-C-K-E-R."

He laughed again and raised his glass. "I'll keep that in mind, Mister Hacker," he said.

MacDuff came back out onto the terrace, this time holding a tray with two large pieces of raw meat. He went over to the huge stainless steel barbecue grill on the far side of the terrace and, opening the top lid, threw the hunks of steak down on the grill which was glowing red with heat. The meat sizzled and immediately began to smoke. My mouth began to water.

An Open Case of Death

"So how is the book coming along?" Harwood interrupted my steak fantasy. "I thought you might have some questions I could help with. I've been playing golf here at Pebble Beach since I was eighteen years old. They actually let us enlisted pukes play for free on Mondays and Tuesdays back in the day."

He paused, reminiscing. "That was before the accountants took over and everything had to be monetized," he said. "Hell, some of us in the Army truck pool would volunteer to work weekends just so we could be here at five a.m. on Monday morning, ready to be first off the tee. Sometimes, if business was slow, they'd let us go around a second time. Can you imagine?"

"Sounds pretty awesome," I said. And it did.

"Afterwards, we'd go into Carmel, hit the bar at the Hog's Breath Saloon," he said. "Beer was seventy cents a glass." He took a sip from his drink. "Man, life doesn't get a whole lot better than that."

I let him sit there with his memories for a count or two.

"I'm just getting started on the book," I said. "Dottie van Dyke has loaded me up with reading material, which I'll probably take back to Boston. But you used to play in the Crosby, right?"

"Oh, sure," he said. "Bing brought his tournament up here in 1947, after the war. He had started it originally down near San Diego, near the racetrack he owned. After the war, Crosby was looking for a new place for his little tournament. I'm sure some money changed hands somewhere, but he brought it up here and all his friends from Hollywood came up to play. The Crosby Clambake."

"I understand the betting was rather ferocious," I said.

"Dear God, you could've funded a small country with what they bet in the Calcutta," Harwood said, chuckling softly to himself. "I didn't start playing until the late 60's...I think my first was 1968. But the stories some of the old timers told me…hundreds of thousands changed hands. Some of the pros got in on the action. Hell, they probably made more betting than they could win on the course. Sam Snead was always buying teams left and right. He liked to make a little on the side whenever he could."

"You ever come close to winning?" I asked.

"Nah," he said with another soft chuckle. "You gotta have one of two things to win the Crosby, or whatever the hell they call it now. One, a pro who goes totally insane and makes everything he looks at all weekend. Or, two: an amateur who cheats like fuck." He laughed. "I was either too honest or too bad to do the latter, and I never had a pro partner who went nutso. But Jeez, win or lose, you always had a good time. And not just with the golf. Every night there'd be a big party, and the entertainment was off the charts. Sinatra would sing, or Dean Martin and Jerry Lewis would do half an hour of their best schtick. Fuckin' Buddy Hackett would have them rolling on the floor. There'd be girls, booze, even some drugs…man, those were the days!"

MacDuff finished grilling the steaks, put them back on his tray and went back inside.

"Guess it's time to eat," Harwood said. "After Bing died, I think it was around 1977, '78, everything changed. Of course, it started changing when they put the tournament on TV, which was back in 1958. Then, like everything else, it became all about the money. Television ruins everything it touches."

"Says one of the stars of the entertainment industry," I said.

"Touché," he said, nodding at me. "But I don't do any of my work for television. Here's how I see it…the old Crosby Clambake was like a bottle of fine wine. See, some people love golf, but don't particularly like pro-ams. Others like coming out to watch the celebrities, but don't know shit about golf. OK? It's an acquired taste. If you liked that kind of thing, like that particular bottle of wine, it was almost perfect the way it was. But then TV came along and took that bottle of fine wine and poured it out on the ground and said 'If you want some of this, lick it up off the dirt.' That's what TV does. Lowest fucking denominator."

"And millions of people licked it up," I said. "Still do. Willingly."

Jack Harwood drained the last of his cocktail and stood up.

"And that, Mister Hacker, is why this country finds itself in the crapper," he said. "Let's eat."

The dining room, perpendicular to the long living room, was also Spanish: high, heavy wooden beams across the ceiling, terracotta floor in hexagonal shapes, and a long wooden table that could have easily held twenty guests. MacDuff had set two places at the far end: Harwood at the head, and one for little old me at his side. We sat down, Harwood poured two glasses of red wine from the crystal decanter next to his place. MacDuff came out and set two dinner plates down: the grilled steaks, a baked potato and a few stalks of asparagus.

He lifted his wine glass toward me. "Salude," he said. We clinked and I took a sip. The red was delicious, fruity, rich and with a slightly peppery finish.

"Nice," I said.

"Thanks," Jack said. "It's from my vineyard. Grapes grow well in the hills up above town. Great country out there. We grow mencía up there and my guy mixes in a little Shiraz at the end."

"You sell a lot?" I had to admit, I had no idea that Jack Harwood was in the wine business, too.

"Nah," he said, shaking his head. "Couple hundred cases a year. It's mostly a hobby. And I like to drink stuff I like, so I just make it myself."

"Good to be the king," I said.

"Amen to that," he said.

After that, we stopped talking and began eating. The steaks were perfect, medium rare. There was a little tub of béarnaise sauce to dabble on the meat. I was hungry, since it had been some hours since lunch, and dug in with relish.

I mentioned that the dining room looked like it hosted some big dinner parties in the past, and Harwood started telling me some Hollywood stories, finishing with a long and hilarious tale of the time the comedian Red Skelton challenged the actor Telly Savalas to a duel over the favors of a certain well-endowed young lady who had come to dinner with someone else entirely. Swords had improbably been produced, taken down from a display on the wall, and a long and drunken fight had ensued, complete with f-bomb laced insults, Shakespearean posturing and a hearty clashing of swords that took the combatants up and over the dining table and all around the house. "It's a bloody miracle that neither of them died that night," Harwood said with his sideways grin. "But it was a great sword fight. I always regretted not having filmed it. It had everything: Dialogue! Action! And the damsel off in the corner hiding her eyes but wanting to see which Lothario was going to win her heart."

He painted the scene so brilliantly that I could envision the two Hollywood figures going at it, sword and tong, knocking dishes off the table and turning over chairs.

MacDuff came in and announced coffee in front of the fireplace, so Harwood and I moved into the living room. He sat in a leather chair next to the fire, while I sat on the plush sofa. MacDuff poured each of us a steaming mug and disappeared again.

Harwood took a sip of his coffee and sat back in his chair, holding the mug on his lap.

"I was sorry to hear of J.J. Udall's passing," I said. He closed his eyes and nodded. "Were you two close?"

"I wouldn't say we were the best of friends," he said, "But I always got along with him. Smart dude. Knew everyone in the sports world. Fun guy on the golf course, which is important in my book."

"Did all of you owners get together regularly?"

He nodded. "Yeah, couple times a year. We'd all synchronize our schedules and find a weekend we could all come up here. We'd review the numbers, ask a few questions. Jake Strauss was usually on hand if there was something big afoot."

"Like what?"

"Oh, you know…" he waved his hand, "Big capital expenditures or some new building that needed construction. Strauss was the banker, so if we needed a banker's opinion on something, we dragged him in."

"How is it going to work now that Udall is gone?" I asked.

He was silent for a beat or two. I wondered if I had asked one too many questions.

"You know, Hacker, I'm not sure," he said. "It's my understanding that all the arrangements were made for how we handle the passing of one of the principal shareholders. After all, none of the four of us is exactly a spring chicken anymore. I think Jake and the lawyers had it all worked out. I guess we'll find out what happens next when we find out."

"You worried at all?"

"Nah," he shook his head. "Investing in this place was rock solid. They don't make places like Pebble Beach anymore. You can't lose money owning a piece of a place like this."

He paused, thinking.

"But I am going to miss J.J.," he said. "You know, I think I was the last one to see him alive."

"Really?"

"Yeah. I heard about his heart attack when I was down in L.A.," he said. "I came up to Frisco as soon as I could, and went to the hospital to see how he was. He was a little weak, and they had him pumped full of drugs, but he seemed to be in good spirits. Gave me the usual ration of shit."

He stroked his chin, remembering.

"I remember, though, something he said just before I left him that night. He told me to be careful. Not to trust anyone."

"About what?"

"Don't know," Harwood said. "He never said exactly what I was supposed to be careful about. I figured he was just a little disoriented, maybe drugged up with something they gave him. He passed away the next afternoon. They told me he seemed to be doing fine. It looked like he was going to recover, get out of the hospital and get on with it. But the nurse checked in on him the next afternoon and he was gone. The docs were surprised. But he was an old coot, his heart was weak, and I guess his time was just up."

He yawned, which reminded me that Jack Harwood was an old coot, too, and that it was time to go. I thanked him, he wished me well on the book, told me to call him if I had any other questions, and I made my way back down the hill, past all the gaily lit mansions and back into the lap of luxury at Pebble Beach.

Chapter 10

I parked my car in the lot near my room, but instead of going inside, I went out on the Terrace Lounge at the rear of the Lodge, to take in some night air, look at the stars, listen to the surf pounding against the seawall along the 18th fairway. There was a fire pit out there, filled with logs burning merrily, throwing out the smell of cedar.

I heard a siren in the distance, which got louder and louder as it got closer. Then I heard another. The klaxons pierced the night air. I heard a noise up above and saw a helicopter flying by. I watched as it headed out to the point of land where the seventh green and eighth tee was located, on that rocky headland extending out into Carmel Bay. The copter flipped on a search light and began circling around. The sirens stopped, but then I could see the flashing red lights of two emergency vehicles driving down the sixth fairway: a fire engine and an ambulance. Something was going on out there. But what? A boat on the rocks?

I heard another siren coming up from 17 Mile Drive, and decided maybe I should go take a look. The old newspaperman instinct, I guess. Get it first, get it fast, get it right. I went back inside the Lodge, then out the front door and turned right towards the golf clubhouse above the first tee. Someone had turned on the floodlights on the clubhouse roofline, and the tee area and cart path area next to the tee was bathed in a pool of golden light. A couple of green, roofed carts were parked there, and a couple of men came bursting out of the clubhouse and down the stairs. I jogged over.

"What's going on?" I asked one guy, who was wearing a white shirt with epaulets and a golden badge over one breast. He looked like a security guard.

"There's been an accident out on eight," he said. "Cart over the cliff."

He jumped behind the wheel of one of the carts. I jumped in next to him. He looked at me, frowning.

"Maybe I can help," I said. He shrugged and we took off.

It took us about five minutes to drive all the way out to the eighth hole, including a couple full-speed jumps over the four-inch asphalt curbing. I had to hand on for dear life to avoid being jarred out of the cart and left to tumble down the green grass. My driver didn't apologize, but kept his foot on the gas.

The emergency vehicles—the fire engine, ambulance and a police cruiser—were parked on the bluff high above the beach when we arrived. The flashing lights washed across the darkness. There are little white posts hammered into the turf along the edge of the cliff up there, with yellow rope strung between. You have to be blind not to see the barrier; you have to be suicidal to drive over them. But somebody had. Two of the posts were dislodged and the rope stretched out towards the edge of the cliff. A group of firemen and a police officer were gathered at the edge, peering down over the side, pointing down with their flashlights.

An Open Case of Death

The security guy and I joined them. The hovering helicopter's search light was now focused on the rocky scrim at the bottom of the cliff, where the orange rocks had eroded off the face of the cliff over the years and gathered on the white sandy beach. The search light was centered on one of the Pebble Beach's dark green carts, crushed nose first onto those rocks, its white plastic roof crumpled and broken off to the side. Whoever had been sitting in that cart was now hanging out what had been the windshield. We could see an arm, the torso and part of a leg. Nothing was moving.

Two police ATV units came buzzing up the beach from the direction of Carmel, blue lights flashing and their single front headlights showing the way. They parked near the crashed cart and the officers went to examine the victim. There was a rasping sound from the radio mic from the police officer standing next to us on the top of the cliff.

"We got a 10-50 here base," the disembodied voice said over the radio. "Victim unresponsive. Appears fatal. No pulse detected. We'll need the meat wagon."

"Roger that," came the response. "10-53 at Pebble Beach, Arrowhead Point. Units responding."

The cop whistled softly to himself. "Hoo, man. Been a long time since someone went over the cliff," he said. "I'm guessing alcohol was involved. Pounded the wine at dinner, found a cart, went for a little joyride, and boom!"

"Isn't there usually a woman involved?" I asked. "Guy showing off, maybe hoping for a little action once he impresses her with his driving skills?"

"Good point," the cop nodded. He pressed the mic on his radio.

"Uh, 1445 … any passengers down there?"

There was a short delay, then the response.

"Negative. One male."

The cop sighed. "I'd better look around. Maybe she jumped out."

He pulled out his flashlight and began sweeping its beam around the area. A couple of the firefighters, with nothing else to do, did the same. They checked all around the clifftop, looking back toward the tee and over towards the sixth fairway. But it was all empty out there. Not a soul in sight.

The security guard had his phone out and was busily calling someone. Probably his supervisor. The death of a guest is always a tragedy. It's also a huge potential liability for a company. There would be hell to pay, and unless the Pebble Beach lawyers could step in quickly, there would be millions in damages to pay as well.

I edged away from the group of first responders and made my way carefully in the dark around towards the eighth green. From there, using the flashlight feature on my cell phone, I was able to make my way to climb down through the weeds and scrub to the beach and then over to the base of the cliff where a small crowd of onlookers had gathered. It doesn't seem to matter where or what time a tragedy occurs, there are always people who come out to gawk.

One of the police officers who had ridden up the beach on his ATV was talking to a young couple holding a dog on a leash. The woman was tearfully relating her story.

"We were just out for a walk with Chippie, and we heard this awful crunching sound," she was saying. "Like a bang and a squish together, y'know? We were way over there…" She pointed down the beach back toward Carmel…but it sounded like it was right next to us, it was that loud. Bobby here ran up, saw the cart, and called 9-1-1."

"Yes, ma'am," the cop said, writing in his notebook. "Did you see anyone else? Anyone up on top of the cliff?"

"N-no," she stammered. "I mean, we weren't looking at anything. We were just walking Chippie and holding hands and talking and then we heard this crunch. It was awful. But no, I couldn't see anyone else around at all."

"Any voices before the crash?" I said. "Yelling? Screams?"

The cop looked at me like he wanted to say something, like *butt out, bub,* but he didn't. The couple looked at me.

"No, sir," the woman said. "I just remember the crash." She turned and looked at the man. "Bob?"

"No, I just remember the crashing sound," her male friend said. "It was quiet before that."

The cop began taking down their names and other information. I edged away and wandered over to the crash scene, which was now illuminated by several flood lights. Several other emergency vehicles had driven down the beach and stopped at the base of the cliff, and five or six of responders were working to extricate the body from the wreckage of the cart. They carefully pulled him through the shattered windshield and carried him over to the beach, laying him down on the white sand.

One of the cops flashed his light on the face. I sucked in my breath. There was an unruly shock of red hair illuminated in the lights.

It was Charlie Sykes, assistant golf professional. And he was very, very dead.

CHAPTER 11

BACK IN BOSTON, the black hole of Christmas sucked in all other activities for the next two weeks. The old town actually looks pretty festive at Christmas: the shops and stores are all nicely lit up, people trade in their usual snarly countenances for something that resembles a smile, and the ice rink on the Commons is filled with kids having some noisy fun in the cold. Maybe not quite the full Dickens with plucked geese hanging in the butcher's window, but close enough.

I returned from Pebble Beach in a somber mood. Death will do that to you. I had given a statement to the police, of course. I had played a round with Charlie that morning, yes. He had won forty dollars from me, yes. I was not angry enough about that to push him and a cart over the cliff, no. I think the cops believed me, because they let me go home. Or maybe because they checked with Jack Harwood who had confirmed that I was having dinner with him at the House of Harwood when young Charlie went over the cliff.

Everyone seemed to believe that it was a suicide. Or maybe everyone wanted to believe it was a suicide. Certainly the Pebble Beach Company wanted to believe that.

An Open Case of Death

Far less liability for that. The police sent the body off to the coroner and promised a full toxicology report in due course.

Then we all went home. Back to our normal lives. It was Christmas, after all. Not the season to be thinking about death. I came home in a foul mood. But Mary Jane helped jolly me out of it. Well, actually, she told me to damn well snap out it, it was Christmas and she wasn't going to let me ruin Victoria's holiday. She was right, of course.

So, once Mary Jane and Victoria were out of school, we did the normal family holiday things: shopping along Newbury Street, buying and decorating the tree, attending a matinee performance of the Nutcracker at the Boston Ballet, drinking cocoa and watching all the Christmas movies on TV. Even Mister Shit the cat seemed to get into the spirit of the season and sought out my lap for a brief midwinter's nap on the afternoon I watched some playoff football games.

On Christmas Eve, we delivered Victoria to her grandfather's house where all her cousins would gather for a traditional Italian feast and midnight Mass. Many of them probably had a lot to seek redemption for. We promised we'd be there bright and early the next morning for breakfast and to see what Santa had brought. Then we went home. I grilled a couple of ribeyes on the balcony hitachi, baked a couple of potatoes, tossed a green salad and opened a nice bottle of Bordeaux. Mary Jane was busy as a bee, wrapping the last few presents and singing carols to herself softly. I smiled.

"I'm feeling rather domesticated," I said when MJ swept through the room, trailing wrapping paper, ribbon and tape in her wake.

"Is that OK?" she asked. "No second thoughts about this whole marriage thing?"

"Oh, hell no," I assured her. "I'm as happy as an unfried clam. It's just all this … *activity* … is a little different for me."

"How did you usually celebrate Christmas?"

I thought back. "When I was a kid, my aunt and uncle never made a big deal out of the holidays," I said. "They had a fake tree from Sears when I was still a little kid. But once I hit my teens, they even quit doing that much. We usually gave each other one gift. I usually got a sweater or a pair of woolly socks. I would buy them a tin of Danish sugar cookies from the supermarket. That was about that."

"How sad," she said, plopping down next to me and picking up a glass of red wine to sip. "I had six brothers and sisters, so Christmas for us was basically unqualified madness from Thanksgiving through New Year's. What did you do for Christmas when you grew up?"

"I'd go out on Christmas Eve and buy a bottle of bourbon and a new book," I said. "And on Christmas, I'd drink the bourbon and read the book."

"That's it?"

"Sometimes I'd splurge and order in a pizza, extra cheese," I said. "That was if it had been a good year."

"That's pathetic," she said.

"I never thought so," I said. "I thought it was nice. Peaceful."

We ate our dinner, washed the dishes and snuggled for a bit on the couch. Then, around ten, we bundled up in our warm coats and boots and went out into the frosty cold. The nearly full moon cast a silvery glow on the narrow streets of the North End, which were also decorated in garlands and Christmas lights.

We strolled arm in arm over to Salem Street and got in the line that had already formed for the eleven o'clock service at the Old North Church, of the "one if by land" fame. They let us file in early to get out of the cold and we sat up

An Open Case of Death

in the balcony on the side of the old church, gazing down at the box pews on the main floor of the sanctuary. Christ Church, the proper name of the Old North, used to sell those boxes to its vestrymen and other wealthy members of the church, and families often passed them down over the generations. Some of Boston's most famous early fathers—Revere, Hancock and others—once worshiped here.

The church was decorated to its arched ceiling in greenery and bunches of candles cast a calming glow. When the service began, the white-robed choir marched in and we all sang the old familiar Christmas hymns and carols. It was pleasant. It was peaceful. We felt connected, for a while, to the rest of the world, both the living and the dead.

When we got home, there was a little of the wine left in the bottle, which we shared. Between that and the residual warm feeling from the church service, we were both glowing a bit. We sat in our darkened apartment, with our tree alight, and the cat sleeping silently in his favorite chair. Mary Jane put something classical on and we enjoyed the peace.

Eventually, Mary Jane put her wine glass down, took hold of my hand and led me into our bedroom. We unwrapped each other like the best present ever, and got into our warm bed. Then we made sweet love until we fell into a deep sleep, dreaming of sugarplums and fairies, holes-in-one and woolen socks.

CHAPTER 12

IN THE WEEK between Christmas and New Year's, I took over our little dinette table, spreading out the file folders and pages of information Dottie van Dyke had sent home with me. I had dutifully underlined and highlighted passages I might need, and the papers and my notes began to spill over onto the floor around my feet. Organized? Nah. But I knew where everything was. Mister Shit came over, sat down on a manila folder, cocked his head and gave me one of those "*you can't be serious*" looks that cats do so well.

I didn't think I was bothering anyone until one afternoon, when Victoria had gone off for a play date with a school mate, Mary Jane walked in with her own armload of papers for a curriculum-planning session, sat down in an empty chair, looked at the mess I had created, cocked her head and gave me one of those "*what the hell are you doing?*" looks that women do so well.

"Sorry," I said, and tried to move some stuff out of her way. "My research is getting out of hand."

"You know, Hacker," she said, glancing at the piles of paper on the table, two of the three chairs and several square feet of floor, "You don't have to go all the way back to Christopher Columbus to write the history of the place."

An Open Case of Death

"Junipero Serra," I said.

"What?"

"Father Junipero Serra," I said. "Now he's Saint Junipero Serra. He was a Spanish priest who founded a Catholic mission in Carmel-by-the-Sea that became the headquarters for all the missions in Alta California. Put the place on the map. The mission has a name..." I began shuffling through some of the papers. "I just had it a second ago."

"Hacker." Her voice was calm, but there was an undeniable undertone of disdain.

"What?" I was still looking for the pages on the Spanish mission of 1752 or thereabouts.

"I'm not a big golfer, and I do like history, but I'm pretty sure the name of the Spanish mission in Carmel has absolutely zero relevance for how the U.S. Golf Association came to hold their national championships on the golf course at Pebble Beach."

She took her notebooks and papers and went into the living room where she sat down on the couch.

"You think I'm overdoing it?"

"Yes, dear," she called, even though she was only about ten feet away.

I sat there and thought about this for a minute.

"So the stuff about how Monterey was once the capital of colonial California, until they discovered gold at Sutter's Mill outside Sacramento in 1848, after which they moved lock, stock and governor ... I should deep-six all that?"

"Don't see how it's important, dear," she said sweetly.

I flipped through a few more pages of notes.

"How about the Pacific Improvement Company?" I asked. "And the plans to develop what is now the exclusive neighborhood of Pebble Beach into an early twentieth-century version of Levittown, with rows and rows of little boxy houses on quarter-acre lots?"

"Well, that sounds partially interesting," she said, although I could tell she was only half-listening. "Tell me more."

"Ah," I said, and reached for my stack of PIC papers. "OK, it was right after the Civil War and the U.S. government decided to build the Transcontinental Railroad across the U.S. of A.."

"Yes," she said. "I heard about that. In seventh grade."

"So these four guys moved out West from New York to seek their fortunes, and they formed a company to build the railroad from Oakland heading east. They got paid something like twenty thousand bucks a mile except for the mountains, for which they got paid twice as much. Naturally, they told the government most of the roadbed was in the mountains. And they used Chinese coolie labor, paying subsistence wages, so they made even more. These four guys ended up as rich as Warren Buffet."

"Ah, yes," Mary Jane said, her head buried in her course planner. I heard her pencil scratching furiously away. "Rapacious capitalists suckling at the public teat while exploiting labor. Kind of the story of America. I believe you'll find it continues to this day."

"It does?"

"You've heard of the military-industrial complex? Same thing."

"Right," I said. It was too early in the day to start drinking, and thus not an auspicious time to begin a political discussion. "So these four rich guys started up a company which began investing its profits in real estate and other companies and all kinds of things."

"Of course they did," Mary Jane said. "That's what rapacious capitalists do."

"Well, yeah," I said. "One of the four used his money to start a university."

"Was his name Berkeley?" she asked.

"Ha ha," I said. "No, it was Leland Stanford."

"Oh, yes," she said. "Heard of that one."

"Anyway, one of the chunks of real estate this company—they called it the Pacific Improvement Company, or PIC—assembled was in Monterey and Carmel," I said. They owned virtually the entire Monterey Peninsula and way up into the Carmel Valley. Thousands and thousands of acres."

"How lovely for them," Mary Jane said. "Are they the ones who wanted to build tiny little houses all over the Pebble Beach golf course?"

"Well, yes," I said. "But you're getting ahead of the story. There wasn't a golf course there yet."

"How about Jupiter Serra?" she asked. "Had he arrived yet on his mission?"

"Junipero," I said. "Pay attention. So the four rich guys bought up all this land, and a bunch of other stuff, and the years go by and the four guys die …"

"Please tell me they weren't murdered," Mary Jane said. "People you know have a terrible habit of getting murdered. Or committing suicide by driving golf carts over cliffs and all."

"Jesus H. Christ," I said. "I wonder if Michael Beschloss or Doris Kearns Goodwin ever had this much trouble relating history."

"Sorry, dear," she said, sounding not sorry in the least. "Continue."

"So now we're up to 1915 or so," I said. "And the heirs of the original four rich guys decide they want more money so they decide to sell off all the assets held by the Pacific Improvement Company. Cash out. Liquidate the lot."

"How nice for them," Mary Jane said. "All that lovely real estate must have been worth a fortune."

"Well, it was 1915 and California hadn't gone as real estate crazy as it is today," I said. "But yes, the assets were pretty valuable. So the heirs of the four rich guys hired a guy to come in and fix up and sell all the companies and stuff they owned. His name was Samuel F.B. Morse."

"Oh," she said. "I've heard of him. He invented the telegraph machine, right? And the code that they used? Dots and dits and all that?"

"Close, but no cigar," I said. "That was another Samuel F.B. Morse, a distant cousin or something of this guy. Back then, there must have been a limit on names, so they had to use old ones over and over. This guy, we'll call him Sam Morse, took a look at the assets the company owned in Monterey and Carmel and decided he wanted to buy them himself."

"He wanted to be a rapacious capitalist, too!" Mary Jane said. "They say it's catching."

"Whatever," I said. "The original four guys had used some of their filthy wealth to build a huge resort hotel outside of Monterey, called the Del Monte Hotel."

"Oh," she said. "Did they also make that delicious fruit cocktail in heavy syrup that comes in the cans?"

"No," I said. "Different Del Monte."

"Too bad," she said. "I loved that stuff when I was a kid."

"During the Gilded Age, the Del Monte was a famous destination resort. One of the original four rich guys started the Southern Pacific railroad and he ran a spur line down from San Francisco almost right to the front door of the hotel, so guests had an easy way of getting there."

"What was his name?"

"Crocker," I said. "I forget his first name … Charles or William or something. In addition to the railroad, he owned a big bank in San Francisco."

"Was his wife named Betty?" Mary Jane asked. "That would be funny. I think she invented brownies in a box."

"Different Crocker," I said. "Now at this big hotel there was golf and tennis and horseback riding. You could ride

An Open Case of Death

in a carriage around the edge of the peninsula, looking at the sea and the rocks and the barking seals and the cypress trees, and over above Stillwater Cove there was a log cabin lodge where they served those three-hour lunches of seven or eight courses and then you could stumble back into the carriage and go back to the big hotel and have another huge dinner of twelve or thirteen courses."

"No wonder President Taft was so big," she said. "Those people ate like draft horses back then."

"Rapacious," I said. "So our Sam Morse decided he wanted to buy that hotel and also have a hand in developing the land around Monterey, including Pebble Beach."

"Did he come up with the plan for all those little houses on little lots?"

"No, he threw those plans away," I said. "He had a vision for Pebble Beach that was more like Newport, Rhode Island, with big mansions on the sea and society people living there."

Mary Jane got up, came into the kitchen and poured herself some coffee. "Well, I guess he did it," she said. "Isn't that what's there now? Big mansions and very rich people?"

"Yes," I said. "Plus the golf course, which took up the best real estate, right on the edge of the sea."

"Ah," Mary Jane said, leaning back against the fridge. "We finally get to the golf course, which is the point of this whole exercise, right? Not that I haven't enjoyed hearing all about Junki Serra, Buzzi Berkeley and Sam the Man Morse Code."

I looked at her. "My draft might need some editing," I said.

"Ya think?" she said, smiling broadly. "OK, tell me about the golf course."

"Well," I said, "The interesting thing there was that when Sam Morse decided to build the golf course, instead of all those grids of streets and houses, he still was operating under his original assignment, which was to fix up all the assets and sell them off to the highest bidder. So, since he wanted to be the highest bidder, Sam Morse cheaped out and just hired a couple of local golfers to lay the holes out."

"No architect?" Mary Jane said, raising her eyebrows. "Was Pete Dye even born yet?"

"I don't know," I said. "I'll have to do some research on that." She groaned, softly but audibly. "There were some famous people building golf courses in 1916—Donald Ross was in his prime, and Alister Mackenzie, who built Cypress Point a few years after Pebble Beach opened, was very active in California. But Sam Morse turned to two nobodies who had won some amateur tournaments in California—Jack Neville and Douglas Grant—and told them to go lay out a golf course."

"Did he pay them?" she asked.

"If he did, it wasn't much," I said.

"Hmmm," she said. "More of your fine rapacious capitalism at work, exploiting the worker."

"OK, Che," I said. "But it worked out pretty well. However they did it, they managed to find a pretty sporty golf course on those cliffs and dunes. Neville once said all they did was cut down a few trees, sprinkle some grass seed around and stand back."

"The simple way is always the best," she said. "So when did the US Golf Association hear about it?'

"Well, the golf course at Pebble opened late in 1918, and they held the California Amateur tournament there the next year. People liked the place so much that the Cal Am returned to Pebble Beach for the next forty-five years in a row. But the first USGA event was the US Amateur, in 1929, or ten years after the course officially opened."

"And did the USGA decide to hold its tournament there because they heard the golf course was so great?"

Mary Jane asked. "Or did the rapacious capitalist pig named Morse lay a big fat donation on their ass in return for the tournament and its national publicity?"

"My, my," I said. "Aren't we Little Miss Cynical this afternoon?"

"Cynical yes, yet pure of heart," she said.

I laughed. "Well, I don't know why they selected Pebble Beach, but I imagine they were looking for some good west coast golf courses they could add to the championship roster," I said. "When the USGA was organized, back in 1895, the only one of the six original member clubs not on the East Coast was Chicago. So holding a national championship on the West Coast was good politics. And the course had developed a good reputation."

"But Pebble Beach wasn't a fancy, male-only, private club where no blacks or Jews were allowed," Mary Jane said. "How did they get over *that* hurdle?"

"That will be discussed in Howard Zinn's forthcoming *History of the Golfing Proletariat*," I said. "In my book, I will merely point out that Pebble Beach was the first non-private club venue for the Amateur in its 35 year history to that point. And the first resort course ever chosen for a national championship."

"Zowie," she said. "That's pretty fucking historic."

"Cynical *and* profane," I said. "How did I get so lucky?"

"If you ever want to get lucky again, bub, you'd better have that table cleared off by dinner time," she said. "By the way, who won the '29 Amateur?"

I shuffled through some papers. "Jimmy Johnston," I told her. "He beat Oscar Willing. Willingly, I imagine."

"Jimmy Johnson the football coach?" she said. "Or the NASCAR driver?"

I laughed. "Neither. Johnston, with a T," I said. "He was from St. Paul, Minnesota, and he made a nice recovery from the rocks on the 18th hole on his way to victory. You know who didn't win in 1929, though, right?"

"1929? Warren Harding."

"Good guess, although I don't think the President played the Amateur that year," I said. "He was getting ready for the stock market crash and the onset of the Great Depression. No, it was Bobby Jones who didn't win the Amateur at Pebble Beach in 1929."

"How come? Disqualified for niceness?"

"He won the medal qualifying, but lost in the first round of match play to a young caddie from Omaha," I said. "Big upset. Jones was gunning for his third straight Amateur. And the next year, he won the Impregnable Quadrilateral."

"The whosy *what?*"

"The Grand Slam," I said. "US Amateur, British Amateur, US Open and British Open. Never been done before, nor since. When he lost at Pebble that year, he went down the road and played the new Mackenzie course at Cypress Point. He liked it so much, he hired the architect to design his new course over in Augusta, Georgia. And the rest is history."

"Well, the history is interesting," she said, "But maybe it's still running a bit long."

"True," I said. "But always bending towards justice."

She snorted. Kinda a laugh. I'll take it.

An Open Case of Death

Chapter 13

FEBRUARY FOUND ME back on the West Coast. Jake Strauss thought I should attend the AT&T National Pro-Am at Pebble Beach, since the USGA would have a small army of officials in attendance making sure the grass was growing properly in anticipation of the US Open in June. I wasn't all that excited about leaving home, since I had managed to get a good bit of work done in January, writing chapters on Shinnecock Hills, Winged Foot and Baltusrol.

Mary Jane told me to go. "Vic and I are fine," she told me one morning. "School keeps us busy. We won't even know you've gone."

"Gee, thanks, I think," I said.

She was about to say something else, when she suddenly held up a finger, turned and ran for the bathroom. I finished washing up the breakfast dishes and making sure Victoria's lunch box was packed. Mary Jane came back a few minutes later. She looked a little pale.

"You feeling OK?" I asked.

"Yeah," she said, "I'm good. I think it's just a little bug I picked up. It's been going around the school."

"We got Pepto?" I said. "I can go get some today if you need it."

"No, we're good," she said. "Book your tickets. Really. We'll be fine."

So I did. This time, though, Dottie van Dyke couldn't find me a free room at the Lodge, or at the Inn at Spanish Bay a few miles down 17-Mile Drive. The best she could come up with was a room at a motel in Monterey where the rest of the press, TV crews and assorted other tournament people were staying. I remembered that place—it was famous for crack whores, Saturday night stabbings and rental car thefts—so I called Sharky Duvall to see if his back bedroom was available for the week.

"Sure, Hack," he told me when I called. "I've got a few other friends crashing here, so one more won't matter. As long as you don't mind sharing the bathroom, you're welcome."

So I flew out to San Francisco on the night of the Super Bowl, rented a car and headed down the 101 to Carmel. It felt a little strange. Once upon a time, I did this almost every week from January to October: fly and drive somewhere to watch professional golfers stage their little weekly dramas. But this time, I didn't need to come up with a column, pages of notes or a final game story. I was just there to … well, truth to tell, I wasn't sure why I was there. But the USGA had paid for my ticket, so I figured I'd just go with the flow.

It was pretty late when I arrived at Sharky's place, but he was still awake, watching a movie on television. He offered me something to eat or drink, but I was pretty beat. He pointed me toward the bedroom at the back of the house.

"There are two single beds in there," he said. "Take the one not occupied."

"Does he snore?" I asked.

"How do you know it's a he?" Sharky said with a smile.

"You do realize I'm a happily married man, right?"

An Open Case of Death

He waved his hand in the air. "Whatever," he said.

I used the bathroom first, brushing the six hours of air travel out of my teeth. I really wanted a shower, too, but decided to postpone that until the morning. The back bedroom was dark as a crypt, but I managed to locate the empty bed, disrobed and crawled under the covers. My roomie stirred slightly, turned over and began a steady, rhythmic snoring that would have made a chainsaw jealous. I spent about two minutes worrying about never being able to get to sleep and then I was gone.

A bright California sun was streaming in the window when I opened my eyes again. I raised my head and looked over at the other bed, which was empty. I lay there for a while until my bladder began to complain, then finally arose, threw on my pants and went in search of coffee.

Sharky was up, bustling around in his small kitchen. He nodded at me when I walked in, turned and poured a mug of coffee and handed it to me. "Cream's in the fridge, sugar's over there," he nodded.

"Thanks," I said. "Black's fine."

The kitchen opened into a large space at the front of the house that was mostly the living room, with the large flatscreen TV hung on the far wall. Just outside the kitchen, separated by a pass-through counter, was a wooden table with six chairs. A man wearing a crimson Stanford T-shirt and some flannel sweatpants was sitting at one of the chairs, sipping his own mug of joe. He was in his forties, with some flecks of gray showing at the temples of an otherwise full head of dark brown hair. He was bent over, peering at the tiny screen of his smartphone.

"Hack," Sharky said, "This is your roommate for the week, Benji Connover."

He looked up from his screen long enough to shake my hand.

"Hope I didn't snore too much," he said.

"I dunno," I said, "I was asleep most of the time."

He went back to his screen, and I sat down at the table. Sharky looked on from the kitchen.

"Breakfast?" he asked me. "I got cereal, granola, toast. There are eggs in the fridge, but you gotta make them yourself. Anything else, just ask and I'll say 'no.'"

"I'm good for now," I said. "Coffee is good."

Benji groaned audibly from the other side of the table. "Shit," he said. "The Pinkston kid from San Diego is going to UCLA. Dammit. His mother never liked me."

Sharky grinned at me. "Benji is the golf coach at Stanford," he said. "It's recruiting season." He looked at him. "You were never going to land Pinkston," he said. "He's Southern California down to his toenails."

"Yeah, you're right," Benji said, shaking his head sadly. "All beach, no brains. But his mother is still a bitch."

Sharky laughed and refilled the man's coffee mug.

"Stanford, huh?" I said. "Did you have Charlie Sykes on your team?"

He put his phone down and frowned. "Yeah," he said. "What a tragedy that was. Geez."

"Have they figured out what happened yet?" I asked.

"They're not a hundred percent sure yet," Sharky said. "The toxology report came back inconclusive. He had some alcohol in his system, he had some weed in his system."

"Like most twenty-somethings," I said.

Sharky nodded. "Indeed. But he also had Valium in his bloodstream," he said. "More than usual. They think he took maybe three or four tabs."

"That much would knock out a good sized horse," I said.

"True," Sharky nodded. "But it would also deaden one's nerves if one had decided to drive an E-Z-Go over the edge of a cliff. So, like I said, inconclusive."

"So he did it on purpose?"

An Open Case of Death

"That's the operating opinion," Sharky said. "But I know some of the boys at the Monterey sheriff's shop, and they're not totally convinced he did himself."

"I'll never believe it, not for one second," Benji Connover said. "Not a chance in hell that kid killed himself."

"Why not?" I asked.

"He had everything going his way," Benji said, sipping his coffee. "He had a great job at a great place. He knew that in another year or two, he would be able to have his pick of a head professional job. We talked about it all the time."

"You stayed in touch with him after college?"

"Oh, hell, yeah," he said. "I keep in touch with all my guys. Charley came from a good family, one with some money. Hell, his Dad knew Harold Meyer, who owns Pebble Beach. That's how he got the job here. His parents live up in Marin County. Good, tight family, no problems. Good job. Good future prospects … no reason to off himself. None at all."

"There doesn't always have to be a good reason," I said.

"C'mon man," Benji said hotly. "Nobody is going to drive a golf cart off a cliff like that unless there's something big going on in his life. Going wrong in his life. Charlie had everything going his way. That's what drives me nuts about the whole thing. It's totally senseless."

"What about a girlfriend? Or boyfriend, if that was his thing."

"Charlie never had any problems getting a girl," Benji said. "He'd had a few girlfriends at Stanford, but none that got serious. He told me that he was waiting until he got a more permanent, settled job before he got serious about anyone."

"Sounds like he had planned things out," I said.

"Yeah, he was like that," Benji said. "He was a planner. Thought things through. He was always very strategic on the golf course. Thought his way around a course as well as anyone I ever coached. Strong mentally. He was ambitious, too. He had a plan, and knew what he had to do to reach his goals. Unusual for a kid that age."

"Yeah, that day I played with him, he talked about being ready in case some opportunity walked in the door," I said. "I thought that was mature for someone so young."

"That sounds like Charlie," Benji said. "He was very aware. I think he knew from maybe sophomore year on that he wasn't going to make it on the Tour. He was good, but not Tour good. There's a difference."

"Was he the best player on his team?"

"Nah. Maybe three or four. He had his moments. He had some game, for sure. But he knew, most days, he couldn't beat Bill Hanniford, who's playing now on the Web.com tour. He couldn't beat Mikey."

"Mikey?"

"Mike Nelson," Benji said. "He was probably Charlie's best friend on the team. They'd room together on the road."

Mike Nelson. Mike N. Fifty-five percent probability. I felt my heartbeat accelerate.

"Where is Mikey these days?" I asked.

"He's working up at the Redwoods," he said. He picked up his phone and started scrolling through his messages again.

I looked at Sharky and raised my eyebrows. "The Ranch at Redwoods," he said. "Super fancy-dancy real estate project up in the Santa Lucia mountains, about twenty miles east of here and a couple of thousand feet higher. Million dollar lots. Twenty million dollar homes. Two golf courses. Horses. Fly fishing. Playground for billionaires."

Time for a road trip, I thought.

"So, Hack, what's on your schedule today?" Sharky said, changing the subject.

An Open Case of Death

"I'm supposed to meet up with the USGA guys later this morning," I said. "The agronomy experts are grilling the greenskeeper. They probably want fairways only wide enough for single-file walking, and he's holding out for two abreast."

Sharky laughed. "Well, if I know Pete Daniels, he'll be able to hold his own," he said. "He keeps that course in pretty good shape, despite the quarter-million players that walk all over it every year."

"How about you, Benji?" I asked. "Going over to the course today?"

"Nah," he said. "I'm meeting someone for lunch. Up in Frisco."

"Hack, I'll ride with you if it's OK," Sharky said. "I've got a parking pass for you. Gets you into the volunteers and officials lot. Pretty close to the Lodge. You need a badge?"

"Nah. The USGA sent me credentials," I said. "I'm an 'Official Visitor.'"

"That'll get you into the Tap Room, anyway," Sharky said with a chuckle. "I think I have a press pass somewhere if you need to get into the press tent. For old time's sake."

"Thanks," I said. "But I'll pass on the pass." I put down my coffee cup. "But I'm calling first dibs on the shower."

Chapter 14

I drove Sharky over to Pebble Beach an hour or so later. Mondays at a PGA golf tournament are usually pretty boring: there is a lot of last-minute bustling going on, with delivery trucks dropping things off at various tents, booths and counters, and people with official badges running around checking on the logistics. There are few actual golf professionals on site as most would be flying into town tonight from Phoenix or wherever they lived. Here at the AT&T Pro-Am, there were a lot of the amateurs—Hollywood celebs, business magnates, some professional athletes—milling about, getting ready to play a practice round on the Pebble Beach course. That was part of the attraction of playing in this event: the chance to play Pebble, and Spyglass, and the Monterey Peninsula Country Club course. They'd get a practice round on each of those, play a tournament round with their pro on each and, if lucky or good at sandbagging, make it into the final round at Pebble on Sunday. Throw in the nightly parties and lavish dinners, and they'd all stagger home on Sunday night in need of sleep and alcohol detoxification.

I knew that any golf writers in town would not be found anywhere near Pebble Beach until Wednesday at the earliest. If any had come up early, they would be out playing golf themselves, at Pasatiempo, or Bayonet at Fort Ord, Harding Park or Olympic up in Frisco, or at one of the fancy real estate projects up in the mountains rising above Carmel Valley. Like the Ranch at Redwoods. But there is nothing newsworthy going on Monday.

I had an hour to kill before I was supposed to meet up with Jake Strauss at some conference room in the Lodge. Sharky had pointed to a couple of mess tents set up off the main pedestrian pathways.

"Those are reserved to feed the tournament officials and volunteers," he told me. "The food is catered by the Lodge and it's always excellent. Also, free. Later in the week, you'll find a lot of players and their caddies eating in there. Far away from the fans and, like I said, the food is great."

I followed his advice and walked up the hill to one and stepped through the tent's entrance. There were rows of mostly empty tables and chairs, and at the back, a long steam-tabled food line. Because it was still morning, there were trays of eggs, pancakes, bacon and sausage, hash browns, Mexican breakfast burritos and platters of fresh fruit, baked goods and more. I grabbed a plate and loaded it up, and poured myself a big mug of coffee.

Looking around for a place to sit, I noticed an older guy sitting by himself a table away. He looked familiar. I walked closer and recognized him: it was Will Becker, former Tour star and one of the four co-owners of Pebble Beach. I pulled out a chair and sat down across from him.

He looked up at me and smiled. "Man, these hash browns are great," he said. "They make 'em fresh, y' know. None of that pre-made, frozen crap that they put in the microwave. I've been down to the kitchen, talked with Chef, watched him make a batch."

I held out my hand and he shook it. "Hacker, Boston *Journal*," I said, figuring a small lie wouldn't condemn me straight to Hell. And it was easier than explaining my entire life history and all the changes that had befallen it.

He nodded and went back to eating. Becker was getting up there in years, and it was starting to show. His head was mostly bald, save for a few hopeful strands of white gray hair crisscrossing his noggin here and there. His skin was patchy, with splotches of red and patches of white, along with some scary looking moles that were beginning to look like angry fighting animals. Those famous Becker eyebrows, that in his youth had distinguished him, made him look like one of the rugged pioneers in the Lewis and Clark expedition across the continent, were now snow white. He was wearing a long-sleeved chamois shirt with one dark, stained spot on the front, and some old-looking blue jeans. I watched him eating his breakfast for a bit, and noticed the tremors in his hands.

Becker had to be in his mid-eighties. He had been one of the lions of the Tour back in the day, contending with Nicklaus and Palmer, Miller and Trevino. His tall, lithe frame, broad bony shoulders, and those knife-sharp eyebrows had made him as much matinee idol as champion golfer. Pebble Beach would roll him out in front of the cameras this weekend to remind older viewers of the golden days of yore when heroes strolled the fairways, men ruled the world and nobody took drugs.

"Those bastards in Boston wouldn't let me play a practice round at the Country Club," Will said suddenly, snapping me back to the present. I realized he had heard me say "Boston" and his memory had dragged up some incident from his more youthful days.

"Really?" I said. "How come?"

He shrugged and nibbled on the end of a piece of bacon. "They said it was too busy," he said. "Members first. It was a freakin' Tuesday morning. I think I was the only one there that day."

"Well, that place is known for being a little snotty," I said.

"I didn't qualify for the Open in '63," he said. "I was just a year out of college then. Julius Boros won that year. He beat Arnie and Jackie Cupit in a playoff. I was pretty much done by 1988, when Curtis Strange won the thing. But I'll never forget when they told me to take a hike."

"Did they know who you were?"

He looked at me, and I could see a flame of pride shoot up in his eyes.

"Sonny boy," he said, "Back in the day, *everyone* knew who I was. Everyone. Will Becker was a name. Kids wanted to be like me. Women wanted to sleep with me. Hell, a lotta *men* wanted to sleep with me, too!"

He thought that was funny and began to harrumph with laughter, which quickly devolved into a hacking cough that made me think I might need to remember how to do the Heimlich maneuver. But he slowly got control of himself, and wiped his streaming eyes with his napkin.

"Well," I said, "When I get back home, I'll go out to Brookline and tell them that Will Becker says hello."

"Nah. Tell 'em Will Becker says to go fuck yourself." He began braying again.

Two guys came up, told Will it was an honor to meet him, and asked for his autograph. He nodded silently, and scribbled his name on each of their golf caps. They thanked him profusely and backed away. When they were out of earshot, he looked across the table at me with a wry smile.

"That was nice, right?" he said. "Except five'll get ya ten that they aren't fans at all. Autograph hounds, prolly. They'll spend the week getting as many guys as they can to sign those damn fool hats and then next week they'll be trying to sell 'em on E-Bay for a few hundred bucks. I'd like to tell 'em to fuck off, but my wife says I should just pretend they are fans. Sometimes, just for the hell of it, I write 'John Lennon' or 'George Washington.' They never notice."

"I get the impression that you've just about run out of craps to give about most stuff," I said.

He chuckled.

"What did you say your name was?" he said. "I like that line. Gonna steal it. 'Run outta craps to give.' Beautiful."

"You still own a piece of this place?" I asked.

He nodded and looked around the tent, as if he could see something to brag about owning, instead of the white plastic tent enclosing a field canteen filled with cheap rental tables and chairs.

"Yeah," he said. "Meyer and Udall got me involved, years ago. Talked my manager into it, really. I had to pony up ten million bucks. Luckily, I had it. I never cared much about the money. I just liked winning golf tournaments. My manager was pretty smart, though he wasn't no Mark McCormack. That son-of-a-bitch made Arnie and Jack into billionaires. But they had to sell their souls to do it. Not me. I never did more than one or two commercials a year. Concentrated on playing golf. Winning. That's what I liked."

"And you did a bunch of that," I said.

"Thirty-one times, bubba," Becker said and sat back in his chair with a self-satisfied smile. "Woulda been thirty-two, except for that time when Joe Dey called me for touching the sand in that bunker down in Tucson. Fuckin' bastard cost me two hundred thousand. Never forgave him. Never."

I vaguely remembered the incident he was talking about, but I was going in a different direction.

"You ever going to sell your share?" I said.

He looked at me, those famous eyebrows going up and down like kids on a seesaw.

An Open Case of Death

"Funny you should ask me that," he said.

"Why?"

He looked around, to make sure no one was lurking and listening in. The tent had maybe seven people in it, total. Nobody but me was listening.

"Well, now that J.J. is gone, there's gonna be some big changes around here," he said.

"Revisions in the ownership deal?" I asked.

He shook his head, took a swig of his coffee and smiled at me.

"That's what they'll say in public," he said. "But the truth is, the big cats are trying to get rid of the little cats and take over. J.J.'s death is just an excuse to clean house."

"Really?" I said. "Who are the big cats?"

"Only one left is Harold Meyer," he said. "Now that J.J. is gone. Jackie is a little cat, like me. We were useful twenty odd years ago. Now we ain't, so out we go."

"How do you know this?" I asked.

He nodded at me with the self-knowledgeable look of the cat that swallowed the canary. "He told me hisself," he said.

"Who did?"

"J.J. Udall," Becker said, rapping the table with his knuckles for emphasis. "I went up to see him when he got sick the last time, in the hospital. He told me to sit down and listen up. Laid the whole thing out for me. Told me to call my manager, call my lawyers and tell them to sit up straight and pay attention."

"Wow," I said, "That sounds serious. What did he say was going to happen?"

Becker sat back in his chair and crossed his arms over his chest.

"Sorry, young feller," he said. "But I ain't telling you that. J.J. said not to trust anyone, not to talk to anyone. He told me to just wait and watch and see."

"So you're not supposed to trust anyone," I said. "That include Harold Meyer?"

"Oh, hell's bells, I ain't never trusted that sumbitch," he said with a barking laugh. "You don't get to be that rich and that powerful without being as dishonest as the day is long. But it ain't just Meyer."

"Who else is there?"

He touched the side of his nose with his finger tip.

"Follow the money, young man," he said. "Follow the ever-lovin' money."

I was silent for a bit, thinking.

"Baruch Brothers?" I said, guessing. But then, they were the money in this deal, even if all of the partners were not hurting for spare cash.

He slapped his hand down on the table so hard, I jumped. So did some of the seven other people in the tent.

"Bingo!" he almost yelled. "You stack my ten million against the kind of scratch those New York scumballs can throw against the wall and it ain't even a close contest. J.J. told me they'd be coming after me, and coming after Jack Harwood, too. He said if my lawyers weren't careful, they'd try to renege on the deal we all had, pay us as little as possible, pat us on the head and send us away. And as soon as that was done, they'd sell the place for a couple, three billion and walk on outta here with greenbacks stuffed in their pockets."

He paused, looked around. A few more people had come into the tent, and were over at the steam tables, loading up plates with food. The number of people paying attention to him was still none. Except for me, of course.

"But I thought J.J. Udall was one of the big cats," I said. "I thought he was on the same level as Meyer."

"He was," Becker nodded. "But he was worried. He knew some shit that I didn't. He knew some stuff was coming down. That's why he warned me not to trust anybody. I think he meant that to include Harold Meyer."

"How about Jacob Strauss?" I said.

"Strauss!" He said the name like he was naming the serpent in the garden of Eden. His sibilant pronunciation was dripping with dislike and disdain. "I never trusted that sumbitch from day one," he said. "He's like all them boys on Wall Street: they're in it to win it. For they own selves. Nothing else."

"What happens next?" I asked. "When is this all supposed to come down?"

"I dunno," Becker said. "Next board meeting is right after the Open, in July. I got my lawyer prepped and ready. Expect Jackie Harwood does as well. We'll see what bullshit they come up with and deal with it then."

He stood up and stretched.

"I gotta go do some meet and greet on the putting green," he said. "Nice chatting with ya, Boston."

He left. I stayed there for a while, thinking.

Chapter 15

PETE DANIELS, THE greens superintendent at Pebble Beach, had been talking nonstop for the better part of forty-five minutes on the subject of *poa annua,* or the strain of bluegrass that was found in the greens on the Pebble Beach golf course. I learned that there were actually some 15 different strains of poa that could be found on Pebble's greens—hence their characteristic splotchy look—and I tried to stay awake as Pete described each of them in some detail, right down to their Latin names. It made me want to go dig up the body of the great Swedish botanist Linnaeus, who had dedicated his life to identifying and naming and classifying every last plant known to mankind, and kill him again.

When Daniels put a slide up on the wall screen which showed a graph comparing the various growth speed aspects of each of the strains of poa found at Pebble Beach's greens, my eyes began to cross. I wasn't sure I really cared that *poa alpigena* grew at an average rate of 0.376 mm per six hours at 75°F (23.88°C), while *poa napensis* sometimes exceeded 0.753 mm.

The rest of the people gathered around the dark wood conference table, a combination of officials from the USGA agronomy department, greenskeepers from the next three Open sites and a few local academics down from Stanford and UCal, hung on Daniels' every word. I started thinking about what he would look like naked. That worried me.

Luckily, Jake Strauss poked his head in the door, caught my eye and motioned for me to come outside with him. I restrained myself from shouting "Yes!" and pumping my fist, and got up. But I did let out a sigh of relief, once out in the hallway.

He chuckled. "Some people get off on that stuff," he said.

"Mazeltov for them," I said. "I was about to start poking my eyes out with a pencil."

"Let's go have some lunch," he said and led me down the hall, a flight of stairs and around the corner until we arrived at the Tap Room. It was crowded, but we found a table over in the corner and sat down. A waiter brought the menus over and we ordered a beer.

"So what's new?" he asked, leafing through the pages of his menu.

"I might have a lead on this Newell person," I said.

"Really?" he said. "Where is he?"

"I didn't say I know where he is. Or who he is. I just said I might have a lead," I said. "I need to chase it down first."

"Don't get cute with me, Hacker," Strauss said. I looked at him, surprised at his aggressive tone. "If you know where this guy is, I want to know."

"And when I find out, I'll tell you," I said.

He sat there simmering. The waiter brought us our beers. I tasted mine. It came from a local craft brewery. It was cold, it was hoppy, it was beer.

"I spoke this morning with Will Becker," I said, changing the subject. "He's not a big fan of yours."

"He's a dumbass," Strauss said. "He used to be a pretty good player. But he's just another old guy with delusions of grandeur."

"His delusions are worth at least ten million bucks," I said. "So maybe not so deluded after all."

Strauss took a sip of his beer. His face got a little red.

"Whose side are you on, Hacker?" he said, his voice low and menacing. "I'm not liking this attitude of yours."

"My *attitude*?" I said. "I'm just doing what you hired me to do. I'm trying to find your mystery heir. I've talked to both Jack Harwood and Will Becker and both of them say that, before he died, J.J. Udall warned them not to trust anybody. And your name came up as someone they should particularly not trust. Maybe I should go see Harold Meyer and make it a trifecta."

The waiter came back to take our orders. I asked if they still had that cheeseburger with the Angus beef and the melted brie. He said they did, but told me it was priced at $40 during the tournament week. I smiled and ordered one. Jake asked for the turkey club.

"First of all, I don't know why you are talking to the partners," he said when the waiter left. "Second, I don't know why they shouldn't trust me. What did I ever do to them, but help make them rich?"

"Hard to figure, isn't it?" I said. "Of course, now that Udall is dead, somebody at Baruch Brothers is going to come in and rejigger the whole management foundation of the Pebble Beach Company. And since that someone is you, maybe they feel like they're gonna get rejiggered right out of the picture. Unpossible, I know, but I think that's what they are expecting."

"My primary fiduciary responsibility is to the corporation," Strauss said. "And that means …"

"That you'll cut off their balls first chance you get," I said. I shrugged. "Don't feel bad, that's what all you capitalists do."

"I have no intention of cutting off anyone's balls," he said. "But the death of J.J. Udall means that changes have to be made to the corporate structure. It's all written down in the partnership agreement. It's all …"

"…perfectly legal," I finished for him. "Yeah, that's probably what has them worried."

Jordan Speith and Justin Thomas walked in, looking like they had just finished a practice round. They saw Strauss and came over to greet him. And me. They pulled up chairs and sat down. The waiter brought out our food, took orders from the two newcomers and went away. Strauss began pontificating on the Rules changes just instituted at the beginning of the year, and the three of them began a spirited discussion of the hows and the whys. My eyes glazed over almost as much as they had during the lecture about poa annua, so I just ate my forty dollar hamburger and listened with half an ear.

When I was finished, I stood up.

"You guys will have to excuse me," I said. "I have some work to do."

I left the Lodge, stopping by the putting green to see if I knew anyone there. I didn't see any professional golfers, but I did see the guy who starred on a CBS sitcom I never watched. He was standing by the ropes, signing autographs and, it appeared to me, flirting with some rather nicely proportioned California girls. Since CBS broadcast the AT&T National Pro-Am on the weekend, they always made sure most of their stars were prominently featured on the broadcast, whether or not they could actually play the game. It's a cynical world.

I wandered up to the press tent and ran into Sharky, who was talking to a police officer. He waved me over.

"Hack, this is Johnny Levin," he said. "He's a detective with the Monterey Sheriff's department. He was just telling me something about the Sykes case."

I shook his hand. He was a big and burly man with broad shoulders and a thick trunk, dressed in a white dress shirt and black slacks. But his wide black belt with gun and holster affixed on one hip gave him away as a cop. He turned to look at me. His head was huge, the size of a watermelon, but his eyes were small and beady.

"Just telling the Shark-man here that forensics found what looked like footprints in the area," he said.

"Up on the clifftop, or down on the beach?" I wondered.

"Up top," he said. "Could be nothing, of course. How many golfers a week wander over to the cliff and look down? Probably a lot. But they have a good print of a left shoe and a partial on the right."

"Do they still think Charlie went over on purpose?" I asked. "Or are you thinking he might have been helped?"

"Way too early to tell," he said. "Officially, it's still ruled a suicide. But if that ever changes, we have the shoe prints on file, just in case."

"Interesting," I said. "Let me ask … when an old guy dies of natural causes in the hospital, do they ever do an autopsy?"

"Almost never," he said. "The medical examiner only looks at bodies when we think a crime has been committed. If some old geezer has a heart attack and dies, especially if he's in the hospital and under medical care, there's no reason to go to the expense. Cause of death is obvious and the case is closed. Why do you ask?"

I shrugged. "I dunno, it's probably a longshot. But I'm wondering about J.J. Udall's death a few months ago."

"The sports guy who used to own a piece of this place?" Levin's eyebrows shot up in surprise.

"Yeah," I said. "He was in the hospital up in Frisco. He had like three or four heart attacks, and was in their care after the last one. The docs said he seemed to be getting better. Then he died. Suddenly. Unexpectedly."

An Open Case of Death

"Geez, Hack," Sharky said, "Udall was something like 85 years old. People that age die all the time. And not unexpectedly. It's called old age."

"I know, I know," I said, "But I've talked to some people who saw him in the hospital, and they said he was worried about something. Warned them. So I just wondered if they might have done any tests after he passed."

"Doesn't sound like it would be likely," the cop said, shaking his head. "Not much in the way of probable cause. Like Sharky said, when an eighty-something kicks off, it's not exactly a surprise, is it?"

I agreed with him and we walked off.

"That sounds like a longshot, Hack," Sharky said.

"Yeah, probably so," I agreed. "Let's try something more tangible. Wanna go with me up to the mountains?"

"The Ranch at Redwoods? Let's do it!"

CHAPTER 16

I DROVE MY car down through Carmel and turned east onto Carmel Valley Road. For about ten miles, we followed the twisty road, which in turn followed the twisty Carmel River, past several golf courses, vineyards, upscale neighborhoods and fancy looking restaurants. Sharky, doing the navigating, told me to turn north on Redwoods Road, which started climbing into the mountains. There were switchbacks, long uphill straights and occasional downhill sections when we crossed over a ridgeline. Despite the name, I didn't see any giant stands of redwoods anywhere: to the contrary, the landscape was mostly open fields of brown grasslands, with occasional woodsy groupings down in the valleys which were drained by streams and creeks. As we climbed, the views got better and better, as rough rows of mountain peaks loomed in a purple barrier to the east, while, looking back as we crossed the many ridgelines, the aching blue vastness of the Pacific filled the horizon to the west.

"Boy, I wouldn't want to try this road out late at night after pounding beers down at the Hog's Breath," I said.

"Yeah, "Sharky said, "If you buy land up here, it's because you really want to get away from the human race."

An Open Case of Death

A small herd of deer scrambled across the road in front of us, skittering down into a wooded copse a few hundred feet below the roadbed.

It was a good twenty minutes of careful driving before we reached the entrance to the Ranch at Redwoods. A big fancy sign in gold leaf, built on a circular walled platform of squarish river rock, told us we were entering "A Community of Distinction."

There was a guardhouse a few hundred yards down the entrance drive. I pulled to a stop in front of the gate and an elderly gentleman in a blue and gold uniform came out of his wooden building and leaned down to speak through my side window.

"Afternoon, gents," he drawled, giving us his best Ranch at Redwoods smile. "Where are we off to, today?"

"We're going to the golf clubhouse," I said.

"And what is the purpose of your visit?"

"Rape and pillage," I said with a straight face. "Maybe some arson, too. But mostly pillage."

The security guard didn't respond, but just smiled in at us as if he hadn't heard what I'd just said.

Sharky leaned forward and spoke. "We're here to see Reggie Davis," he said. "Meeting him at the clubhouse."

"Right, Mister Davis," the guard said, as if glad that someone had finally spoken the magic word. I half expected a stuffed Groucho duck to descend from the skies above. He went back into his guardhouse and came back out a few second later with a green sheet of paper announcing us as verified and approved guests. He reached in and place it on the sill of my front windscreen.

"Golf course is second drive on the right," he said. "About a quarter mile on up. You'll see the sign. You gentlemen have yourselves a grand Redwoods day."

He stood back and gave us a two-fingered salute off the brim of his cap as I pulled away.

"Must be lonely up here," I said. "Probably doesn't get many visitors."

"Pillage?" Sharky said.

"Who is this Reggie Davis chap?"

"Owner and developer," Sharky said. "Always good to drop the name of the big chief."

"Do you know him?"

"Nah. I've seen his picture in the paper, though."

I found the turn off to the golf course and we soon pulled up at the sprawling clubhouse facility. The exterior was more of that dark, reddish river rock. The building's red tile roof was massive, swooping down in front and on both sides in wavy lines, almost like melting chocolate. There were heavy wooden beams and lots of brass appointments everywhere. The architecture spoke of exclusivity and wealth. I pulled up at the front and a kid in black slacks and a white oxford shirt came running out to valet-park the car.

"Welcome to the Links at Redwoods," the kid said, handing me a ticket. "Do you have clubs to drop off?"

"Nah, we're just here scouting the place for a heist," I said. "We won't be long."

The kid looked at us like I had spoken in Swahili. Sharky said "We're meeting someone in the pro shop." He led me up the entrance steps and into the dark depths of the clubhouse.

The lobby was elegantly appointed, with soft upholstered chairs scattered in conversation groups here and there. A big circular desk stood in the middle, manned by a lovely young thing in a Redwoods polo shirt and dark skirt. We nodded at her and Sharky pointed at the pro shop, which was off to the left in its own wing. I could see a large dining room off to the right, with tables set with glistening silver and china before huge picture windows looking out over the golf course and the mountains beyond.

An Open Case of Death

The pro shop was, like the rest of the place, elegantly appointed. The fixtures for clothes and other golfing gear were made of rich mahogany. Brass sconces cast pools of light onto the dark green walls which were hung with prints showing ye olde golfers bashing balls around Scotland with their mashies and niblicks. Soft music of an indeterminate kind played softly in the background.

Yet another beautiful California woman stood behind the desk, smiling at us. Tall, blond, she wore a white monogrammed polo, pressed chinos and had a swishy little pony tail thing going on. I made myself conjure up a mental picture of Mary Jane. But I still had one or two carnal thoughts sneak through.

"Hi guys," she said enthusiastically. "You have a tee time?"

Sharky answered before I could say anything. He was probably worried about what I might come up with next.

"We're looking for Mike Nelson," he said. "He around today?"

"Sure is," she said, tossing her head towards a window. Her pony tail swished behind her. "He's out on the range. Giving a lesson to Mrs. Wallbeck."

"Thanks," Sharky said, smiling at swishy girl. "We'll go find him."

We wandered out onto the huge deck behind the clubhouse. It was flagstone, with a painted metal railing all around and filled with wooden tables and chairs. All the tables were empty, save for one off to the right, where two white-haired women were enjoying a pitcher of what looked like margaritas and a huge plate of nachos covered with cheese and chili. Luckily, I had just eaten lunch an hour earlier, or I might have made a move on them. The nachos looked delicious.

"Not a lot of people enjoying life at the Ranch today," I said to Sharky.

"I think if you lay out ten or twenty million for a home up here, you kinda expect not to have a lot of riff-raff around," he said.

"Are you the riff or the raff?" I wondered. He didn't tell me.

Beyond the flagstone deck, a large pond extended out several hundred yards. There was a green ribbon of fairway winding along the edge of the pond to the right, and off to the left, a kind of stepped terrace of lawns ran down to the edge of the water. Here, they had set up the practice area, with yellow ropes, metal stands for clubs, ball washers and buckets of water for club washing, and neat little triangles of stacked balls waiting for someone to come along and whack them into the pond. Out in the water, they had colored flags anchored to provide targets and distances.

"Floaters for the practice range, huh?" Sharky said, looking at the set-up. "Kinda cool."

I agreed. Way down at the far end of the range I could see a young man gesticulating as he explained some fine point of the golf swing to an elderly woman with slightly bluish hair. I guessed we had found Mike Nelson and his student, Mrs. Wallbeck.

We decided to wait until the lesson was over. We sat down at one of the tables and in short order, a waitress came out. I asked for some iced tea and Sharky nodded his agreement. She went away and came back in short order with two glasses filled with ice and slices of lemon and a big pitcher of tea. She placed a little paper and pencil down next to me. I signed the name "Reggie Davis" and in the space where it asked for my membership number, I wrote "XXIV."

Sharky watched with a smile playing at the corners of his mouth. He looked at me with raised eyebrows.

"Oldest member," I said. "Signs his chits in Roman numerals."

Sharky chuckled and we sat and sipped our iced tea and enjoyed the warm sun and the nice views for about fifteen minutes. We watched as Mike Nelson finished up the lesson, helped Mrs. Wallbeck load her clubs on the back of her golf cart and wave as she drove away.

The young man walked back to the clubhouse, and when he was approaching the deck, we waved him over. He put on a friendly smile, peeled off his white golf glove and walked over to our table. I pushed out a chair for him.

"Golf teaching is thirsty work," I said, "C'mon join us for a spell."

"Don't mind if I do," he said and sat down. He looked at his watch. "Mr. Geddes, my next lesson, isn't due for another forty minutes." The ever-vigilant waitress came out with another ice-filled glass. Of course, we were the only customers, except for the two dears demolishing the plate of nachos on the other side of the deck.

"I'm Hacker and this is Sharky Duvall," I said. "We'd like to talk to you about Charley Sykes."

His body stiffened. He drank some tea and then sat back in his chair, crossing his legs.

"You guys cops?" he asked.

Interesting response, I thought.

"Do we look like cops?" I said.

He smiled. "Not really," he said. "Why do you want to talk about Charley?"

"We're trying to figure out why a young man with a bright future would kill himself," Sharky said. "And since you were his best friend in college, we thought you might have some ideas about that."

"Look, I told the Monterey cops last December everything I knew," he said. "Charley and I went our separate ways after college. He had a nice gig down at Pebble, and I've been working up here. We didn't see each other much…maybe once or twice in the last year. He seemed

OK to me. Liked his job. Was working on his game. We were going to play in a couple NCGA events this summer."

"NCGA?" I asked.

"Northern California Golf Association," Mike said. "They run some tournaments around here. A lot of assistant pros sign up, try to keep the competitive juices flowing."

"Did he have a girlfriend?" Sharky asked.

Nelson shrugged. "I really don't know," he said. "He never mentioned anyone. Listen, why do you want to know all this stuff? Who are you again?"

"I'm a writer," I said. "Working on a piece about Charley. Young man with promise, takes his own life. Our readers want to know why."

"Mmm," he didn't look convinced. My answer was paper thin. I wouldn't have believed me, either.

"Sorry," he said. "I can't give you much. Like I said, we kinda went our own ways after Stanford. All I know is that it's a goddam shame. Charley was a great kid. A good friend. I'll miss him."

He stood up. The interview was apparently at an end. I stood up too, and extended my hand.

"Well, thanks anyway, Mr. Newell," I said. "Appreciate the time."

"It's Nelson," he said.

"Oh, right, sorry," I said. "Thanks again."

Sharky and I retraced our steps to the entrance, collected my rental car, gave the valet kid a few bucks and drove off. But I only went a few hundred yards and pulled in to one of the hundreds of empty parking spaces at the far end of the lot.

"What are you doing?" Sharky asked.

"Just wait a sec," I said.

It was more than a sec. It was about four minutes before we saw Mike Nelson come out of the clubhouse, rush down the stairs and head off around to the left, out of sight. But shortly, we saw an old black Nissan SUV come out of a back lot and head back down the main drive. Mike Nelson was behind the wheel. I waited a few seconds and then followed.

Chapter 17

NELSON WAS MOTORING pretty damn fast as we went down the main drive. He blew past the gatehouse entrance doing about 40 mph. I was going fast enough to keep him in sight, and as we approached, I watched the uniformed guard come out and yell something at the speeding Nissan as it disappeared in the distance, screeching its tires as it turned right with a nice little fishtail maneuver onto the main road.

I slowed down as we went past the gatehouse, dropping my green visitor's pass out the window as we went through. I looked in the rearview mirror and saw the guard chasing the paper as it blew around in the air currents.

"Where do you think he's going?" Sharky asked as I picked up the pace on the main road.

"Dunno," I said. "I just hope he makes it. He keeps driving like this, he's gonna end up wrapped around a tree."

I managed to get within about two hundred yards of the speeding Nissan. I kept that distance as we descended down the long valley. I don't think Nelson was paying too much attention to what was going on behind him—he was bound and determined to get where he was going as soon as possible.

I was beginning to think we were going to trail him all the way back to Carmel Valley, when he suddenly slammed on his brakes and swerved onto a dirt and gravel access road that branched off to the right. The Nissan disappeared in a cloud of yellow dust that swirled up behind it.

I slowed down as we approached the spot where he had turned, pulled ahead of the dirt road and stopped. The access road dropped downward on a nearly parallel angle to the main road, and ended after a hundred yards at a double-wide trailer at the bottom. The trailer rested in a shady spot along the bank of a rocky creek that flowed behind it. Across the creek was a flatland of golden grass and a few bushy shrubs.

"Casa Nelson," I said. "Out here in the boonies."

"Very peaceful," Sharky said.

The Nissan had stopped in front of the trailer. The driver's side door was open. There was no sign of Mike Nelson. The cloud of yellow dust had mostly dissipated, with just a few swirls left in the air.

The door to the trailer flapped open with a bang and we watched as Nelson came out, holding a phone to his ear. He was waving his other hand around wildly. He paced back and forth forcefully as he spoke.

"Who do you suppose he's talking to?" Sharky wondered out loud.

"Dunno," I said. "But he doesn't look happy."

"No, he does not."

"What do you think set him off?"

Sharky chuckled. "Well, if I were a betting man, I'd guess that somebody calling him 'Mr. Newell' might have done the trick," he said.

"Yeah, he did kinda react to that, didn't he?" I said. "That, and he wanted to know if we were cops."

"You think he's the one who wrote the letter?" Sharky asked.

"I'd say he's the leader in the clubhouse," I said.

"Shall we go down there and ask him?"

"I don't think so," I said. "Might prove injurious to our health. Anybody who lives out here in the boonies likely keeps a shotgun by the front door. I know I would. Besides, I'm more interested in who he's talking to right now."

"Who do you think it is?"

"Just guessing," I said, "But I'll go with one of the three surviving partners in the Pebble Beach Company. And since Jake Strauss pretty much told me that Jack Harwood and Will Becker are going to be bought out, that leaves one Harold Meyer as the leading candidate."

"I'm betting he's talking to a woman," Sharky said. "There's always a woman involved in stuff like this."

I thought about that. Sharky had a point. I pulled my car forward a ways, turned it around and pulled up on the side of the road facing back down towards the trailer, down in the hollow below the road. I turned off the engine.

"Let's wait a bit and see what happens," I said.

"Okay," Sharky said. "But let's not wait too long. I've got some iced tea floating around that's gonna need to escape pretty soon."

I motioned over my shoulder. "Lotta woods out there," I said. "Long as you don't piss on a bear."

While we waited, I kept one eye on the trailer down below us to the front, and one eye on the road coming up behind us. It was about fifteen minutes later that I saw a red pick-up heading our way. I told Sharky and we both ducked down as it drove past us, slowing and turning on the dusty access road down to the trailer. We sat up again and watched.

An Open Case of Death

The truck stopped behind the Nissan, and Mike Nelson came out of the trailer again. The pickup's door opened and a woman got out. She looked to be in her twenties. She had dark brown hair and was dressed in blue slacks and a matching polo. She and Nelson hugged.

"Told you," Sharky said. "The femme fatale."

"Good call, Garth," I said.

We watched the couple talk. At a couple of hundred yards away, there was no way to hear what they were saying. After a few minutes, Nelson fumbled in his pocket, pulled out his phone and held it up to his ear. He began nodding and talking. He seemed to ring off, put his phone away, and, after saying something to the girl, they hugged and each got back in their vehicles. They drove up the access road, and Nelson blasted away towards the Ranch at Redwoods.

The pickup turned in our direction, heading back the way it had come. Sharky and I ducked down again, but I kept my head high enough to read the plate on the front bumper. I read it out loud, so one of us could remember. The truck whooshed past us and disappeared down the road. I sat up and wrote the plate number down.

Sharky got out his phone and dialed.

"Johnny Levin, please," he said. He waited. "John, it's Sharky. Can you run a license plate for me? Yes, I know it's illegal or unethical and all that, but I need to know who's pickup it is." He read off the plate numbers. "Thanks, man," he said. "Let me know."

He hung up and looked at me.

"That was a good afternoon's work," he said. "Let's go get a beer."

CHAPTER 18

WE WENT BACK to Steinie's in Monterey, and Sharky, after a visit to the men's room, took up his position at the far end of the bar. We ordered up a couple of beers. The crowd was a little bigger and more boisterous than it had been the other night. The Warriors were playing the Bulls back in Chicago, and some of the bearded biker dudes were apparently rabid fans of Golden State. I thought of doing a poll to find out which golfer the bikers in Monterey preferred among all others, but decided that while that might be funny, it might also be somewhat dangerous to my health.

I was talking to Sharky about something or other when I noticed his eyes light up as he was looking over my shoulder. He smiled and nodded his head. I turned to look. A pretty woman, in years way beyond the hot-babe phase, dressed well if still casually, with shortish pixie hair spiking in all directions and a pair of bright twinkling eyes, was making her way across to us from the front door.

She came up, draping an arm on the back of each of our stools. "Hiya, men," she said, her mouth breaking into a wide grin. "Room for one more?" She leaned over and gave Sharky a kiss on the lips and turned to look at me.

An Open Case of Death

That grin, those eyes bright with life and even the spiky do, all made for a pleasant package. Here was someone you'd like to get to know.

"Hacker," Sharky said by way of introduction. "This is Aggie. Short for Agatha."

I got up and gave her my bar stool. "Delighted," I said. "I hope your last name is Christie because Shark and I have been trying to solve some of the many mysteries of life."

She smiled her thanks at me as she hung her big straw bag over the back rail and perched her athletic rear end on my stool. "Sorry," she said. "It's Lindstrom. I know a lot about medical things, and nothing at all about murders on the Orient Express."

She was, I learned, an ER nurse at the Community Hospital in Monterey, the largest medical facility on the Peninsula. And though no one told me, I could tell that she and Sharky were something of a couple. Maybe it was that kiss hello. Maybe it was the way he looked at her, with equal parts longing and admiration.

"So, how was your day, hon?" she asked Sharky, waving at the bartender for him to bring her a beer. Maybe it was that she called him 'hon' and asked about his day. My powers of deductive reasoning are pretty awesome.

"Meh," he said. "The usual. Dealing with other people's problems."

She turned those sparkling eyes on me. "And how about you, Hacker?" she said. "You have to deal with problems all day?"

"Me?" I said. "Nah. In my world, it's all unicorns and gumdrops."

She chuckled. "I'd go live in your world, if I wasn't spoken for," she said.

"Don't believe him, Ags," Sharky said. "His world is just as dark as any other."

On the television over the bar, Stephen Curry drained a three-pointer from the corner. Kevin Durant then stole the inbounds pass, tossed it back out to Curry, who drained another three. The bikers in the bar roared their approval.

"I have a medical question," I said, when the crowd calmed down. Agatha looked at me. "You know who J.J. Udall was?"

"The guy who ran the Olympics?" she said. "Know the name. Didn't he pass on a little while ago?"

"Yeah," I said. "He had a heart attack and then died a few days later. He wasn't in your hospital, was he?"

"No, I don't think so," she said.

"I think he was up at UCSF, in Frisco," Sharky said. "I remember reading that in the newspaper."

"Makes sense," Agatha said. "Udall lived in the Bay area. And being a rich and famous dude, he'd likely be taken to the best hospital in the state. That's UCal, San Francisco. Why do you ask?"

"I'm trying to decide if I think there was some funny business with his death," I said.

"OK," Agatha said. "What do we know?"

"He was in his mid-eighties," Sharky said. "He'd had three heart attacks already, this was his fourth. They got him stabilized, resting comfortably."

"He had visitors," I chimed in. "At least two. They reported he seemed to be his usual self, except for a little weakness and fatigue from the attack itself."

"On the day he died, he seemed fine at nine in the morning," Sharky finished up. "They found him dead at three in the afternoon."

"They said it was from natural causes," I said.

"And you wonder?" Agatha smiled at me. "Old guy, weak, past history ... I dunno, Hacker, when the man upstairs calls your number, most of the time the jig is up."

"What kind of medications would they give him?" I asked.

"Well, after a heart attack, they usually are on warfarin," she said. "That's a blood thinner. And they put them on aspirin, to keep the platelets from binding together. Neither one of those would be fatal in any normal dosage amount."

She thought a bit. "They might have put him on digoxin," she said. "That's if he had a-fib ... sorry, that's atrial fibrillation, for his ticker. Too much of that stuff will kill you, for sure." She shrugged. "Those are the normal things. Of course, he might have had a billion other things going wrong, and his docs might have had him on something weird. Hard to tell unless you're in the room."

"I wonder how one would go about getting a peek at his medical records," I said.

"Almost impossible," Agatha said. "California laws are pretty strict about privacy. You'd need a court order and even then the hospital would likely protest. Could take years."

"Oh," I said. "I guess that's not gonna happen, then."

"Or," she said, "You could buy a girl dinner and another beer or two, and said girl might be willing to call a friend of hers who works in the ICU at UCSF Medical Center and see if she can shake something loose."

"Done," I said. "Where do you want to go?"

"Hoo, boy," Sharky said, shaking his head sadly. "Hope Jake Strauss's expense account has no limits."

"Oh, I wouldn't do that to your friend," Agatha said, with a sparkle in her eyes that said, oh yes she would. "But I haven't been over to La Bicyclette in ages. Let's go there!"

And so we did. The restaurant was in Carmel-by-the-Sea, that lovely little, tree-shaded town by the beach. In Carmel, every tree is considered sacred or something like that, so even thinking about cutting down a tree requires a permit; and the people of the town decided long ago that having street numbers on each house or place of business was un-American or something. So we parked along 8th Avenue and walked down the crunchy, leaf-strewn sidewalk to the corner of Dolores and 7th. That's the address of La Bicyclette: "the corner of Dolores and 7th." One reason California has so much smog is that people trying to ship things to Carmel cause the United Parcel Service computers to overheat.

La Bicyclette was a charming little French bistro of a place, with four tall, arched windows (one containing a bicycle) in the front, and inside, dappled walls, barn-siding table tops, chalkboard menus and soft lighting all of which looked like it had been flown in direct from Montmartre. With all the celebrities in town for the golf tournament, the place was busy, but we were seated after a short wait in the little bar in back.

Agatha ordered the duck, Sharky had one of their wood-fired pizzas and I went with the charcuterie sampler of cured meats with some fromage on the side. They told me they had a special on a bordeaux from St. Emilion, so I ordered a bottle.

There was a handful of recognizable Hollywood celebrities dining around us, and we were enjoying being some of the Beautiful People out for a night in Carmel, when Sharky's phone rang. He took the call, nodded a few times and hung up.

"Johnny L," he said, looking at me. "Got a name to go with the plates. One Cassie Conway. Lives up in the Valley. Works at one of the vineyards, in the tasting room."

"Salude," I said, holding up my glass of red. "In my business, we call that a clue. The game is afoot!"

My dinner companions clinked glasses.

"It's gonna be the butler, isn't it?" Agatha said, eyes alight with delight. "It's always the butler that did it."

An Open Case of Death

"I don't think there is a butler," I said. "But I'll keep my eyes peeled for one."

Chapter 19

Finding Cassie Conway had been my main priority for the next day, but she had to wait. When I got out of bed, Coach Connover was already up, and when I made it into the kitchen, he was back at the kitchen table, eyes locked onto his telephone screen. Sharky and Aggie were also seated at the table, sipping their coffee and looking rumpled and happy. My amazing powers of deduction suggested that they had had an enjoyable evening while I was fast asleep from an overdose of beer, wine and good French food.

My phone rang and I saw it was Jake Strauss calling.

"Crap," I said. "He'll be wanting to know if I've found Mike Newell yet."

I answered.

"Have you found Newell?" he said. Not even a hello, first.

"Maybe," I said.

"Maybe? You're giving me *maybes*?"

"There are still a few things to check out before I know for sure," I said. "These things take time."

"Well, hurry the fuck up," he said. "I can't wait forever."

"You'll be the first to know," I said.

"Listen," he said, "How soon can you get over here to the Lodge? I'm supposed to go up to San Francisco and meet with Meyer this morning. I want you to come along."

"Why?"

That took him aback. He probably wasn't used to having people question his decisions.

"Well … because … oh, I don't know," he stammered. "I thought you'd want to interview him for the book."

"Oh, yeah, the book," I said drily. I didn't tell Strauss that the chapter on Pebble Beach was mostly done. I didn't think I needed anything more from Harold Meyer. "OK. I'll be there in thirty minutes."

"Make it twenty," he said and rang off.

I looked at the others.

"Maybe it's just me, but I'm beginning to think Jacob Strauss is something of giant asshole."

"Nah," Sharky said, refilling my coffee cup. "I think most people in golf think he's an extra-large anus."

It was more like forty-five minutes before I arrived in the lobby of the Lodge. I'll admit I dawdled a bit getting dressed and out the door. Sharky's coffee was pretty good and Agatha Lindstrom was fun to talk with. More fun than Jake Strauss would ever be. Plus, she laughed at all my jokes.

I parked in the designated lot and walked down to the hotel. There was a long stretch limo idling in the turn-around drive by the front door. Jake Strauss was inside the lobby, phone glued to his ear as he paced back and forth in front of the huge windows that looked out over the golf course. The lobby was abuzz with pre-tournament excitement, and a lot of people were gathered on the narrow deck beyond those big windows, looking down on the 18th green. There was nobody on the green, but I guess it was nice to look at.

A Hacker Golf Mystery

Strauss hung up his phone and motioned for me to follow. For a split second, I thought about grabbing hold of one of the beige columns framing the front entrance and making him drag me, but I decided to act like an adult instead. Besides, I was actually looking forward to going to San Francisco and talking to Harold Meyer. He was the last of the surviving Amigos I had yet to meet.

Instead, I grabbed a to-go cup of coffee from the urn placed on a cart near the front desk, and I was fiddling with the lid when I climbed into the back seat of the limo. Strauss gave me that impatient, *where the hell have you been* look, but he was already on another call. I smiled at him and settled back into the plush leather.

Strauss stayed on the phone almost all the way up to San Francisco. I ignored him and leafed through the magazines tucked into the seat divider. The driver picked up the 101 north of Salinas and followed it through San Jose and up through Palo Alto and San Mateo into the city. We skirted the Mission District and followed the signs to the Golden Gate, but turned off near the Presidio and climbed one of San Francisco's many steep hills. I saw a street sign at an intersection that said we were on Vallejo.

At the crest of the hill, the limo swung into a narrow entrance, sliding through some wrought iron gates that had magically opened for us, and stopped at the front door. I got out and looked up at a massive gray stuccoed mansion. It was three stories tall, featured lots of ornate molding at the roof line and stained glass windows in the front. It looked just like the kind of place where one of the richest men in the world would live.

We walked up the marble steps with the curved brass railing and the front door silently swung open. A uniformed butler—black pants, narrow tie and one of those little white coats nipped in tightly at the waist—ushered us into the inner sanctum. The marble foyer was bedecked in mirrors and brass and the ceiling extended all the way to the roof, three stories up. But an elegant brass chandelier dropped down two of those stories. There were banks of fresh flowers, all in white, stuffed into brass urns on all the tabletops. A flight of white marble stairs rose at the back of the space and spiraled its way upwards to the other floors.

"Mister Meyer is on the sundeck," the butler announced. His voice sounded a bit more Hispanic than Jeeves, but it was still authoritative. He gestured toward the gold-paneled elevator doors to the right of the great hall.

"Shall we walk?" I said. "I could use the exercise after sitting in the car."

"Shut up," Strauss snapped, and we took the elevator.

The sundeck on the roof of the mansion was almost totally enclosed in glass, save for one wall which contained a wood-burning fireplace and a floor-to-ceiling stonework mantle. There was a huge, U-shaped white sofa arrayed in front of the fireplace, and several other tables and seating groups scattered across the rest of the space. At the far end, the glass roof had been pulled back for some 20 feet on a system of chains and pulleys, and the sunshine and cool fresh air filled the room. As we gazed out at the Bay, the Golden Gate Bridge rose above the greenery of the Presidio forest to the left, the low-slung cellblocks of Alcatraz clung to their rocks directly across from us, and the impressive skyscrapers of downtown San Francisco towered off to the right. You could say this house had a million-dollar view, but that would be shorting the price. By a lot.

Over in the sunny, open area a solitary figure was sitting in a plush wicker chair. Harold Meyer was a tiny little man, with an impressive shock of snow-white hair. He was wearing a gold paisley smoking jacket of some kind—the fabric was shiny—and a pair of black slacks, with black loafers. His tiny face was mostly obscured by a pair of large-rimmed glasses with darkened lenses. On the table in front of him sat a silver tray with a large pitcher of what looked like iced tea, an ice bucket and two tall empty glasses. He had already poured himself a glass.

As we approached, he didn't get up—the sign of the alpha dog—but motioned us to sit down.

"Hullo, Jacob," he said, his voice surprisingly deep and resolute. "Have some tea. It's an herbal blend. Supposed to be good for the prostate."

He looked at me.

"And whom do I have the pleasure of meeting?" he said.

"This is Hacker," Strauss said, sitting down and pouring himself a glass. He looked at me.

"Sure, I'll have some," I said. "Can't be too proactive about the ole prostate."

"You joke, Mister Hacker," the old man said. "But for some of us, prostate problems are very real. I myself have battled with prostate cancer for years. I had a tiny radioactive seed implanted in mine two years ago. In Thailand. Cutting edge therapy."

"And is the old block and tackle doing OK?" I said. I heard Jake Strauss make a choking sound that he quickly modified into a cough as he took a sip of his herbal tea.

"Quite well, thank you for asking," Meyer said.

He looked at Strauss.

"What is the purpose of your visit with me today, Jacob?" he asked.

"I have some papers prepared for you," Strauss said, burrowing down into the depths of a leather briefcase he had brought with him. "I think everything is in order. And I wanted you to meet Mr. Hacker, here, who is writing the book on the history of Open courses for us."

He passed the sheaf of legal documents over to the old man, who glanced at them and tossed them down on the table in front of him. He looked at me through the lenses of those thick, darkened glasses.

"You are a writer, then, Mr. Hacker," he said. "Is that right?"

"I sure hope so," I said. "Otherwise the 50,000 words I've already got down on paper are gonna disappoint the hell out of someone."

He didn't react.

"How can I be of service for your work?"

I took a sip of my herbal tea, felt it washing me all the way down to my prostate. I felt like a homeless bum, in ragged clothes and smelling of alley, dropped against his will at a fancy soiree where everyone else is in black tie and tiaras. But then, I've felt that way most of my life.

"I was hoping to draw a parallel between Samuel F.B. Morse and the current ownership," I said, making it all up on the fly. "Explore the connection between Morse's desire to repurpose the Monterey Peninsula for recreation and real estate, and your current business plan, which is to …"

I had hoped that my unspooling bullshit would end at some appropriate place, but I ran out of concepts I could pair with 'business plan.' Luckily, Meyer jumped in.

"Our business plan is to maximize return while providing our guests with the utmost in a luxury resort experience," he said.

"Exactly," I agreed, nodding my head with vehemence. "Maximizing the experience." Which is not what he said, of course. But I think they teach you in business school to just repeat back the words that your target says, so they think they're brilliant. And then, feeling brilliant, they'll buy whatever bull you are slinging.

"Of course," he said, "I have no idea what concept Samuel Morse had for the property."

"Making lots of money," I said. "As much as humanly possible."

He paused and looked at me to see if I was perhaps trolling him. I was, but I gazed back with my head cocked, as if I was hanging on his every word.

"Well, that goes without saying," he said.

"Naturally," I said, nodding in agreement. "Of course. Absolutely."

Meyer turned to Strauss.

"Have you made any progress on that letter?" he asked. "Do we know if it's real or not?"

"Nothing to report yet, I'm afraid," Strauss said. "Hacker here is looking into that as well."

"Is he now?" Meyer smiled at me. "A little investigative work, eh?"

"Yes," I said. "Just like when I was at the newspaper, digging up stories. It's second nature to all of us journos, digging into people's private lives, finding all their dirty secrets."

"And have you had any success to date?"

I shrugged. "I've got a few leads I'm following," I said. "But nothing definitive as yet. I'm still not sure I understand why it makes a difference if J.J. Udall had a secret son."

"Quite simple," Meyer said. "Under the partnership agreement, Udall's interests in the Pebble Beach Company close out upon his death. His estate will be paid the current value of his investment. The transaction will be simple and clean. But if it turns out he has an heir, which nobody who ever knew J.J. had an inkling of … well, then the potential is there for litigation that could conceivably drag out for years to come."

"And that would screw up your plans to reorganize the company with you as the sole owner," I said.

Meyer paused for a moment or two, then broke out in a soft chuckle.

"I can see that you have excellent analytical skills, Mr. Hacker," he said, smiling. "Perhaps when you are finished with your current assignment, you would consider joining the Meyer Companies. We're always in need of good thinkers, people who grasp complicated concepts with ease."

"How very kind," I said. "I will take your offer under advisement."

"What offer?" Jake sputtered next to me. "Hacker is a former reporter with skills of being a pain in the ass and occasionally ferreting out some hidden facts. Which is hardly the same as quantitative business analysis."

This time, Meyer turned his whole head and upper body to look directly at Strauss.

"Come, come, Jacob," he said disapprovingly. "I would have thought all those years at Baruch Brothers would have better sharpened your skills at personnel assessment. I think your Hacker here would be excellent. Most excellent, in fact."

I gave Strauss a knowing glance, even though I wanted to say *neener neener* to him.

"Tell me something," I said to Meyer. "How did this partnership work, internally? I'm asking for the book. You had four wildly different personalities. Two of you were business guys, each with his own expertise and resources. Two of you were celebrities, and again, each from a different world. How did all four of you agree on anything?"

Meyer smiled at me, showing off his twin rows of tiny, pointed teeth. They were not the dangerous choppers of a predator, designed to quickly tear, open and kill, but rather they looked like teeth designed to nip, chew and destroy, to make the victim scream in pain as his life slowly ebbed away.

"It was often quite difficult," Meyer said. "I depended on J.J. Udall to back me up on the important questions. The other two would fall into line if we two agreed."

"And did he agree with you most of the time?"

"No," Meyer said, shaking his head. "J.J. could be very difficult. Hard headed. Impulsive. He was good at certain things, but he thought he knew more than he really did. His own success was based more on luck and good timing than on any innate abilities, in my opinion. So I did have to spend quite a bit of time making sure I got Udall on my side."

"Do you think he trusted you?" I asked.

Meyer shrugged. "I have no way of knowing that, one way or the other," he said. "I never entirely trusted him. But one never enters a deal or makes a decision based only on trust. You've got to have hard numbers, or something concrete, to back it up."

I turned to Jake Strauss. "Why did you set up the management this way?" I asked. "It seems like it was designed to fail. Four very different personalities, each with his own priorities. Seems to me that in the long run, it was going to fall apart eventually."

"But it didn't, did it?" Strauss said, smiling. "Somehow, they found a way to work together. And the company has done better with every passing year."

"Until now," I said.

"The company is still doing big business," he countered. "It was the sudden death of J.J. that created this crisis, if you can call it that. It's really just a simple problem of evolving leadership. Every company would have to face something like this if a principal member of ownership passed away."

"Have you had a chance to speak with Will Becker yet?" Meyer asked. "It's important that we handle that matter well."

"I've called him a couple times this week," Strauss said. "His wife said he's too ill to come to the phone. She's lying, of course…he is avoiding me."

An Open Case of Death

"Keep after him, Jacob," Meyer said. "If the public thinks we're throwing a former PGA great over the side, we'll never hear the end of it."

"But you are," I said. They looked at me. "You are throwing Will Becker over the side. You know it. He knows it. And what about Jack Harwood? He knows something is up, too."

"Harwood is my concern," Meyer said. "He's dealt with Hollywood moguls for years. He knows the score. You fight when you can, and you take the money and walk away when you can't. He won't be a problem."

"If this were the movies, he'd drop down onto your roof from a helicopter, blow us all away and escape with the girl," I said.

"This isn't the movies," Harold Meyer said. "And there isn't any girl. I can handle Jack Harwood."

He sounded like he believed that. I didn't.

Chapter 20

"Is it your goal in life, when you wake up every morning, to see how many people you can piss off before the day is done?" Strauss seemed a little unhappy. We had gotten back into the big limo, driven down to Palo Alto and parked outside an upscale Mexican restaurant for lunch. We went in, sat down at the bar, ordered food and Coronas, and sat there looking at the high-techies at the tables around us, most of whom were staring blankly at their laptops. Strauss had been mostly silent, although I could tell he was upset.

I turned in my seat and looked at him. But didn't say anything.

"I mean, Harold Meyer is a very powerful and important man," Strauss said, waving his hands in the air for extra emphasis. "You don't smart off to someone like that."

"I didn't smart off," I said. "I thought we had a nice conversation."

"About his prostate?"

I shrugged. "He brought that up, I didn't," I said. "I just went with the flow, so to speak."

Strauss blew out a breath in frustration. "You are a very stupid man, Hacker," he said.

An Open Case of Death

"Maybe so," I said. "But my heart is pure. And he may own half the real estate in San Francisco and he may soon own the entire Lodge at Pebble Beach, but he doesn't own me."

"He could if he wanted to," Jake said. "And he could hire an army or two of goons to make you do what he wanted. With a snap of his fingers."

"So I'm supposed to just roll over and say 'yes, Master' just because he has a lot of money? Or because he could have me beaten up?" I shook my head. "Nope. I don't work that way."

"You have a contract…"

I cut him off. "My contract is with the United States Golf Association," I said. "The name Harold G. Meyer does not appear on it, anywhere. So, like I said, I don't work for him."

He shook his head, folded his arms across his chest and went silent again. And stayed that way when our food arrived. We ate in silence, which was fine with me. My fish tacos were pretty darn good.

"When do you think you'll know something about Mike Newell?" Strauss asked me after a while. I guess he got tired of giving me the silent treatment.

"I don't know," I said. "I've got someone to talk to tomorrow. Should know a little more after that."

"Well, let me know as soon as you can," he said. "It's important."

"What can you tell me about Huckleberry Hills?" I said.

He was getting ready to lift a corner of a taco to his lips. After my question, he seemed to slip and the taco seemed to crumble, and he had to do a quick move to keep his food from flying all over the table. He managed to get it mostly into his mouth, but needed a napkin to mop up.

"Why the hell are you asking me about that?" he said when he could talk again.

"Because I learned about it doing some research, and I'd like to know what you know about it," I said.

"It's a real estate development project that the Pebble Beach Company first proposed more than ten years ago," he said. "It has gone before the California Coastal Commission for permit approvals, and they sent it back with some suggested changes. Pebble Beach has put the plans on the shelf for the time being, but may seek to reopen them at some point in the future."

"What are the changes the CCC asked for?"

"They thought we needed to lower the density of the project," he said.

"How big a project are we talking about?" I asked.

He shrugged. "Ten years ago, it was around four to five hundred million," he said. "I don't know what it would be today."

I whistled. "That's a lot of money," I said.

"In California?" Strauss smiled. "On the Monterey Peninsula? That's petty cash money."

"Why does Pebble want to get into the real estate business?" I asked. "Isn't that a business fraught with risks?"

This time he laughed, unusual for Jacob Strauss. "Risk?" he said. "For an upscale, luxury condo development? In California? On the Monterey Peninsula? Overlooking Pebble Beach and Carmel Bay? You've got to be kidding. Whatever it costs, it will pay for itself quickly and make a profit. And why Pebble Beach? Why not? How many golf resorts around the country sell real estate? Many of them do."

"Then why is it on hold?"

"Partly for solid business reasons," he said. "To do Huckleberry Hills will take a lot of capital."

"Four hundred million," I said.

"At least," he agreed, nodding. "Probably more. So we are waiting until the time comes when we have the capital resources we need to do the job. But there's also a strategic component. The timing has to be right, too."

"And when is the right time?"

"Well, there are several answers to that question," he said. "But for me, the right time will be when we can get approval from the CCC. Without that, the project isn't going anywhere."

"And how do you get to that point? Do you think the day will come when the Coastal Commission will willingly approve your plan?"

He smiled. "Willingly? No, they will never willingly approve it. But there might come a time when they agree to our project in return for our doing something they want. That's the strategic part."

"Is that realistic?"

He nodded. "About twenty years ago, we wanted to build a seawall along the frontage of the 18th hole," he said. "The entire fairway was in danger of being washed away. Every time there was a big storm, the waves came over the rocks and flooded the fairway. We lost the green once or twice. So we found some engineers who said they could build artificial walls made from blown concrete that would repel the waves, even in most storms. Great, right?"

I nodded.

"But of course, that was introducing all kinds of artificial stuff on the waterfront. Which is completely against the very foundational ideas of the CCC, which exists to protect and preserve Nature on the California coastline. So, what to do? We had a need, they had a coastline to protect, so, after some discussions that went on for years, we arrived at an agreement."

"You had to give something up," I said.

"Yes we did," Strauss nodded. "We gave up an entire golf course that we had planned to build. Deep-sixed it completely. They gave us our seawall. Life went on."

"So what do you have to bargain with for the condo project?"

He shrugged. "Don't know," he said. "Something will come up. It usually does. Or maybe we can convince them to see the light."

I thought about that for a minute.

"That sounds like payola," I said.

"You ready to go?" Strauss stood up to leave. "Business isn't about right and wrong, Hacker. It's about getting what you want for as little cost as possible."

Chapter 21

THE NEXT MORNING, the hubbub at the golf course got louder. All the pros had arrived, joined up with their celebrity partners and the practice rounds were taking place at all three golf courses on the Peninsula.

Sharky and I messed around until lunchtime and then set off up Carmel Valley Road once again. But this time, instead of branching off into the high country where the Ranch at Redwoods sat, we kept straight on, eventually reaching an area of low hills spreading up from the banks of the Carmel River. The hills were mostly treeless, save for the occasional copse here and there, and covered in brown, waving grasses. And when we pulled into the drive of the Radiata Vineyard, we found a hundred or so acres of grape vines planted on the hillsides.

In February, the plants were still leafless, and the vines had all been cropped back against the wire guides strung between wooden posts. They were mulched with round river rocks and some kind of narrow hosing fed steady streams of water, or fertilizer or a combination of both to the roots of each plant in the rows. Growing grapes is supposed to be Nature's work, but out here near Silicon Valley, they leave nothing to Nature's chance, but use technology to deliver the proper molecules to the proper root at the proper time.

We parked outside the vineyard's tasting room, which was housed in a dramatic lean-to-like building that was all windows and granite ledges on the front, looking back down the valley towards the distant sea. Inside, the slate floor, granite counters and rough-sawn wood siding created a rustic look. Several displays showed off the various vintages made by Radiata, and, behind the tasting bar, rows of crystal glasses hung from a wrought-iron fixture that dangled from thick chains affixed to the high ceiling.

"My theory," Sharky said as we stood in the lobby looking around at all this architectural extravagance, "Is that the quality of the wine is in exactly opposite relation to the fanciness of the place where it's made."

"This place is pretty fancy," I said.

"Agreed," he said. "I'll bet the wine sucks."

We got in line behind a half dozen other wine tourists and eventually made our way to the registration desk.

"Good afternoon, gents," said a friendly young woman behind the desk. "Are you interested in the tour of the vineyards, the bottling operations, or are you just here for the tasting experience?"

"Oh, we're always up for a tasting experience," I said. "But we were also wondering if Cassie Conway was here today."

"She sure is," the young woman said. "I think she's doing the vineyard tour right now. We had a bus come in from Sacramento. She should be back in about thirty minutes."

"Well, we'll just taste some wine until then," I said.

I paid the money and we sidled over to the tasting bar, behind which three employees, two young men and a woman, were dispensing small dollops of the Radiata varieties, along with tasting notes.

An Open Case of Death

One of the young men came over, put down two wine glasses and dribbled out half an inch of a purplish red.

"This is our Radiata Shiraz," he intoned, sounding bored like he had to repeat the same words a thousand times a day. "It was one of the first grapes planted here at Radiata Vineyard when we opened fifteen years ago. The grapes were originally thought to have been cultivated in the ancient Persian capital of Shiraz in Iran and brought to France by the Phoenician mariners around 600 BC. But modern genetic testing has demonstrated that the grape, also known as Syrah, can actually be traced to the northern Rhone area of France at least four thousand years ago."

Sharky and I tried some. Sharky did the whole swish and spit bit, swirling his tiny sip around in his mouth like it was mouthwash for a ten seconds or so, and then spitting it out into a waste pitcher our helpful tasting guide placed on the counter. I just sipped and swallowed. I'm a simple kind of guy. It tasted like wine. Red wine.

"Nice peppery finish," Sharky said.

"Yes, that's the Shiraz variety's claim to fame," our tasting guide said. "Most people mention notes of coffee, chocolate and black pepper."

"What do you get, Hack?" he asked.

"Wine," I said. "Red wine. Chewy."

"I think your notes are out of tune," Sharky said.

Tasty Boy poured us some cabernet and something called tempranillo, which he said was a Spanish grape. "It comes from a region in Spain with a climate much like our own," he said. "Arid, temperate, chalky, sandy soil, some marine influence. I think you'll like it."

I actually did. It was a deep purple wine, smelled fruity and it tasted like purple, fruity wine. I told Sharky what I thought.

"You are probably the world's worst oenophile," he said.

"I'm number one!" I said.

A fairly large crowd of people began filing in. At the head of the group was the woman Sharky and I had seen with Mike Nelson up at Redwood the day before. Dressed in slacks and a polo shirt featuring the logo of the vineyard, she was speaking in a loud, outdoor voice and gesticulating like a flight attendant explaining where the exit rows are located.

"Okay, people," she said, "Please take a position along this counter. Our wine guides will serve your samples and answer any questions you might have. When you're done, don't forget to visit our wine and gift shop, so you can take home any of our fine wines to enjoy with your friends and family."

Her charges obeyed her orders and she turned away, looking somewhat relieved. I went up to her.

"Cassie?" I said.

She looked at me blankly.

"I was wondering if you had time to answer a couple of questions for my friend and me."

She peeked at the watch on her wrist, frowned, but nodded.

"I've got another group in ten minutes," she said. "But shoot."

"Did you know Charlie Sykes?" I asked.

"Or Mike Nelson?" Sharky had come up next to me.

Her eyes went from me to Sharky and back again, and her face paled. One of her hands came up to her throat and began fiddling with the charm on her necklace dangling there.

"Oh my God," she said, almost to herself. "You are the guys who went to see Mike the other day."

"Yup," I said. "We are."

"What do you want?" she said. "Why can't you just leave us alone?"

I looked around the room. There was a small patio off to one side of the building, with some plastic chairs and tables.

"Maybe we should go outside," I said, nodding at the patio. "We can talk privately there."

She nodded and led the way. Outside, the midday sun felt good on our backs as we all sat around a clear-topped table.

"So we know that Charlie and Mike were besties up at Stanford," I started. "How did you come to know them?"

She looked at us, studying me first, then looking at Sharky.

"You aren't cops, are you?" she said. It was a statement, not a question.

"No, ma'am," Sharky said. "We're investigating a letter someone sent to Pebble Beach. We think it might have been Mike Nelson."

She shook her head sadly.

"I told those guys it was a big mistake," she said. "I told them it would backfire."

"Maybe you should start at the beginning," I suggested. She did.

She had met, and briefly dated, Charlie Sykes at Stanford. They were friends first, she said, and although she had been interested in taking things further, Sykes had demurred, telling her he needed to concentrate on his academics and his golf. But it was all very friendly and not awkward, so they continued hanging out. And since Mike Nelson was Charlie's best friend, he became part of the circle of friends. Which meant that Cassie grew fond of Mike, too, and he returned the feelings. Pretty soon, they had a nice little threesome going.

"Not a sexual thing, really," she said to us. "There was one night when we all got pretty hammered and high, and we all fell asleep on the same bed. There might have been a little drunken groping that night, but, again, it was all cool."

After graduation, the three of them found work on the Monterey Peninsula: Charley rode his family connections into the job at Pebble, Mike landed a job at the Ranch at Redwoods, and Cassie began working at Radiata, planning to move into marketing and promotions after serving her time as a tour guide.

Cassie had all but moved into Mike's trailer up in the hills, they were planning to make it official soon, and Charley was a frequent visitor. Like most twenty-somethings, they partied together, went to concerts, ski weekends in the winter, hiked in the mountains some … the usual work-hard, play-hard lifestyle of people their age. Life was good.

"Did Charley have any girlfriends?" I asked.

She shook her head. "Nope. He told us he was waiting for what he called 'the big score' before he even thought about settling down," she said. "Charley was goal oriented. He knew what he wanted and he was going to get it. He wouldn't let anything else get in his way."

"What was the big score?"

"I don't know," she admitted. "I don't think he knew. He just believed that something big would come along and he wanted to be ready to cash in when it did."

So Cassie, at least, was not surprised when Charley came out to their trailer toward the end of last year and asked them to help him write a letter. He told them he had learned about something that was going on at the Pebble Beach Company, and that what he had learned could easily result in making him lots of money.

"He found his Big Score," I said.

Cassie nodded.

"What was it?"

She shook her head. "He wouldn't tell us the details," she said. "He said he wanted to protect us, keep us out of trouble. We helped him come up with a fake name. Mike has a cousin in Idaho named Newell, so we used that."

"How did Charley expect to score a lot of money by pretending to be Udall's long-lost son" Sharky asked.

Cassie looked at us blankly.

"What are you talking about?" she said. "What long-lost son? That's not what the letter was about."

Sharky and I looked at each other.

"What was the letter about?" I asked.

"Mike and I never saw the actual letter," she said. "Charley wrote it. But he told us he was going to tell them he knew what was going on and would tell the authorities what was going on unless …"

"Unless someone paid him to keep quiet," I said.

"Yeah, that was basically it," she said. "I told him he was crazy and that he could get into serious trouble. But he thought he could pull it off. He said he had all the information he needed. He said it was a slam dunk."

"And then he went over the cliff," I said. "Not the kind of slam dunk he was thinking about, was it?"

Her eyes filled and she looked away.

"He told us he was going to collect the money," she said. "That was the night he died."

"Do you think he killed himself?"

She shook her head vigorously, but could not speak. A few tears ran down her cheek.

"After he died, did you say anything?"

"No," she said in a gasp. "I told Mike we had to keep this quiet. Either we'd get in trouble with someone for knowing about Charley's plan, or someone would think we were somehow involved. And …"

"And you could be in danger yourselves," I finished for her.

"Probably a good call," Sharky said.

"Are you going to tell on us?" Cassie's voice wavered. "Is Mike going to get in trouble?"

"I don't know," I said. Because I didn't know. "If someone pushed Charley Sykes over the cliff, that's homicide. I think we've got to tell the police what you just told us."

"Can't you just leave Mike and me out of it? Tell them to find the guy Charley wrote his letter to."

"But you don't know who that is," I pointed out.

"Oh, yeah," she said.

I took out my wallet and fished out a business card.

"Why don't you have another little talk with Mike," I said. "Maybe you could help him try and remember if he ever heard the name of the guy who got the letter. Anything would help. How Charley met the guy. When and where? Did they meet in person, or on the phone? Or did he send an email or a text? Anything like that could help us track the guy down. If we get him, we don't need you."

"I will," she promised, and flashed us a weak smile. "I'll try."

She got up and left. Her next tour group had arrived. Sharky and I sat there in the bright sun.

"Strauss showed me a copy of the letter," I said. "It said nothing about blackmail. It was all about being a long-lost heir to Udall and that he wanted his share."

"Do you think Cassie was lying to us?"

"No," I said. "I don't. Do you?"

"Didn't feel like it," he said. "We gotta tell Johnny Levin what we know," he said. "It's material evidence of a possible crime."

"Yeah, I know," I said. "But do we have to tell him today? If Cassie can squeeze some information out of Mikey, we might be able to shed a little light on what really went down."

"Johnny would say we should tell him right now," he said. "But I don't think waiting a day or two is gonna thwart justice all that much."

"Right," I said. "We're not thwarting justice, we're just letting it simmer for a bit."

"And like Oliver Wendell Holmes used to say, justice simmered is justice …"

"Made more delicious," I said.

CHAPTER 22

THE AT&T PRO-AM officially began at the crack of dawn on Thursday, but Sharky and I decided to ignore it until around noon. Then he drove us down 17 Mile Drive to the course at Spyglass Hill, one of the three courses utilized in the tournament, along with Pebble and one of the courses at the Monterey Country Club.

Sharky told me that he'd been invited to watch the golf from the comfort of the balcony outside the offices of the Northern California Golf Association, which perch above the 9th and 18th greens on the course.

"Open bar, good eats, indoor toilets," he said succinctly.

"Sounds good to me," I said.

It was a cloudy day, damp and chilly, with the wind coming in strong off the cold Pacific. Little bands of mist blew in with a scattering of rain, draping the trees in smoky clouds that hung, drifted and were blown away again. Very atmospheric, especially out at Spyglass Hill, which even on a nice day can feel otherworldly. Most of the holes are built beneath a cathedral of tall pines along a ridge above the ocean. But the first hole, a long par-five, drops out of the cathedral into an open, treeless plain where the rocky sea is visible just across 17 Mile Drive, and you can often hear the seals barking away on the rocks where they gather just offshore. Down there, the fairways and greens are bordered by thick, impenetrable stands of ice plant and sedge, and the ocean breeze is always a factor. Soon, the course climbs back up into the forest and I've never played Spyglass without having a herd of deer materialize suddenly from some dark thicket, prance around the fairway, and run off into some other part of the woods. Part of the magic of the place.

I rode with Sharky since he had all the required parking passes. Gotta love a guy with resources. He pulled into a lot right behind the NCGA offices and we made our way inside. Sharky was busy greeting everyone, shaking hands and exchanging hugs. That happens almost everywhere Sharky goes, so one gets used to it.

Eventually, we made our way out to the redwood deck which, as advertised, overlooked both finishing holes of the nines. White jacketed crew were busy setting up a full bar on one end of the deck, and chafing dishes for the luncheon on the other. Tables and chairs were scattered everywhere.

Sharky brought me a beer. "This is the way to watch golf," he said.

"If that's what you call it," I said, and motioned down to the ninth green, where one of the amateurs in the foursome, a country musician of whose work I was unfamiliar, was blading shots back and forth across the green, from bunker to bunker until his professional partner told him to pick the goddam thing up and get out of the way.

"Reminds me of me," Sharky said with a chuckle.

Somebody wearing a knee-length black cape, a pair of filigreed cowboy boots and a ten-gallon Stetson hat, strolled out onto the deck, saw Sharky and me standing next to the railing, and came over. His boots rang out on the wood decking, a sound which made the grumpy golf pro down below us break away from the putt he was about to make and shoot a dark and angry glance up the hill at us.

"Hack-Man!" said Andre Citrone when he came up, cape aflourish. "Wassup?"

"Sheriff Dracula, I presume," Sharky said, under his breath but loud enough for Drey to hear. He turned and looked at Sharky.

"Hello, Lawrence," he said. "Are you out of rehab again?"

The dripping condescension in Drey's voice was arresting. Until that moment, I never knew Sharky's real first name. I had never heard anyone use it before. And the shot about rehab was the final low blow. I looked around for a place to stash my beer when the fisticuffs broke out.

"Citrone," Sharky said with a sneer, flashing the fakest smile at him I had seen in a while. "I enjoyed your piece last Sunday. Oh, no wait, that was somebody else. I don't buy your paper. Sorry."

"Now, boys," I said. "Can't we all just get along?"

Neither of them answered, which I took as a definitive 'no.'

"Have you talked with Jake Strauss?" I asked Andre. "I told him you were looking for a word."

He shook his head. "I left word," he said. "He hasn't called me back yet." He looked at Sharky.

"You haven't heard anything about the Pebble Beach Company being put up for sale, have you, Lawrence?" he said. He put a little emphasis on the name. "My sources tell me a sale is happening pretty quick."

Sharky looked at Citrone. I could hear the wheels spinning in Sharky's head as he decided just which body part would receive the sudden thrust of the dagger. Almost reflexively, I stepped back a bit.

An Open Case of Death

"This place is always for sale," he said. "Meyer and his group would sell it this afternoon if someone came along and offered them the number they're thinking about. So you should go ahead and write the story. It might not be accurate today, or tomorrow, but one day it will happen, and you'll have nailed it."

Drey glared back at him, but kept silent. He turned and looked at me.

"I understand you're interested in the Huckleberry Hill project, Hacker," he said. "Give me a call sometime. I've got loads of material on that abortion."

I looked at him over the top of my beer bottle while I took a sip. He was looking at me with a little smirk. Take that, he seemed to be saying.

"That's the second time you've asked me about something I discussed privately with Jake Strauss," I said. "Which one of us do you have wired?"

Citrone laughed and turned away a bit to take a glass of red wine from the tray of a waiter passing by.

"A good reporter never divulges his sources, Hack," he said. "You should know that."

"Yeah, but we're talking about you, Drey," Sharky said. "That rules out the good reporter part."

Citrone's face got redder and I began to envision not just fisticuffs, but a full-blown, chair-slinging brawl.

"Hey," I said, "Look who just walked in! The man himself. Drey, you can ask him anything you want."

I nodded over at the door to the deck, and we all saw Jake Strauss come outside, in the company of three other guys in suits and ties. I waved, Jake saw me, and headed our way.

"Mr. Strauss," I said when he walked up. "I think you know Sharky Duvall here…" They nodded at each other. "…And this is Andre Citrone of the Chronicle. He has a question for you."

Strauss turned and looked at Andre. I saw him give the man's ridiculous outfit a head-to-toe scan and gave him credit for not bursting out in laughter. Strauss smiled and cocked his head to the side, waiting.

"Um, right," Drey hesitated, then decided to jump right in. "My sources have been telling me that you're out here brokering the sale of the Pebble Beach Company," he said. "True?"

Strauss' smile widened a bit, and he paused a bit before answering.

"No, not really," he said.

"Not really?" Drey jumped. "What part is true, then?"

"I love this cape," Jake said, reaching out and tugging at the shoulders. "I don't know why more men don't wear capes. They seem so useful."

"Most men don't want to be seen as fashion morons," Sharky said. "But that's just one reason for most men. Having an ounce of self respect is another."

"Shut up, you fat fuck," Andre growled. "Who asked you?"

"Now, now," Strauss chuckled, holding up his hands. "I said 'not really' because I know that Pebble Beach gets offers all the time. Probably two or three a month. Unsolicited. At least, that's what I've been told. I'm not in that business anymore, Drey. I'm in the business of growing the game of golf and running our tournaments."

He reached out and brushed a bit of pine needle that had fallen onto Drey's shoulder. "So it sounds like your sources may have jumped the gun a bit," he said. "Or maybe they just misunderstood. But I'm glad you asked. I appreciate the chance to set the record straight."

That was Jake Strauss to a T. Polite, transparent, authoritative. He would have made a good politician, except he wasn't corrupt. Or, not corrupt enough.

"Why do I think you wouldn't tell me even if it was true?" Drey said.

Strauss chuckled again. "Now, Andre, that sounds rather cynical," he said. "Have I ever told you something that was untrue?"

"You told me that writing this goddam book would be easy," I said. "That's turned out to be, shall we say, a bunch of bull hockey."

Strauss laughed out loud at this. *HaHa*. He looked at Sharky. "My goodness, Mr. Duvall," he said. "I am under attack from all sides. Perhaps I'd best find more congenial company."

"I'm still working this story," Drey said, sounding a bit menacing. "My sources are solid."

Strauss merely shrugged and stayed silent. Drey exhaled loudly in frustration, turned on his heel and stomped away, boots ringing angrily. We watched him go.

"How good are his sources?" Strauss asked me when Drey had left the deck. "What does he have?"

I shrugged. "Sharky says he's tight with Harold Meyer," I said. "So he may be getting good information. He seems to know about everything you and I talk about."

"Really?" Strauss said. "Duly noted." He looked at me. "Where the hell is Mike Newell?"

I shrugged. "The lead I was following proved inconclusive," I said. I hoped that sounded legitimate. Strauss looked at Sharky. He shrugged. Strauss shook his head.

"I'm planning on flying back to New York tonight," he said. "I've got the Gulfstream coming in to the Monterey airport around ten. Would you like to fly back East with me?"

"Sure," I said, "My wife misses me and I should really be working on the book, not hanging out here in the land of fruits and nuts."

We made plans on where to rendezvous, shook hands all around and Strauss went off to make the rounds with the NCGA people.

"Still letting justice simmer, I see," Sharky said, smiling at me.

"I'm not gonna throw those kids under the bus until I figure out what's going on," I said.

"And why Jacob Strauss showed you a fake letter."

"And why he has been banging on about that letter being some kind of threat to the management arrangement at Pebble Beach," I said. "Not to mention that he's leaking to Andre Citrone about everything I'm doing.

"Lotta questions," he said.

"Not many good answers," I said.

"Geez," he said. "I hope I can rent your room out for the rest of the weekend."

"Hope you can get at least what I was paying for it," I said.

"Oh, yeah," Sharky said. "Forgot about that."

A waitress carrying a tray of hors d'oeuvres stopped in front of us. I was hungry, but I resisted the urge to just take the whole tray and make her go back to the kitchen and get another one. Instead, I took one toothpick stabbed into a square of cheese, and another holding together a bacon-wrapped barbecued shrimp.

"The longer we wait, the worse it may be for those kids," he said. "Not to mention us. Cops generally don't like not being told about important stuff. Especially in murder cases."

"I hear ya," I said. "But I need to know more. It appears to be a strong case that someone out there shut up Charley Sykes."

"He was most definitely shut up," Sharkey said. "Permanently."

"And those two kids, as you call them, would be next in line," I said. "Wouldn't be fair to leave them unprotected."

"Not a fair fight," Sharky said, nodding.

"Let's wait and see if we can find out more."

A burst of cheers from down below interrupted us. One of the pros had made a nice long putt for birdie. He walked across the green, pulled his ball from the hole and waved his acknowledgment for the cheers.

"Oh, look," Sharky said. "They just put out the fried calamari. It must be lunchtime."

CHAPTER 23

Sharky, Aggie and I had a farewell drink late that afternoon. We met at Steinbeck's, not for old times sake, but because they sold beer there.

"Will you miss me?" I asked.

"Only if you stay gone," Sharky said. But he smiled.

Aggie rummaged around in her bag and pulled out a notepad with some notes written on it.

"I heard back from my friend up in San Francisco," she said. "She worked in the ICU when that Udall guy was there. She wouldn't—or couldn't—send me his files, but she told me what was in them."

She riffled through her notebook.

"Udall had advanced congestive heart failure," she said. "Four events in five years. They had him stabilized and monitored and his prognosis was guardedly positive."

"What does that mean?" I asked.

"They had every expectation that he would recover and be released within a week at the most," she said. "His life expectancy was not great. But they all felt he had more time left in his ticker."

"Guess they were wrong," I said. "Do they know what actually killed him?"

"No," Aggie said, shaking her head. "Again, no post-mortem was performed. Nor was one indicated. Still, their notes indicate that it was a pulmonary edema that killed him."

"And that is …?"

"His lungs filled with fluid," Agatha said. "His heart was not strong enough to help eliminate the fluid. He basically drowned."

"Is that unusual?"

"No," she said. "Patients with severe heart failure often present with edema. That's why the usual treatment is to give the patient diuretics. In most cases, they give the patient a water pill every three or four hours and monitor the amount of urine to make sure that fluids are coming out. In severe cases, the patient gets an IV solution with the diuretic flowing directly into the bloodstream. Udall was getting 20 milligrams of furosemide every hour in intravenous saline."

She looked up from her notebook.

"However, Patty noticed something when she was reviewing the records," she said.

"What?"

"There was a notation that said there was a clamp found on the IV tube," she said. "After Udall died, they were unhooking all the equipment and monitors they had him on, and one of the nurses noted how much saline and other medicines were left. Part of the usual records they keep. But there was a note that there was a clip found on the IV tube. It didn't say it was blocking the flow of saline, or that anyone put it there deliberately. Just that there was a clip found on the tube. Patty told me that was a bit unusual, and had she been there, she might have asked a question or two about it. But Udall's death was not deemed unusual, so nobody paid much attention."

"If someone did clip off the IV tube and Udall wasn't getting his diuretic infusion, what would have happened?" I asked.

"His lungs would have quickly filled with fluid and he would have drowned," Aggie said.

"So it's possible that someone killed him," I said.

"Possible, but pretty hard to prove," Aggie said. "When he goes Code Red, alarms start going off and nurses and doctors rush to his bedside to see what they can do. Then, when he's declared dead, everyone leaves, and one junior nurse begins cleaning up the room, taking out all his IVs, making notes of the last readings from the machines, that kind of thing. No one is looking for evidence of murder. It's more like 'How fast can we clear out this patient and bring another one in?'"

"I wonder if they have security cameras in that hospital," I said, thinking out loud. "Maybe we could see who was the last one to visit Udall before he died?"

"I thought of that," Aggie said, nodding. "I asked Patty and she said she'd ask someone. He died more than six months ago, so I doubt if they keep security videos around that long if there's no reason."

"Yeah," I said. "Probably a dead end. But thanks for asking."

I finished my beer, bid them farewell and then I drove out to the Monterey Regional Airport, dropped off my rental car and had them take me over to the private air terminal. The airport at Monterey handles mostly small puddle-jumper commercial planes working their way up and down the Pacific coastline, but does a big business in private aviation.

Strauss hadn't arrived yet, so while I waited in the comfortable lounge, I called Mary Jane to tell her I'd be home in the morning, probably around eleven. I'd have to make my way from Teterboro in New Jersey, where Strauss' plane was going to land, over to LaGuardia and catch a shuttle up to Beantown.

"I'm glad you're coming home," she said. "But I'm working tomorrow, so I won't be able to meet you at the airport."

"I'm ready to be home again, too," I said. "Not to worry. I hear Boston has good public transportation."

"Yeah, I've heard that too," she said. "Be safe. See you tomorrow."

Strauss came into the terminal, dragging his suitcase behind, with his big leather briefcase draped over his shoulder. I noticed how people began to jump into action when he came in—they had pretty much ignored me just a few minutes earlier. I guess it's good to be the King. With a high net worth.

In short order, we were walked out onto the tarmac, climbed in his Gulfstream, slammed the door shut, taxied out to the end of the runway and blasted off into the night sky.

"I kinda miss the experience of being groped by some TSA guy," I said.

HaHa.

There was seating for eight on the plane, so we had plenty of room to spread out. And we had Jilly. She swore that was really her name, even after I accused her of stealing it from some Bond girl. She fit the Bond girl stereotype: she was tall, ginger-haired, slender, curvaceous, well-dressed and had a smile that could light up Piccadilly Circus. She brought us each a cocktail, which she made to order, and then began working at a galley at the rear of the plane.

"We have a nice chicken alfredo and pasta," she said, "With a green salad. And a very nice pinot noir from Napa. It'll be ready in a jiff."

Strauss pulled a big wad of papers out of his briefcase, but sat there looking at it with an expression of boredom.

"So what did *you* learn this week, while I was off chasing after dead ends in the Carmel Valley?" I asked him. And hoped he wouldn't ask any follow ups.

"Well," he said, "Pebble seems to be ready for the Open. Unless they have terrible weather this spring, the course should be in good condition by mid-June. The new greens they renovated are looking like they've been there for decades. All the logistics seem to be well in hand. It's not their first rodeo, and almost everyone at Pebble Beach knows what their job is. So I'd say they're as ready as they can be at this point in time."

"And if Andre Citrone breaks his story about the sale?"

"It's not a sale," Strauss said. "It's a partnership realignment. Partial buy-out. But the basic ownership structure stays the same. There's nothing that needs to be filed in public, at least at this point. And since the Pebble Beach Company is privately held, it's no business of the SEC or any other regulatory agency. So if they have nothing to declare, they have nothing to deny. He really doesn't have a story."

"What if Will Becker or Jack Webber go public?" I asked. "They could tell Citrone they've cashed out. He could use that, couldn't he?"

"Dottie van Dyke has been instructed to deny everything," Strauss said. "Mr. Citrone will get a great big 'no comment.'"

"Like that's ever worked," I said, mostly under my breath.

Jilly brought each of us a tray with a linen cloth, real silverware, a china plate and crystal wine glass. Then she wheeled over a serving unit with the food on it. We helped ourselves while she poured us each a glass of wine. It was delicious.

An Open Case of Death

After dinner, she cleared the dishes away, passed around a basket of freshly baked chocolate chip cookies and dimmed the cabin lights. Strauss made another effort at his stack of paperwork, and then fell asleep, snoring softly. I tried to watch a movie—there were several tablets on board, each pre-loaded with about twenty recent features. But I couldn't concentrate. Too much stray info was buzzing around in my head. I finally turned the movie off.

Jilly noticed and came over.

"Sleeping pill?" she inquired.

"Seriously?" I said.

"Absolutely," she said with a smile. "Our job is to get you to your destination, well rested, alert and ready to rumble."

I thought about it. Fine chemicals for better living. I think one of the DuPonts once said that. What the hell. I nodded. She put a little white pill in my hand and gave me a glass of water. I swallowed. And by the time we hit the Rockies, I was dead asleep.

It was closer to one o'clock the next afternoon when I finally walked in the door of my apartment in the North End of Boston. Mister Shit the cat raised his head from his sleeping place on the arm of the couch and looked at me. He was so excited to see me, he yawned, dropped his head and went right back to sleep.

I put my bag in the bedroom, kicked off my shoes, got a cold beer out of the fridge and picked up a big stack of mail on the kitchen counter. I took it back to the couch and began to sift through it, separating the bills from the junk. There were no envelopes containing checks. There rarely are.

I went to put my drink down on the end table and saw a little paperback book resting there. I almost just ignored it, putting my drink down on it as a coaster substitute, when I noticed the title.

BABY'S JOURNEY: THE STEPS TO MOTHERHOOD.

I picked it up and began to read. It was quite interesting, what with the illustrations showing the size of a tiny fetus at four weeks, eight weeks and twelve weeks. And lots of information about exercise and nutrition and sleep.

I was still reading at three, when Mary Jane and Victoria came bounding in from their day at school. They were both laughing at something as they came through the door, saw me, and came running over for a group hug.

Mary Jane noticed me holding the book, my thumb stuck in it halfway through, keeping my place. It was the chapter about all the wonderful changes to a woman's body that could be expected to happen from the tenth through the twentieth weeks of gestation.

"Oh, crap," she said. "I wanted to tell you in person."

"*We're gonna be a mommy!*" Victoria shrieked, loudly enough to cause Mister Shit to jump off the arm of the couch in alarm and run away into the bedroom to hide under the bed. A part of me wanted to go with him.

"You mean…" I started to speak, but found I was suddenly breathless. Mouth was dry. Felt a little dizzy.

"You are *not* going to faint on me, Hacker," Mary Jane said sternly. "I won't have that. You're in this with me up to your fetlocks, so buck up."

"I…" I tried speaking again. "I'm …"

"*You're gonna be a daddy!*" Victoria shrieked again, and began jumping up and down. "Hacker's a daddy! Hacker's a daddy!"

Mary Jane grinned at me. "Surprised?" she said.

"Just a bit." I finally managed a complete sentence. But my mind was spinning away again, eleventy thousand different thoughts competing, trying to fight their way through to the vocalization part of the brain.

AN OPEN CASE OF DEATH

I finally gave up. I dropped the Mommy book on the floor and grabbed my wife in an embrace that threatened to go on forever.

"Easy, big boy," she said finally, after a long, long while. "I'm hugging for two, now."

"Is that why you were puking every morning like clockwork?" I asked.

"My man, ace detective," she said with a smile.

"When did you find out?"

"I saw my OB/GYN about ten days ago," she said. "I knew before you went west, but I decided to wait until you got back. Didn't want you stumbling around out there like a zombie."

"When are we due?"

She laughed a little at the editorial 'we.' "I don't know when you're due, but I expect to be squeezing your little brat out of me sometime near the end of September."

I shuddered. "I think *I'm* going to puke, now," I said.

"Are you going to collapse at the first sight of blood?" she asked.

"There's going to be blood? Nobody told me there was going to be blood."

"You'd better finish that book," she said. "The good stuff happens at the end."

"The Vickster seems pleased," I noted.

MaryJane laughed. "She's been busy composing names this week," she said.

On cue, Victoria came bounding into the room. She held a lined notebook and a pencil.

"How's this?" she said. "Abena Adelaide Hacker. That's if its a girl, of course."

"Abena?" I said.

"It's from Ghana," she told me. "We've been studying the nations of Africa in school this month."

"Well, I suppose it's better than Idi Amin Hacker," I said.

"Silly," she said. "That's a boy's name." She skipped off back to her room.

I looked at Mary Jane. "Do we know what sex it is?"

She shook her head. "Another month or so. I have an ultrasound scheduled for mid-March. You can come with me and see for yourself." She paused. "There shouldn't be any blood."

Hacker, ace golf writer, now signed up for ultrasounds at the OB/GYN. *Yeah*, I thought, *that qualifies as change.*

Chapter 24

By April, the book was mostly finished. I shipped off what I had to an editor in New York, and she began sending me back chapters with her notes and suggestions. Most of them were very good. The publisher had found an art director who was laying in the old timey photos. When the Masters rolled around the second week of the month, we had more than three-quarters of the manuscript finished and ready to send off to the printer.

It felt more than a little weird not to be going down to Augusta for the annual flower show and golf tournament, but I managed to gut it out. I remembered the stories of Lincoln Werdell, the golf writer who had covered the first forty years of the Masters for the New York Times. The year after he finally retired, he had called down to Augusta National to see if he could get a press pass to come back and say hello, or good-bye, to all his fellow writers, the pros he had covered, and the members he had befriended over the years.

"*No*," the club had written back. "Working press only."

Such sweet, sweet people. I didn't even try to get credentialed, knowing their response would begin with "F" and end in "you." Despite all I did for them!

Instead, we went and had Sunday dinner with Carmine Spoleto out in Milton. It was his birthday, more or less, so the house was once again filled with a bevy of happy, noisy family. Everyone seemed thrilled to learn that Mary Jane and I were expecting, even though there was absolutely zero Spoleto bloodlines in our little growing buglet. Mary Jane spent most of the afternoon getting hugged by every woman in sight, and I endured more than a few semi-painful congratulatory whacks on the back. I think there's a lot of passive-aggressive genes in big Italian families.

As at Thanksgiving, Carmine eventually led me into his study, shutting the door against the cacophony going on outside. He poured us each a small glass of brandy.

"*Salute*," the old man said, raising his glass at me. "It is an honorable thing to have a family," he said. "My own son, may he rest in peace, was not an honorable man, but he redeemed himself when he created our Victoria. He lives on through her, and that is how it should be."

I did not mention that I hoped to whatever God was listening that Victoria did not retain a single characteristic in her own life and personality that recalled that small-time hoodlum, whose life skills included pistol whipping, loan sharking, prostitute running and general lowlife-edness. I didn't say that, but I thought it.

"How is your book coming?" he asked.

"Almost finished," I said. "It will be officially launched at the U.S. Open in California in June. There'll be a big party. You should come out."

He smiled and waved his hand. "Thank you," he said," "But I think my traveling days are over," he said. "But I am happy for your success."

We chatted for a bit about Mary Jane and her teaching position, and about how Victoria was doing in school. He cocked his head and looked at me.

An Open Case of Death

"How are things in Cali?" he said. "I trust you haven't run into any trouble out there?"

I laughed, a little ruefully.

"Well, there was a murder when I was out there last time," I said.

He clucked his tongue, a sound that seemed to mean *Oh, really? Do tell.* His eyebrows went up.

"Officially, they say it was a suicide, but I think someone killed the kid," I said. I explained briefly what had happened.

"*Dilettante*," Carmine said, sipping his brandy and sneering just a bit. "Amateur."

"How's that?"

"If you need someone to be dead, you make him dead," he said. "You don't go fooling around with pushing men over cliffs in silly little cars. Two shots to the head is faster and less trouble. The one who did this is not a killer. He is pretending."

"You're probably right," I said, nodding my agreement. "But now there's a twist. Maybe more than one."

"With you, Signore Hacker, there is always one of these…what did you call it? … *twists*," he said, a smile playing at the corners of his lips, eyes dancing. "What is it?"

I told him about the death of J.J. Udall and the arrival of the letter from Mike Newell, claiming to be his heir. And how Strauss had asked me to find the letter writer. And how I had discovered that the letter wasn't from an heir, but was blackmail.

"And you found him," Carmine said, his eyes narrowed.

"I did."

"But you didn't tell this Strauss that you found him."

I blew out a breath. "No," I said, "I didn't."

"And why is that?"

"I don't know who to trust," I said, and realized that I was admitting this to myself for the first time.

"And why is that?"

"Well, there's a lot of money at stake," I said. "And then there's the letter thing. The letter I was shown was all about claims of a mystery heir. But the girlfriend of the letter writer says it was more of a direct attempt at blackmail. This Charley Sykes guy supposedly found out about something illegal going on and probably asked for money to keep quiet about it."

"And so he was killed," Carmine said.

"Yeah," I said. "I think that's what happened. So why would Jake Strauss give me a fake letter?"

"Because he is the killer, and he wants to find the others who know, and have them killed as well," Carmine said. "And he thinks you can find them. Which you have."

"But did the letter go to Jake Strauss?" I wondered. "Or did it go to one of the surviving owners? Like Harold Meyer, who probably stands to benefit the most. Maybe Meyer gave Strauss a fake letter. Or maybe Meyer told Strauss to make up the story about the heir. Maybe Meyer had Sykes pushed off that cliff."

"Or maybe it was someone else entirely," Carmine said.

"But who?"

He shrugged. "You tell me this company of the rocks …"

"Pebble Beach," I said, smiling.

"…Whatever…" he waved his hands. "This company you say is worth many millions of dollars, no?"

"It is indeed. Add in the real estate and it's probably more than a billion dollars."

"That is millions of reasons for someone to kill," he said. "I have seen men murdered for much, much less. But there is another problem I see."

"What?"

"This Pebble company, it is worth a lot. But here is the thing. You cannot easily take cash out of a company like that. Even if the worth of all the property is, say, two billion dollars, how does one take that money away?"

"Legally? You'd sell the property," I said.

He smiled.

"And then what happens?"

"You have to find a buyer. Who has the money or can borrow it," I said.

"And then?"

"The sale is recorded, money changes hands, the government comes in and takes it's share. State, local, federal …"

"In other words, lots of paper," Carmine said. "Lots of documents. Having lots of documents is not good if you are trying to steal the money. Also, little pieces of the whole are taken off … three percent for him, eight percent for her…pretty soon, the two billion is less. Pretty soon, it is all gone." He sipped his brandy and smiled. "That is not a good plan for someone trying to pocket the money."

"How would you do it?" I asked.

"Ah," he said, "That is a good question." He paused, thinking. "Do you know the town of Nahant?"

"On that little spit of land on the causeway off Lynn on the North Shore?" I said. "I know where it is. Can't say I've ever been out there."

He waved his hand dismissively.

"*Non importante*," he said. "There used to be a bar and restaurant out there, called Rick's Place. Opened many years ago by my friend, Enrico Corvo. He was a great man, Enrico. Came over here from Napoli after the war against the *fascisti*. Started his bar, married a fine woman, raised his family. He had three boys, I forget all their names. I am growing old, and my memory is not as it was. In any case, Enrico died, as we all must. His three sons could not decide what to do with his place, this Rick's Place, on the beach in Nahant."

He paused, thinking. "They came to me and said 'Zio'—they called me uncle because I was close to their father—they said 'Zio, we cannot decide what to do with our father's business. We cannot agree on how to proceed so that we are all happy. Help us, please, Zio.'"

He smiled at me. It was the smile of a hungry lion just before he leaps upon the back of the helpless wildebeest: feral, pitiless, determined. And doing just exactly what it was put on earth to do.

"That very night," Carmine said to me, "There was a fire at Rick's Place. My friend's bar burned to the ground. It was a total loss."

"That's terrible," I said.

"Yes," the old man said. "Terrible. And yet, they had the insurance, because my friend Enrico was smart in the ways of the world and of the men who live in it. And the boys were able to split that money up into portions for them all, even some for their sisters. And so, it was not so terrible in the end. In a way, it was a blessing."

"Did they rebuild the bar?"

Carmine Spoleto reached over and patted my knee.

"Of course not," he said. "None of those boys wanted to own a bar. Enrico had made sure they all had their education. They had all made their way in the world, far from the little town of Nahant, and the little business that their father had started. To them, the business was a problem, not an opportunity. They wanted the money, not the place itself. I helped them understand that. They were very happy, in the end."

I thought about that silently for a while. Carmine had taken none of the insurance money for himself after torching the business. That wasn't how it worked. Instead, the three brothers knew that one day, they would get a call from their Zio Carmine, either from him personally or from one of his *capi*, and they would be asked to perform a little favor. Drive a car up to Gloucester and leave it there. Or purchase some blankets and pots and pans for a safe house. And the boys would do it, automatically and gratefully. Just as they would send Zio Carmine a nice card on the Feast of St. Joseph, or light a candle in memory of Carmine's late wife on her saint's day. That was how it worked.

"I'm not sure I understand how that story relates to the situation at Pebble Beach," I said finally.

He shrugged. "They don't care about the business, my dear *genero*, they care about the money. *I soldi*."

CHAPTER 25

AT THE BEGINNING of May, I was invited to a lunchtime get together with some of my former colleagues at the *Journal*. A weep and greet if you will. I wasn't all that excited about attending, since weeping has never been my strong point, and there weren't all that many of my former workers I missed that much. The ones I really regretted not being able to see and talk with again were the ones who were dead.

But Mary Jane told me I needed to go.

"Maybe some of them miss *you*," she said. "Stop thinking of yourself first in everything."

She was probably right. And against the remote possibility she was wrong and I had a bad time, I could always come home and blame her rampaging hormonal influenza. Silently, of course, since I do not have an advanced death wish.

So I put on some clean pants and a semi-pressed shirt on the selected day and began walking over to the Quincy Market, a place the city fathers had helped renovate a few decades ago, turning what had been a row of rat-infested warehouses, empty and crumbling next to the once-horrible elevated highway that had split downtown Boston, a

An Open Case of Death

highway replaced by the Big Dig, which had enriched generations of labor bosses and politicians. The Market was now a nice tourist attraction filled with food shops, cafes, restaurants and shops, all in the shadow of Faneuil Hall, where historical things had once happened. Of course, in Boston, historical things had once happened on virtually every street corner, which the city fathers had wisely decided not to memorialize with lots of signs and plaques. JOHN QUINCY ADAMS SPAT HERE IN 1789!

I came out of my building. It was one of those sunny but raw spring days in Boston. The wind was out of the northwest, which means it was coming straight down from Canada, crossing Lake Erie where it picked up enough moisture to pack a punch, and then whistled straight across New York and New England in relentless cold gusts. Winter was over, but not by much, even here in May.

I set off at a brisk pace, thankful I had put on my windbreaker, did a few zigs and zags through the neighborhood streets and was strolling down Hanover when I noticed ... no, *felt* ... someone behind me. So, at the next storefront window, I stopped, looked inside, then spun around fast.

Standing there, looking at me stupidly, was Mike Nelson. He had to stop suddenly to avoid running into me. His face reddened. He was wearing jeans, a thick sweater and a San Francisco Giants baseball cap. The latter item did nothing to help him blend into the background. Not in this town.

"Well, well, well," I said. "Fancy running into you here on the mean streets of Boston. You wouldn't be following me, would you?"

"I ... no ... I mean ..." he stammered. "Hacker, I need to talk to you." He finally got the words out.

Gennaro's Cafe was a few doors down. I motioned at him to follow me and led him into the warm, brick-and-beams space. The aroma of roasting coffee filled the air, competing with the wonderful smells of baked good coming out of Gennaro's brick ovens. Sorry, Dunkin Donuts, you lose!

I ordered us each a large espresso and led Nelson to a table in the back, against the brick wall. I took the chair facing the door. One surprise a day is my quota.

"What are you doing in Boston?" I asked when we sat down. "And did you bring Cassie with you?"

"I need to talk to you," he said. "Cassie's still in California. But she had your business card. So I came east."

"Did you ever think about calling me on the telephone?" I asked. "It's a great modern invention. Can save a body from flying across the country sometimes."

A waiter, an older Italian gentleman with a wonderful bushy gray walrus mustache, came over with a tray containing our coffees. He set them down with a flourish, nodded at us silently and disappeared.

Mike sipped his coffee gratefully, like a man who hasn't had much good lately in his life. He closed his eyes, savoring the taste. He opened them again and looked at me.

"I couldn't use the phone," he said. "I think they were listening in."

"Who?" I asked. "The CIA?"

He sipped some more coffee. He did look thinner than the last time I had seen him, working in the lap of luxury at the Ranch at Redwoods. I figured I was going to have to spring for some food to get him to talk to me.

"They tried to kill me," he said.

Not much you can say in response to that. *Oh, gee, really?* Or *Well, I see they missed* are probably not proper comebacks. So I didn't say anything, waiting for him to tell me.

He did. About two weeks ago, he had finished up his work at the golf course, told his co-workers he was going home and headed off. But on the way, he had suddenly decided to go see Cassie, and had continued on to the vineyard where she worked. They went out for dinner, and then he decided to stay at her apartment for the night. None of this was unusual.

His cellphone woke him up at three in the morning. The county cops were calling to tell him his trailer had gone up in smoke. Burned to a crisp. They said preliminary information was that a big old Molotov cocktail had been pegged through his front window, and did he know of anybody mad enough at him to try to kill him?

Of course, he demurred. Even when Johnny Levin of the Monterey sheriff's office had noted that Mike Nelson had been longtime best friends with the late Charley Sykes, who had met an ugly and as yet unexplained end at the bottom of the cliff at hole number eight at Pebble Beach back in December.

Mike had sworn there was no connection, and then he had gotten the hell out of Dodge.

"I hitched a ride with a trucker," he said. "Got as far as Chicago. Then I found another who took me to Hartford. Got into Boston two days ago."

"You been on the streets?"

He nodded.

"Hungry?"

He nodded.

I waved for the old Italian gentleman and asked him for a menu. I ordered some calzones and a pepperoni pizza. And more coffee. I called the woman who had organized the weep and greet and told her something had come up and I was going to have to cancel.

When the food came, steaming hot out of the oven, I mostly sat back, ate a slice of pizza and watched Mike devour the rest. I think he had been hungry.

Once he was finished, he sat back with a groan of satisfaction.

"How did they find you?" I asked, while he wiped the tomato sauce off of his face and hands. "Did you tell anyone about Charley and the letter?"

"No," he said, shaking his head vigorously. " I swear, neither one of us has said a thing. I don't know how they found me."

"Nothing out of the ordinary?"

He started to shake his head again, but stopped. "Well," he said, "There was this phone call…"

"Tell me," I ordered.

"It was a few weeks ago," he said. "I was home one night and my phone rang and the person said 'Is this Mike?' I didn't recognize the voice. It was a man, with a deep voice. But it sounded kinda fake to me. So I said 'You have the wrong number' and hung up."

"Guess you didn't fool him," I said.

"Guess not," he said. His shoulders sagged. "I'm fucked, aren't I?" His voice wavered a bit, but he was doing a good job holding it together. I imagine the calzones and pizza and the coffee helped.

"Not fucked, necessarily," I said. "But in a spot of bother, for sure. I would imagine whoever is chasing you has discovered that you and Charley Sykes were besties at Stanford, and maybe put two and two together."

"Will they go after Cassie, too?" He looked anguished at the possibility.

"Don't know, kid," I said. "Anything's possible."

"I left without calling her or anything," he said. "Haven't called her since I left. So if they're listening in on her phone, they can't trace her back to me."

"That's probably a good thing," I said. "Though she may be a bit worried."

"Can you call her?" He looked at me with big sad eyes. Like a puppy whose been lost for a week. "Tell her I'm OK?"

An Open Case of Death

"Probably not a good idea to say it exactly like that, in case someone from the dark side is listening," I said. "But I can probably think of a way to get her a message. But more important to me right now is, what are we going to do with you?"

The sad puppy eyes came back. "Well, I was hoping I could crash with you for a few days," he said. "Until we came up with a plan. I don't mind sleeping on a couch or something. Really. Even the floor would do."

I was shaking my head now. "Can't do that, sorry," I said. "Got a pregnant wife, a daughter, a mean cat and no extra room."

"Oh," he said, shoulders slumping again. "Well, I can try the shelters. I had some soup over at a church yesterday, and they told me about some place on Pine Street or something."

"Pine Street Inn," I said. "Fancy name for Boston's best homeless shelter. But I might be able to do a little better than that."

I got out my phone, looked up a number in my contacts and dialed. When someone answered, I identified myself and asked to speak to the boss. "Have him call me back when he can," I said. "And be sure to tell him that his daughter and grand-daughter are fine. This is not an emergency. Thanks."

I hung up and waited. Mike waited too. What else was he going to do? In about five minutes, the phone beeped.

"Hacker?" Carmine Spoleto said. "What can I do for you?"

CHAPTER 27

ON TUESDAY EVENING, we all spiffed ourselves up nicely and drove back into Carmel. The bookstore was on Dolores Street, between 7th and 8th. It was called Zen and Sons and featured a nice little stony garden out in the back, with benches for meditation and little trickling fountains designed to make the wounded whole and heal the sin-sick soul.

The fountain bit didn't work with Mary Jane. "I gotta pee," she said when we walked out there to look. She disappeared inside. Victoria and I admired the peace and quiet.

Inside, Jake Strauss had arranged for a nice little cocktail party surrounding a white cloth-covered table covered with stacks of my book. Victoria looked at my name printed on the bottom of the cover photo (an old black and white shot of Pebble Beach) and gave me one of her sly smiles.

"They spelled your name right, at least," she said.

"Shut up," I whispered.

The blue-blazered USGA crowd was out in force. I hoped Strauss had told them they had to show up or get fired. But there were a few other people there I knew: a couple of golf writers I used to work with, some of the foreign golf officials in town for the US Open, and I even spotted one or two of the Tour players. Most everyone was gathered around the tables that had some finger-food laid out in trays, or were standing in line to get a glass filled with California wine or hand-crafted beer.

At the appropriate hour, Jake Strauss called for attention, gave a brief history of the book project—making sure to mention the early work done by Dick Steinmetz—and thanking me for my talent in creating this wonderful pictorial history of the courses of the U.S. Open. Everyone applauded.

I sat down behind the book table, pulled the top off a felt-tip pen and got ready to sign for the masses.

Naturally, nobody left the food table, nor got out of the free drink line. I had designated Victoria to be my in-line assistant, telling her to ask people to whom they wanted the book dedicated and to tell me when that person made it to the place in front of me. Instead, we stared at each other.

After about five minutes of waiting, I must have looked outwardly the way I was feeling inside. Which was something along the lines of *I wish I could disappear.*

Victoria looked at me. And sighed.

"This is totally bogus," she whispered to me. Then she turned to look at the crowds standing around the other tables.

"Have you people forgotten that this is a book signing?" she called out, using her outside voice. She has a very loud outside voice. "Hacker can't sign any books unless you buy one!"

The crowd turned to look at the little girl, as one. They fell silent. Someone giggled. But slowly, first one, then another, they began to come over to my table, pick up a book and hand it to me to be autographed. The bookstore people were standing by to record the sales. I was kept busy for the next hour or so: Victoria would chat with the people in line, tell me what to write in the flyleaf and then I signed my name. Sometimes, people I knew would stop and chat. It was nice. I felt like a writer.

Strauss had pulled up a chair nearby for Mary Jane, and she sat there, cradling her belly, sipping a glass of club soda, and smiling at me the whole time. People spoke to her as well, and she did a lot of smiling and nodding.

It was around nine o'clock when the room began to empty out. People were heading off to dinner. Sharky and Agatha were two of the last to go through the line. I tried to arrange for Sharky to be given a free book, but he insisted on paying for it like everyone else.

"If it's bad, I want to be able to say it sucks," he said, a smile playing around the corner of his mouth. "Can't do that unless I pay for it."

I gave up and signed his copy. Then I kissed Agatha and thanked her for coming out.

"Where shall we go eat?" I said. "The author is buying."

Just then, an older woman standing over by the hors d'oeuvres began to wheeze and gack, her hand flying to her throat. Her face turned red and she was in obvious distress.

"Hacker," Mary Jane said urgently, "She's choking!"

I started to move towards her, but was bumped out of the way. Jake Strauss leaped across the room, grabbed the woman, spun her around and locked his hands tightly beneath her breasts.

"Exhale!" he said and then gave her a hard squeeze.

"Again!" Another squeeze. A piece of half-chewed something, about as big around as a half dollar, came catapulting out of her throat. It flew about ten feet through the air and landed with a plop on the floor.

Strauss helped the woman into a chair that someone brought over. She was still gasping and crying and breathing in and out and trying to say thank you…all at the same time. Strauss grabbed her wrist and felt for her pulse, counting silently to himself.

"Good strong pulse rate," he announced, mostly to himself.

An employee of the book store came running over. "Do we need to call 9-1-1?" she asked anxiously.

"I don't think so," Strauss said. "Her pulse is strong, her breathing is unimpeded and her color is back to normal. I think she's fine. But if you'd like to ride to the hospital and let them make sure …?" He left the question for the woman to answer.

She held up her hand. "No, no, I'm fine," she said. "I'm very grateful to you, sir. That last bite just went down the wrong way."

"Yes," Strauss said. "A simple tracheal impediment. Usually pretty easy to dislodge, if you know what you're doing."

I stared at him, impressed.

"The doctor is in," I said. "Twenty-five cents."

He laugh-barked. *HaHa*. "Had the training," he said. "Four years in the Navy as a medical corpsman. I could've done a tracheotomy if I'd had to. But I'm glad I didn't." He turned to the woman, "Are you sure you're OK?" he asked.

"Very sure," the woman said, nodding. "Thank you again."

"Pretty good night, Hacker," Strauss said as we were leaving the bookstore. "Sold about forty books and saved a life."

Out on the sidewalk, Mary Jane announced that she and her daughter were heading back to the hotel.

"I'm beat," she said, "And the little one here is sleepy. You guys go and have a good time. We'll be fine."

"I'll get him home by midnight," Sharky promised her.

We walked the five or six blocks over to the Hog's Breath Inn, once owned by a famous actor. We waited for a table in the bar and finally were seated. Sharky ordered the sand dabs, Agatha had a salad and I went for the Australian lamb chops for no good reason other than that sounded good and I was in the mood to splurge.

"So, I've been nosing around a little to find out more about Huckleberry Hills," Sharky announced after we'd eaten and were enjoying some coffee.

"Good," I said. "I've been wondering what the story was with that project."

"It's odd, isn't it?" he said. "Everyone else in town thinks it's as dead as Tiger's A-game, but everyone connected with Pebble Beach seems to think it will someday—years down the road—get built. So I started thinking about why that is."

"Why what is, hon?" Aggie asked.

"Why people like Jake Strauss and Harold Meyer want to believe that Huckleberry Hills is still a viable project," he said. "There's gotta be a reason for them to cling to it."

"And what did you come up with?" I asked, knowing he'd come up with *something*.

He smiled that evil little Sharky smile at me. The one he keeps in reserve until he has something really juicy.

"You ever hear of an EB-5 visa?" he asked.

I looked at Agatha and she looked at me. We shook our heads simultaneously. "Nope," we said in unison. And laughed.

"Not surprised," Sharky said. "Not many people do, even immigration lawyers. But it's a pretty cool thing."

He told us how the EB-5 visa program worked. It had been set up by Congress to encourage foreign investments in the United States, especially investments in low income areas, like inner cities or rural wastelands.

"Basically, the deal is that if a foreign investor ponies up enough money for a new development project in the

An Open Case of Death

United States, and if that project generates jobs here, the investor gets fast-tracked to get a green card."

I whistled softly. "Dang," I said, "Those things are valuable. Everybody wants to get a green card. *Everything free in America!*"

"How much do they have to invest?" Agatha asked.

"Typically, at least one million dollars," Sharky said. "But in certain cases, like for projects in low income areas, a half-million will do just fine. And here's the kicker—the government usually doesn't do much checking up on these projects. You set up a company, tell all your foreign friends from China and Indonesia or wherever that you're accepting investments under the EB-5 program, they write you a check, you cash it and it's all legal."

"You don't have to have an actual development going on?" I said.

"Only if your investors want to get their green cards," he said. "But your US company can just *say* they're going to invest in some buildings in East Central LA, or the Mission District in Frisco, or in uptown Harlem, and the government will fast-track the visa. You file some paperwork and then just start collecting checks."

"Sounds like a program made for fraud," I said.

"Yeah, pretty much," Sharky said. "And the G-men have started to crack down a bit. I found some cases where indictments were filed here and there around the country, and some members of Congress have started complaining about it all. But no one knows how many of these little deals have been set up."

I sat up, interested.

"And you think Huckleberry Hills might be an EB-5 visa fraud?" I said.

"It fits the profile, to a T," he said, nodding. "Harold Meyer has the international connections. Hell, Jake Strauss does too, from his time at Baruch Brothers. They could be taking in millions from *investors*"— he made air quotes with his fingers—"help them obtain their green cards and just salting the cash away."

He smiled at me.

"It's a beautiful set up," he said. "Almost free cash for as long as they want to collect it. They know that Huckleberry Hills will never get past the Coastal Commission. They don't care, as long as they can keep selling points to foreigners. And they can keep selling points as long as they can offer green cards through the program."

"Wait a minute," Agatha jumped in. "Aren't both of those guys already as rich as fuck? Why would they do something like this sort of fraudulent deal? Just for the money? *More* money?"

Sharky and I looked at her. Then we both burst out laughing.

"Why does a cow eat grass?" I said, still chuckling as I paid the bill. "Ain't because he likes the taste. Because that's what cows do."

I sat in the back seat as Sharky drove me back to Spanish Bay.

"How can we test our hypothesis?" I said, thinking out loud. "Knowing Strauss and Meyer, they've probably got this thing buttoned down tight. They probably only accept new investors that are known to one of them, or someone they know. It'd be too dangerous to accept money from anyone off the street."

"Yeah, I thought the same thing," Sharky said. "It'd be a great little sting, but I don't know how we could pull it off."

"Shit, I'll bet Charley Sykes found out about it," I said. "He tried to finagle his way into the deal. Thought it was his big score. That's probably why he did a header off the cliff."

"Quite likely," Sharky said. "But we still don't know who pushed him."

"Strauss was worried about me mouthing off to Meyer," I said. "He told me Harold could easily have me beaten up, or worse."

"He does have a mysterious and slightly tawdry reputation," Sharky said.

He pulled into the hotel drive and dropped me at the door.

"Thanks guys," I said, getting out. "It was a great night. We sold some books, saved a life and came up with another harebrained theory that can't be proved."

"All in a day's work," Sharky said. He and Aggie were laughing as they waved and drove away.

CHAPTER 28

THE U.S. OPEN is different. You can try and step back from the hype, take in the view from thirty thousand feet and convince yourself that it's just another golf tournament. Another weekend of four rounds, field of a hundred fifty good golfers, nice pot of money waiting at the end. Just another weekend on the links. Tee 'em up boys, let 'em fly and may the best man win.

You could try that, but it won't work. The Open is a different animal altogether. It might be the history, or the tradition, or the artificial designation as one of "the majors." All of those things are important, but I think it goes deeper. Or maybe more basic.

Professional golfers play the game for money. We who watch them tend to forget that. Those who play do not. The USGA puts about twelve and a half million on the table. The winner gets two and a quarter mil. Every player in the field mentally deposits that cash before he tees it up on Thursday. That's why they're there. That's why they've constructed their lives around the game. All the practice, all the exercise, all the travel, all the swing coaches and mental gurus and physical therapists ... it's all because someone has put twelve million bucks on the table and invited them to go for it.

But there's more. All who play also want to be remembered. Like we remember Old Tom Morris. (Actually, we should probably remember and revere Willie Park, Senior, who won the first British Open in 1860, beating Old Tom and a field of a couple dozen at Prestwick.) But professional golfers want their names to be recalled along with Braid and Taylor and Vardon, with Bob Jones and Sarazen and Hagen, with Hogan and Snead and Nelson, with Jack and Arnie and Gary, with Tom Watson and Johnny Miller, with Tiger.

Nobody remembers who won the Memphis Open of 1965 or the Greater Milwaukee Classic in 1987. But if you win the U.S. Open, or the Open Championship or the Masters or the PGA, your name gets etched on the trophy and in history *forever*. People remember the name. Win a few of them and you become an immortal. *Immortal.* Like everlasting life. Like Zeus and Hera and Odin and Thor and even Yahweh. Yeah, that would tend to get you out of bed in the morning and off to the range.

And that's why the U.S. Open is different. Why the air is filled with electricity. Why the silence that descends upon a green rimmed by thousands of breathing souls becomes like that of the tomb, at least until the putt is struck. Why every shot, from the 250-yard approach to a two-foot knee-knocker, becomes so vitally important as to tear your guts out. It should be that way. It's immortality on the line.

On Thursday afternoon, with half the field already done with the first round and in the clubhouse, I wandered out to the fourteenth green at Pebble, making my way slowly through the crowds, enjoying the electricity and the silences and the cheers as I went. Mary Jane and the Vickster were off to visit the Monterey Aquarium, where Sharky had a friend who promised to take them on a backstage tour to watch while some of the animals were fed.

The weather was what it always is on the Monterey Peninsula in mid-June: foggy, cloudy, cool and damp. Most of the players wore sweaters or windcheaters. The usual suspects from the morning draw had turned in good scores: DJ, Speith, Koepka were all three or four under par. This afternoon, Tiger and Phil and Bubba were trying to match that, with varying degrees of success. One of the Molinari brothers tore up the front nine in five under, but made a few mistakes on the back side and had fallen back to earth.

Out on fourteen, I admired the renovated green that had been installed for this tournament. The green had always been small, like many at Pebble Beach, and appropriately so for a par-five. But fourteen green had always been a tough one on which to find four good pin placements. The traditional Sunday pin goes on the left-side plateau, tucked behind the big deep front bunker. But finding three other places to put a pin was always tough, since not even the tortuous bastards from the USGA tournament staff could figure out a way to stick the hole on the side of the steep slope that ran down to the right.

So they had flattened out the green quite a bit, and now they had some good places to put the hole. Today it was back right, with the bunker over there coming into play. I watched a few groups play through, and nobody got their approach closer than about ten feet. Chalk one up for the course.

I wandered over behind the bunker on the right, beneath one of the gnarly-limbed oaks, and managed to wiggle my way down close to the ropes. With the pin cut on this side, I figured a few of the players would end up in the bunker and I looked forward to watching them struggle to make par.

An Open Case of Death

Somebody next to me elbowed my in the ribs.

"Your name is Hacker, isn't it?" he said.

I turned. The man was wearing a gray wind jacket, a floppy, wide-brimmed hat with straps that he had tied underneath his chin, and a huge pair of amber-colored aviator sunglasses that covered about half of his face.

"Last time I checked," I said.

He smiled and lifted his huge glasses so I could see more of the face underneath. It was Jack Harwood. He winked at me.

"Don't say anything," he said. "I'm trying to go incognito."

"Right," I said. "Your secret is safe with me."

He nodded, pleased. One of the golfers down the fairway hit his approach shot. I lost it in the cloudy sky overhead, but we all heard it zip into the green about twenty feet beyond the pin, and we saw it bounce once, stop and spin back to about fifteen feet. We all applauded.

Harwood leaned back. There was a small man standing next to him, bare-headed, engrossed in watching the golf.

"Hacker, this is Chin Wan Ho," Harwood said. "Friend of mine from Taiwan. Chin...this is Hacker."

I reached past Harwood and shook the man's hand.

"Been out here long?" Harwood asked.

"Came out about a week ago," I said. "Had a book signing on Tuesday night in town."

"Oh, right," Harwood said, nodding. "Dottie van Dyke told me about that. I would've come by, but Chin and I were talking about a movie he wants me to do for him. We lost track of time."

"Just as well," I said. "If you'd shown up, my wife would have delivered the baby on the spot. It's not due until September."

He laughed. "A baby," he said. "Congrats." I nodded

my thanks. "You want to go get something to eat? Chin and I were talking about grabbing a bite."

"Sure," I said. "I hear the dogs aren't too bad."

"Oh, I think we can do better than hot dogs," he said.

We wiggled our way through the crowds gathered around the ropes again and Harwood led us down the right rough of the 15th hole, the par-four that moved gently downhill and then turned to the right at the green. Behind the green, backed against 17 Mile Drive, was a large white tent. Above the entranceway was a sign identifying it as "The Centennial Club."

"Does my badge work here?" I wondered.

"Not to worry," Harwood said. "Remember, I own this place."

It's good to be the king, and Harwood quickly arranged for Chin and I to gain access to this premium area, designed to give the hoi polloi a place to escape from the unwashed masses, eat and drink in style, and pee someplace other than a Port-A-Johnie. Once inside, I noticed that Jack kept his floppy hat and sunglasses on. I guess he didn't want to be bothered by the hoi polloi types either.

Inside the tent, the floor was carpeted, seating groups and dining tables were scattered everywhere and there were probably two dozen big screen TVs running the Fox Sports feed from the tournament. Two large stand-alone bars were placed at either end, and the entire back wall was covered with booths from vendors offering a wide variety of food. Mr. Chin made a bee-line towards a sushi station, while I saw another booth down a ways from a famous steakhouse chain, offering sliders and fries.

"Yum," I said. "Much better than hot dogs."

We all went and ordered food and carried our trays over to one of the table-clothed dining tables. Harwood caught the eye of a waitress and ordered beers for everyone.

An Open Case of Death

The TV told us that Phil and Tiger were struggling at a couple over par, and that a young kid from Kansas, Freddie Hollister, was now the leader at five under par. But it was only Thursday, and as the man says, there was a lotta golf left.

"So, you're in the movie business?" I said to Mr. Chin as we ate our lunch.

He nodded.

"Have you ever acted? Or are you just the money bags?"

Harwood laughed.

"There's about a thousand different jobs in the movies," he said. "It's not just actors and executive producers."

"No, no," Chin said, somewhat in protest. "It is a good question. I have never acted. I have been an extra before. But it is something I would love to do if I were good at it. I'm afraid I am not."

"But he is good at making money," Harwood chimed in. "Lots of it."

"Too bad," I said. "I could use a good Asian actor."

Harwood laughed again.

"You producing, too?" he said. "Hell, everyone wants to be in the movie business."

"Naw," I said. "I'm not making a movie. I'm trying to catch Harold Meyer in a sting."

Harwood took off his wide brimmed hat, removed his humongous amber specs and sat back.

"You have officially captured my attention," he said. "Do go on."

So I told him. All about Huckleberry Hills and the EB-5 visas and my suspicions that Meyer was running an investment scam. Halfway through my dissertation, Harwood signaled the waitress for another round. Mr. Chin sat there listening, too. Inscrutably.

"Jesus, Mary and Joseph," Harwood said when I was finished. "No wonder they want me and Will Becker out of the way. They know that we'd never approve anything like that. How long has this been going on?"

"Don't know," I said. "In fact, I don't even know if they're really doing this. But it all makes sense."

"And you think one of them, or someone hired by them, pushed that poor kid over the cliff?"

"I do," I said. "And I suspect—although I can't prove it—that someone might have fiddled with J.J. Udall's medications when he was in the hospital. My friend is trying to track down any security tapes that might exist."

"Holy crap," Harwood said. "Are you sure we shouldn't be calling in the cops, or the FBI or someone? This sounds pretty goddam serious."

"If we called in the authorities now," I said, "I don't think they could find any kind of evidence that would seal the deal. But if I can get someone on the inside, someone they think is ready to invest a lot of money in the deal in return for a green card, then we would have some hard evidence of what they're up to. Then the cops can be called in, start applying the thumb screws and wrap the whole thing up."

"I'll do it," Mr. Chin said.

"Now wait a second, Chin," Harwood said. "Before you agree to do what this crazyman is asking, you need to think about it. It could be dangerous. If what Hacker here believes is actually true, these guys have already killed one, and maybe two people already. I couldn't forgive myself if anything happened to you."

"I'll do it," Chin repeated. "Danger is my middle name."

"This isn't a fucking movie, Chin," Harwood said. "I can't yell 'cut' and have everything stop. You gotta think about this, my friend."

"Jack … Jack," Chin said, smiling. "Life is an adventure. Isn't that what you tell me all the time? Live to the fullest, you say. Seize the moment. I have a chance to do something important here. Help you and Mr. Hacker to find out what is going on. If these others are doing bad things, I want to help make them stop. Yes?"

"Sounds good to me," I said.

Harwood was frowning and looked like he wanted to say something more. But a woman walked up to our table.

"Omigod!" she gushed. "Aren't you Jack Harwood? Omigod! I'm your biggest fan! Would you sign my program?"

"No!" he snapped.

The woman's face fell and her shoulders slumped. It looked like she might begin weeping.

"Oh, hell," he said, "Gimme." He reached out for the program, scribbled his name and handed it back.

"Oh, thank you, Jack," she said. "Thank, you, thank you, thank you!" She floated away on the wings of happiness.

Harwood turned back to his friend.

"Now listen, Chin…" he started in again, finger raised.

"No, my friend," Chin said. "I will do it. It will be fun. And maybe you can get something from it to put in our movie!"

Harwood turned and leveled that famous glare at me. It made the hair on the back of my neck stand up. "If anything happens …"

"It'll be OK, Jack," I said. "Mr. Chin will tell them he's looking for a place to park some money. They'll respond however they respond. Obviously, they'll know he doesn't have a million bucks on him, so there will be a need for another meeting so they can have him checked out. He'll be fine."

Mr. Chin nodded. "I'll be fine," he said. "Chill out, Jack."

For some reason, that made me laugh.

CHAPTER 29

THE NEXT MORNING, Sharky and I drove down 17 Mile Drive from the Pacific Grove end and Sharky took some back roads up into the hills above Pebble Beach to Jack Harwood's hacienda. When Mary Jane found out where we were going, she almost stopped talking to me.

"So you can drag me through the wilds of Scotland where it's rainy and cold and I almost get killed by Russian agents, but you won't take me to Jack Harwood's house?" she said. "You are not a nice man."

"I promise I'll introduce you to him when this is all over," I said. "But we've got things to discuss today."

She was somewhat mollified by her plans for the day. Sharky's girlfriend Agatha had volunteered to take the girls up to San Francisco. They planned to lunch at Fisherman's Wharf, do a little shopping, ride a cable car up a hill—the San Francisco treat!—and maybe ride the ferry over to Alcatraz.

"Why do I want to go visit a prison?" Victoria asked. Nobody had a good answer to that. Mary Jane suggested maybe they'd substitute a ride up the elevator on the Transamerica pyramid building instead. Or a visit to Ghirardelli Square to eat some of their chocolate treats.

An Open Case of Death

"OK," Vickie said, "Chocolate is good."

When we arrived at the House of Harwood, we were escorted into his huge dining room. Jack and Mr. Chin were there, along with another gentleman I didn't know.

Harwood waved us in.

"Hacker, this is Charles Bentley, senior counsel for the California Coastal Commission," he said. "I asked him to stop by this morning to talk about Huckleberry Hills."

Bentley stood up and shook my hand. He was tall and patrician looking, dressed in tan slacks and an immaculate silk sweater that looked like it had been knitted directly on his body. A pair of those little half-pane bifocals perched on the end of his nose, and his graying hair was finely combed and held in place with some glistening substance.

"Hacker," I said. "And this is Sharky Duvall."

"Mr. Harwood and I were just discussing what appears to be a slight discrepancy in understanding about the project under discussion," he said. He had deep lawyerly tones, every word sounding like a pearl drop. I wondered if they taught that in lawyer school.

"What's the slight discrepancy?" I asked.

"The California Coastal Commission reached a memorandum of understanding with the Pebble Beach Company about the property known as the Huckleberry Hills condominium project more than seven years ago," Bentley said. "The memorandum was quite clear, at least from our perspective. The CCC had determined that no future development in the Monterey Forest would be approved, including this project. That decision was deemed to be final."

"Why?"

He removed his half-glasses, tilted his head back and stared at the wooden beams in Harwood's ceiling. "The Monterey pine, Latin *Pinus radiata*, is an endangered species," he said. "In addition to this peninsula, *Pinus radiata* can be found in only three other places on the earth. Because of a troublesome canker that first appeared in the late 1960s, the extant population of these trees has been steadily declining, both here and elsewhere."

He stopped looking at the ceiling and looked at Sharky and me.

"Think of it as like the Dutch elm disease that practically wiped out all of the once abundant elm trees in the eastern United States," he continued. "The disease is irreversible. Once it affects a tree, that tree will soon die. In order to prolong the life cycle of *Pinus radiata* the Coastal Commission has voted to halt all further development of any kind anywhere in the Monterey forest on the Monterey Peninsula. In short, gentlemen, there is no way that a project like the Huckleberry Hills condos would be approved." He looked at Harwood. "None, whatsoever. I'm afraid that is final."

Jack Harwood's lips tightened.

"The board of the Pebble Beach Company have been told that Huckleberry is just on hiatus," he said. "We were told that in a few years, when the economic conditions are ripe, we could begin development."

"Who told you that?" I asked.

"Harold Meyer," Harwood said grimly. "Backed up, early on, by Jacob Strauss, acting as our financial advisor. Of course, he left Baruch Brothers five years ago to go work with the U.S. Golf Association. But neither Will Becker nor me was ever told that the CCC had nixed the deal. They kinda kept that an official secret."

"Is that actionable, by the CCC?" Sharky chimed in.

Charles Bentley thought about that for a bit, chewing on the end of his glasses frame.

"In and of itself, no, I don't think so," he said finally. "As long as the Pebble Beach Company does not take any action that could be deemed as active development on the property in question …such as building a road or clearing any underbrush ... I do not believe that the CCC could bring any formal legal action."

"What if we were selling lots for future development?" Harwood asked. "Is that OK?"

"That sounds more like a fraudulent transaction," he said. "That would be a matter for the state investment authority or someone in law enforcement. I do not believe that constitutes a matter for the CCC to adjudicate."

"That's fucking great," Harwood said. "I'm apparently a party to an investment fraud." He shook his head sadly.

"Alleged fraud," Bentley the lawyer said, holding up a forefinger. "So far, I have heard only speculation and innuendo. But there must be evidence."

Harwood stood up and put his hand out towards the lawyer.

"Thanks, Charlie," he said. "Thanks for stopping by. Are you heading down to the golf course?"

"Indeed I am," the lawyer said. "I think Tiger tees off in forty minutes."

"Sounds like the Hollister kid might be more fun to watch," I said. Indeed, the Kansas Flash, as the press were calling him after his excellent first round, where he had finished at six-under. Of course, there's almost always an unexpected flash-in-the-pan in the early rounds of a major. When they start to realize what they're doing—leading the worldwide field of seasoned, experienced golfers—they tend to blow up fast on the weekend.

Harwood walked Bentley out to his car. I poured myself a cup of coffee from the sideboard. When Harwood came back in, he was steaming.

"Those fuckers had no right to get me involved in this," he said, his voice tight with anger. "I'm gonna nail them to the wall."

He picked up his phone and dialed a number. He waited until someone answered.

"Jake?" he said. "Jack here. Yes, I'm fine. Look, the reason I'm calling ... I've got a business associate in town for the tournament this weekend. Great guy. Mr. Chin from Taiwan. We might be working together on a movie soon. Yeah, yeah...but listen, reason I'm calling ...Chin has told me he wants to move some funds into the States. Yeah, things can get dicey over there. Nobody knows what those fucking Chinese will do next, right? Anyway, I told him he ought to talk to you. I know, I know ...you're not in that business anymore. But would you sit down with him for half an hour, have a drink and hear him out? Maybe give him a few off-the-cuff ideas? As a favor to me?"

He paused, listening.

"That would be great, Jake," he said. "Four o'clock in the lobby bar at the Lodge. I'll bring him down myself, let you guys talk in private, OK? Fine, fine. Thanks a lot, Jake, I appreciate everything you do...."

He rang off and looked at us.

"Game on," he said.

An Open Case of Death

Chapter 30

HARWOOD'S PLAN WAS pretty simple. He would escort Mr. Chin into the lobby at The Lodge, find Jacob Strauss, introduce Chin to him, then leave the two alone for thirty minutes or so before circling back to pick Mr. Chin up.

"It's a public place," he said. "And it'll be just a half hour. There's nothing bad that can happen to him in that place and timeframe."

"Sharky and I will be in the crowd out on the balcony," I said. "We'll keep an eye on him, too."

"I will be fine," Mr. Chin said, smiling at us. "Please not to worry."

Despite his bravado, we were all secretly worried. Big crowd of people milling about, golf tournament in the background, a very public place, might provide some kind of guarantee of safety. But it could also provide an opening for unseen chaos. Anything could happen, and none of us were smart enough to think of all the possibilities. That was dangerous.

At three, Sharky and I left the House of Harwood, drove down the hill and parked in the volunteer's lot up above the practice range. We walked down past the range, through the retail section, around the practice putting green and into The Lodge. The lobby was humming with life. People milled about everywhere, moving from the lobby down through the Terrace Lounge and out to the open-air deck in the back and back again. The small intimate lounge in the lobby was busy, and a larger temporary station out on the balcony was also three-deep.

We found a place along the marble railing that offered a reasonably clear sight line back inside. There were tables and chairs outside, most with wood-and-canvas umbrellas providing shade. We could see the bartender at the Terrace Bar inside and about half of the bar itself.

It was about a quarter to four when I saw Jacob Strauss walk into the lobby. He was accompanied by an older woman who seemed familiar to me. I couldn't place her, couldn't come up with her name. She just looked like someone I'd seen before.

Sharky nudged me.

"Look," he said. "Mister Big just got here too."

We watched as Harold Meyer strolled in. He was by himself, dressed in an immaculate double-breasted white suit that would have made Tom Wolfe envious, shiny two-toned oxford shoes and a jaunty straw boater. He held an ebony shafted cane in one hand, which he used to limp up to Jake Strauss. Through the window pane, we watched them shake hands. Strauss found one of the upholstered seating groups in front of the bar and helped Meyer sit down in one of the loveseats. He then turned back to the bar and stood behind a couple waiting to order some drinks.

The woman stayed by Strauss' side. He was wearing the standard USGA uniform: blue blazer, white button down with a striped rep tie and gray slacks. She wore a patterned summer dress, strappy sandals and had her hair up in a bun pinned to the back of her head. She looked to be in her fifties, maybe a bit older.

"Is that his wife?" Sharky asked, standing next to me.

"Dunno," I said. "I've seen her somewhere, but I can't remember where."

There was a loud roar from the crowd around the 18th green, just fifty yards away. Someone had apparently drained a nice putt for an eagle on the last. The sound made all of us on the balcony turn our heads to look. It was Phil Mickelson, who was high-fiving his caddie. The electronic scoreboard off to one side told me that he was now one-under. That would get him into the weekend, but with a long, long hill to climb.

Sharky nudged me again.

"It's showtime," he said, whispering.

Through the pane glass, we watched as Jack Harwood and Mr. Chin approached Harold Meyer's sofa. Chin was dressed formally in a suit, while Jack was wearing an unstructured sport coat over a polo shirt and a pair of black slacks. He wasn't wearing his floppy hat and sunglasses disguise today. Jake Strauss, having placed his drink order, sidled back over to the group, leaving the woman to collect and pay for the drinks. There were handshakes all around, Mr. Chin bowing and smiling.

Jack said something, then turned and walked away. The woman brought the drinks over and passed them around. Mr. Chin sat down across from Meyer. Strauss and Meyer turned to each other and began speaking, Strauss nodding. He got up and walked away.

"Where's he going?" Sharky said.

"Don't know," I said.

Meyer and Chin chatted for a few minutes, then Strauss returned and said something to Meyer. He and Chin stood up, collected their drinks and they all followed Strauss as be began walking through the lobby.

"Shit," I said. "They're going somewhere else to talk."

"That wasn't in the plan," Sharky said.

"It is now," I said. "You go after them. I'll stay here and watch for Harwood to come back."

"Right," he said and disappeared into the crowd.

The woman, who had returned to the bar, watched the men walk away. She smiled at the bartender, spoke to him, and watched as he filled a tall glass with ice and poured a soft drink of some kind for her. She thanked him, picked up her glass and glanced out the pane glass windows, toward me. She went to the door and came out on the crowded balcony.

I watched as she did a quick scan of the people milling about. Was she looking for someone? I couldn't tell. She walked out into the sunshine—the morning fog had burned off just after lunch—and went to stand by the railing about fifteen feet away from me, on the far side of the staircase that fanned downwards to connect with the grassy lawn that ran down toward the green, smiling pleasantly at some of the other fans nearby.

That's when I remembered where I had seen her before. The Harvard Club, New York. Just before I had met Jake Strauss for the first time, for lunch. She had come into Harvard Hall with him. Probably his personal assistant. Given what I had just seen, that made sense.

I was congratulating myself on my eidetic memory when a strange figure walked up the stairs from the lawn, which was filled with people watching the golf, and made a beeline toward the woman, Strauss's assistant. He was dressed in a puffy-sleeved pinkish shirt, a rawhide leather vest with all kinds of leathery straps dangling here and there, some flared black trousers that were pretending to be gaucho pants, shiny black cowboy boots and an odd flat-topped cap of black, with vertical stripes all around in every shade of the rainbow.

Who else, but America's fashion-plate sports columnist, Andre Citrone? He went up to Strauss' assistant, gave her a big hug and a kiss on her cheek and began talking to her animatedly. Her face lit up when she saw him. She rested her hand on his shoulder while they talked.

Well, well, well, I thought, *This here looks like a clue.* It suddenly occurred to me that this was how Drey Citrone had known all about my business. How he had known I was about to sign a book deal to write about Pebble Beach. How he had known about Huckleberry Hills. It had been Jake Strauss' assistant who told him.

I walked over to where they were standing.

"Drey!" I said, clapping him on the back like we were best buddies. "Wassup bro? Nice vest." I turned to the woman. "Oh, hello," I continued. "I'm Hacker, from Boston …"

Neither one of them spoke for a few beats. I did see them exchange a glance with each other. Guilty? Couldn't tell.

"Oh, hi Hacker," Drey finally said. "This is my aunt Chrissie."

"Very nice to meet you," I said, giving her my best friendly smile. "Say, I'm looking for Jake. Have you seen him?" Letting her know, letting both of them know that I knew the relationship.

She hesitated and then smiled back. "He's in a meeting," she said. "Upstairs in the conference room. He should be finished in a few minutes."

"Okay, great," I said. "I'll just hang out here for a while. Turned out nice, didn't it?" I waved at the crowded scene between the Lodge and the 18th green with the seawall beyond. The sun was now shining brightly. The ocean out in Stillwater Cove had turned a magnificent shade of deep blue.

I glanced at Andre. He was standing there with a foolish smile on his face. Busted.

"H-how did your book signing go the other night?" he said finally.

"It went pretty well," I said. "We sold a bunch of books." I turned to Aunt Chrissie. "What was the final count?"

"I think it was forty-three copies," she said. "Mr. Strauss was quite pleased."

"Forty-three!" I said. "How about that! I'll bet I can afford to buy a round of drinks. Anybody interested?"

"Uh, thanks, Hack," Drey said. "I've got to get back to work. Got a deadline in an hour. But thanks."

"No problem, my friend," I said. "Next time. Aunt Chrissie, it was very nice to meet you! See ya later…"

I turned and walked away, going back through the door and into the Terrace Lounge area. Inside, I ran into Sharky, who was looking around for someone. Probably me.

He looked at me, then did a double-take.

"What?" I said.

"If you had a dictionary and looked up the word 'shit-eating grin' there would be a picture of your face right now," he said.

"Oh," I chuckled. "I just solved a mystery."

"Nice work, Sherlock," he said. "Meyer and Strauss have Mr. Chin up in the Lobos Conference room. I couldn't hear anything through the door, but it doesn't sound like they're working him over with brass knuckles."

"Naw," I said. "They're taking his measure. See if he has enough money to contribute to their little scam."

I led Sharky over to the bar and ordered us a couple of beers. I figured we should look like ordinary fans, and most of them around us were drinking something. The TV screens that were set up all around the room told us that the second round was nearing its end. The Kansas Flash, Freddie Hollister, had not folded, yet, and was leading by a couple of strokes, chased by the usual suspects.

Jack Harwood came back into the lobby, saw us, and walked over. We pretended to be seeing each other for the first time in a while and I bought him a beer. We were standing there talking and drinking when Meyer, Strauss and Mr. Chin came back down. They saw us standing there with Harwood and came over.

"Ah, the great author!" Jake said. "Jack, remind me to send you over a copy of Hacker's book. It's really wonderful."

"Thanks, Strauss," Harwood grumbled. "He's already given me one."

"Oh, great," Strauss said. Somebody waved at him from across the room and he excused himself.

"Ready to go, Chin?" Harwood said.

He nodded. The two of them left, heading for the main door.

Harold Meyer watched them go, his eyes locked on the backs of their heads. He turned back and looked at me, eyes narrowed.

"You two good friends?" he said.

I laughed. "Me and Jack Harwood? Oh, yeah," I said. "Like this." I held up one hand with my fingers twined together. "C'mon, Shark."

We left, following Harwood and Chin.

When we got outside, Sharky let out a long breath in a rush.

"That guy scares me," he said. "Watch your back, Hack."

CHAPTER 31

WE ALL WENT back up to the House of Harwood to debrief Mr. Chin. When Sharky and I arrived, Chin had shucked off his suit coat and was sipping some iced tea.

"It was all rather straightforward," he said when we had all gathered around him. We were sitting on Harwood's expansive outdoor deck. The sun was low over the Pacific and shadows lengthened across the expansive lawns of Jack's wealthy neighbors.

"They wanted to know about my company in Taiwan," he continued. "How I was involved with Jack here. How much money I was thinking of investing. How fast I was ready to move."

He paused, thinking, remembering.

"The older one...Meyer? He wanted to know how quickly I could raise the capital. He was the more forceful of the two. Mr. Strauss was quieter, did not ask so many questions. I think Meyer is the boss, for sure."

"Good observation," Harwood said. "Harold Meyer controls every room he is in. Always has."

"What did they tell you about the deal?" I asked.

"They were not forthcoming," Mr. Chin said. "Mr. Strauss spoke in general terms. He said that he and Meyer had both had many Asia-based clients over the years. He said they had helped many people successfully move money into the U.S.A. and make that money work."

"Did they mention Huckleberry Hills? Getting an EB-5 visa?"

"No," Chin said. "It was more general. They said they could put my funds into some growth platforms. That is what they called it: 'growth platforms.'"

"What's the next step?" I asked. "What do they want you to do next?"

"I told them I am staying here with Jack until Monday," Mr. Chin said. "Meyer said they would give me a call before then. He said he had a particular platform in mind that might be good for me."

We all sat there and thought about that. Harwood's man Friday came out with a tray of cocktails. Bourbon Old Fashions. Harwood winked at me. The cocktail I was handed had five maraschino cherries in it.

"I think it may be time to call in the cops," I said. "Tell 'em what we know, what we don't know. Let them decide what to do with the next meeting. They might want Mr. Chin to wear a wire. They might want to arrest all of us for obstructing justice. But I think we've got reasonable evidence that something fishy is going on. Let's let the experts take over."

Harwood sat there and listened. When I was finished, he nodded.

"Hacker is right," he said.

Sharky held up his phone. "I can call Johnnie Levin," he said. "Set up a meeting."

"Let's do it," Harwood said. "See if he can meet in the morning. Tell him he can come over here if he wants."

Sharky went out to call his friend with the Monterey Sheriff's department. The rest of us sat there and drank our cocktails. I ate one of my cherries. And wondered what would happen next.

Lt. Levin told us all to meet him at his office in Salinas at nine the next morning. I brought a box of a dozen doughnuts as a bribe. Sharky knew Levin's favorite kinds. I bought a half dozen cups of coffee, too. In my long experience, cop house coffee is always execrable.

Mary Jane and Vickie said they'd spend the morning horsing around the pool at Spanish Bay, and maybe take the short drive over to Seal Rock to look at the hundreds of lazy seals sunning themselves on that rocky outcropping just offshore. The churning surf kept humans off their rock, so the seals had free reign. Most of them spent their time sleeping in the sun. But others—mostly the young ones—would flop around and bark at each other, so there was always a fascinating din echoing back onto the mainland.

At the police station, we met up with Jack Harwood and Mr. Chin. Levin came out to greet us, and walked us back into the bowels of the building, escorting us into an interview room with a metal table in the center, and chairs set against the windowless walls. He grunted with satisfaction when he saw the doughnuts, and cracked open one of the containers of coffee.

"OK," he said, leaning back and taking the four of us in. "Talk."

Harwood took the lead. He and Levin knew each other, as Jack had long been a friend of the local cops. He had donated funds for injured police, appeared at fund raisers and generally did what he could to help the local men in blue.

For about thirty minutes, Harwood unspooled the story. I noticed he presented it as a narrative whole, with a beginning, a middle and an end. I figured that was how an experienced Hollywood actor and director mentally arranged things. Levin sat there silently, occasionally sipping his coffee and once reaching in to the box for another doughnut.

Harwood finished his story with the meeting we had set up the day before with Mr. Chin, who smiled when his role was described.

"And that's what we got," Jack said, bringing it to a conclusion, albeit not a blockbuster with a last-reel shoot-out and the guy getting the girl and riding off into the sunset. "Meyer and Strauss seem to have cooked up this investment fraud, using the now-dead Huckleberry Hills project to siphon big bucks from foreign investors in return for those EB-5 visas."

Levin stood up and stretched. He stood behind his chair, hands on the back and thought for a minute or so.

"Well, let me see," he began. "I think I heard about seven violations of the laws of Monterey County, the state of California, and, bugger me if I'm wrong, the United States of America, too."

"Now, wait a minute..." I started to protest. Levin wheeled on me.

"You!" he said. "When did you meet this Mike Nelson fellow in Boston?"

"About a month ago," I said. "He's still there. My father-in-law, sort of ..."

"That's interference with a police homicide investigation," Levine interrupted. "Keeping a material witness under wraps. I'll have to ask the D.A. if the fact that you didn't tell us about him for four weeks is an acceleration of the original offense."

He turned to Harwood.

"And you, Jack...you should know better, for Christ sakes. Sending this gentleman..." He nodded at Mr. Chin

… "in to speak with alleged miscreants who may or may not be conducting a fraudulent act against the visa laws of the country. Jesus H. Christ on a pickle. What were you thinking?"

Finally, he turned to Sharky.

"And you, Duvall." He shook his head sadly. "All the times I bailed your sorry ass out of trouble over the years. And all the time this shit was going down, you never once thought it was smart to give me a call? I'm disappointed in you, son. Very disappointed."

We were all silent. He was right, of course. Even though we could all claim that stuff was happening in real time and we were just doing what we thought best, we didn't do things "by the book," and now he was threatening to toss that book right at us.

Levin exhaled, loudly.

"OK, here's what I'm gonna do," he said. "I'm gonna make a few phone calls, talk to a few people. Once I get done with that, I'll feel better about knowing what we're gonna do."

"Can I make a suggestion?" I said.

I watched as Levin's knuckles grew white as he grasped the back railing of his chair. His face began to redden dangerously.

"I know, I know," I said, holding up my hands. "You should take me out back and work me over with the brass knuckles for an hour or two. But my suggestion is to contact the U Cal San Francisco Hospital and ask to review any security cameras on the ward where J.J. Udall died."

"And why in the name of Jehovah would I want to do that?" Levin asked, his voice tight with held-in emotion.

"Udall was visited by several people in the day or two before he died," I said.

"I was one of 'em," Jack Harwood chimed in.

"Will Becker, another co-owner of the Pebble Beach

An Open Case of Death

Company told me that he, too, visited Udall in the hospital," I said. "I think there was at least one more visitor. I'd like to know who it was. Because there are questions about whether Udall died of natural causes, or was helped along."

"And do you have any evidence of that?" Levin said. "Because if you do, that's another count of interference with a police investigation."

"No, I don't," I said. "But the hospital report on Udall's death noted the presence of a clip on his IV tube. That might be important."

"Or it might just be a clip," Levin said. "Hospital rooms are full of them."

"Be good to know," I said.

Levin looked like he wanted to throw his chair across the room. But he didn't.

"You all are free to go," he said. "Thank you for coming in."

We all stood up and left.

CHAPTER 32

SHARKY AND I went down to the golf course. There wasn't much else we could think of to do at this point, and besides, it was Moving Day at the Open!

Freddie Hollister, playing in the last group, made the turn out at nine clinging to a two-shot lead. He had made three early birdies on the front side, as one must at Pebble Beach, but gave back two of them with a double-bogey on eight when his approach shot drifted right into the deep grass just above the beach. His drive on nine found the fairway bunker, but he managed to get up-and-down from the front of the green for par. Shaky, but still alive.

Hollister had become the story of this Open, this young, unknown kid from America's heartland, his cornstraw-blond hair blowing in the Pacific breezes, a big happy smile on his face. He was playing in that metaphysical Zone that appears out of nowhere, hangs around a while and, usually, disappears with a sudden, gut-wrenching crash when the weighty importance of the moment strikes home.

But so far he was surfing the wave and enjoying the ride. Hot on his heels, Dustin Johnson, Jon Rahm and Willie Franklin were two back, and ten other golfers were bunched three and four shots behind. The afternoon promised high drama, with Sunday's nail-biting round yet to come.

Sharky and I walked out to the sixteenth green, just below the tee box on three, and found a shady spot under the canopy of trees to watch for a spell. Sixteen is an odd hole which runs straight downhill towards the sea, then turns hard right. The green is fronted by a deep, sand-filled barranca and is surrounded by an ocean of deep rough and a couple of bunkers. And the green itself is small and slopes hard from right to left.

Most of the players hit long irons or fairway woods over a big round island bunker in the middle of the fairway, then have maybe an eight or nine iron into the green. Nobody hits driver, since the downhill slope of the fairway would kick the ball on through the fairway and into horrible trouble beyond.

But standing around the green was a good place to watch them hit their laser-like approach shots, or, failing that, try to make a tough up-and-down recovery. Plus, it was shady and, just across the way and back up the fairway, there was a concession stand selling beer.

"What do you think Levin is going to do?" I asked Sharky as we watched the next group getting ready to hit into the green.

"I've known him for years," Sharky said. "He's a pretty fair guy for a cop. Lots of bluster but he usually does the right thing."

"So we won't get arrested?"

"Not for anything we did here," he said with a smile.

Brooks Koepka and Ricky Fowler, out in the fairway, both hit nice shots: Koepka to about six feet, Fowler about twenty feet from the hole. The pin was cut in the front left, near the edge of the green, which meant almost all putts were downhill, curvy and fast as hell.

"So why do you still look worried?" I asked Sharky.

"Do I?"

"Yeah, pretty much," I said as the two golfers walked onto the green amid steady applause from the gallery. "Your forehead is all scrunched up, and I think you're running out of nails to bite."

He chuckled. "Still got ten toes," he said.

"You take off your shoes, bucko, and I'm outta here."

Fowler's putt rimmed the hole but spun away three feet. The crowd groaned in unison. The golf groan. Koepka took his time with his birdie and rammed it home. There was an explosion of joyful noise. The putt moved him to five under par, just two back of the leader.

"So what's got under your skin?" I pressed, when they walked off toward the seventeenth tee.

Sharky shrugged. "Just a feeling," he said.

We watched two more groups play through. Most of them made par, except for Matt Kuchar who found the bunker across the green from us, had to come out softly to keep the ball on the green, and was left with a fifteen footer for par, which he missed.

"Let's go get a brewski," I said. I nodded at the concession stand across the barranca and a little way back up the fairway, off to the right. He nodded, and we slowly made our way through the crowds, around the green and up the cart part back towards the tee.

I bought a couple of overpriced Budweisers—is there any other kind?—and we stood there drinking, checking out the posterior attributes of the female fans walking past and occasionally looking at the golfers playing the hole. Being that we were in California, some of the posterior attributes were deserving of our careful attention.

Sharky nudged me suddenly.

"Hack," he said in a whisper. "Two guys at two o'clock."

I looked and immediately saw two large men coming our way, up the hill from the green. It's funny, but I could tell immediately that these two were not here at Pebble Beach to watch the golf.

The tallest of the two was just over six feet, had a heavy five o'clock shadow on his face and his eyes were darting around the crowd of people. He was looking for somebody, or something. He wore black jeans, heavy soled work boots, a navy windcheater jacket and a dark knitted cap. Not your typical, let's go watch some golf kind of outfit. Plus, he had black fingerless gloves on his hands.

The other one, following a step or two behind, was shorter and rounder, with a heavy, florid face. He was dressed in jeans and a sweatshirt.

They were stopped about fifty yards away. The tall guy was still scanning the crowds. But they were still in search mode, it seemed to me.

"You know them?" I asked.

"The fat guy is a bouncer at a strip club over in Salinas," Sharky said. "Don't know the tall one. But I'm pretty sure I saw him yesterday in the lobby when Mr. Chin was meeting with Meyer and Strauss."

"Well, that doesn't bode well, does it?" I said.

"I'd say it bodes badly," Sharky said.

We were standing next to the fairway ropes, just a few steps away from the concession stand. A large green Club Car vehicle pulled up next to the stand. It had a flat bed on the rear filled with some cardboard boxes and several cases of beer. Reinforcements. The black guy driving the cart, wearing his official neon yellow "I'm a worker" jacket, stomped on the brake, making a loud squeal, got out, grabbed a box and headed over to the stand with it.

We looked down where the two guys were. The sound of the brakes had made them look in our direction and they were now looking right at us. The tall guy turned and said something to the short fat guy, and they began striding more purposefully right at us.

"I believe we have been spotted," I said. "I wonder what they want."

"Don't think we should wait and see," Sharky said.

"Why don't you zig thataway," I said, pointing off to the right beyond the concession stand. "And I'll zag thisaway. Meet you at the car in thirty."

Sharky didn't bother to reply. He just vanished, silently. For a guy with a big beer belly, he could move fast when he had to.

I glanced at the two hoods, who were getting closer. They had to push through or step around the crowds of people, most of whom were flowing in the opposite direction. That slowed their progress and gave me a few seconds to think.

I looked over at the cart filled with beer and boxes. The delivery guy had left the key in it. And why not? Who would steal a golf cart full of beer and food in the middle of the U.S. Open?

In two steps, I was at the cart. I grabbed one of the heavy boxes off the flat bed, dropped it onto the gas pedal and turned the steering wheel a bit to aim it down the hill. The cart shot off like a rocket, careening down the path and right at Mutt and Jeff, who were now about ten yards away and closing fast.

"Hey—!" I heard the tall one shout. But I didn't stick around to watch. I hightailed it up the hill towards the tee box, dodging my way through the tide of people. When I got there, I kept going.

I heard some women screaming behind me, but didn't stop or turn around. There was a temporary fence across the cart path between the course and 17 Mile Drive. I leaped over it, turned left and ran down the Drive. Luckily, they blocked and redirected most traffic on the usually busy road for the tournament, so I had clear sailing as I ran the half-mile or so back towards the Lodge. Ignoring the sage advice of the great Satchel Paige, I turned around once to look back, but no one was gaining on me. So I slowed down to a brisk walk.

Back among the safety of the crowds milling around the practice green, retail mall and Lodge entrance, I found a hidden nook next to the Ralph Lauren shop and waited there to see if anyone was still coming after me. After five minutes, seeing no one, I figured I was in the clear.

While I was standing there, I heard some sirens in the distance. Some people walking past were talking to each other.

"Did you hear?" one was saying. "An out of control golf cart ran into the crowd back on sixteen. Couple people are hurt."

"Geez," the other one said. "Hope it wasn't terrorists."

I laughed, silently, to myself. Al Qaida Hacker. Then, I thought *Hope Johnny Levin doesn't hear about this.*

CHAPTER 33

LATER THAT NIGHT, Mary Jane and I were lying on our bed in the hotel room, watching TV. Victoria was fast asleep on the bed next to us. Sharky had driven me back to the Inn at Spanish Bay, laughing hysterically all the way when I told him what I had done to thwart the two hoods. The hysteria part was understandable.

I had rendezvoused with my girls, listened to all their adventures of the day, taken them to dinner at the Inn's main restaurant which featured mostly inoffensive food that even eleven-year-old girls liked, and we had watched a fireworks display that the hotel had laid on for the Open. We had all oohed and aahed over the colors exploding over the darkening Pacific, churning out there amid the rocks and the seals.

The news came on, and the lead story was about a runaway and driverless golf cart that had mysteriously slammed into spectators on the sixteenth hole at the Open that afternoon. Officials said a heavy box had fallen onto the cart's accelerator causing the vehicle to lurch forward into the crowd of spectators. Two people had been hurt enough to require transport to the Community Hospital in Monterey; one with a broken leg and the other with contusions.

An Open Case of Death

"Hacker," Mary Jane said.

"Hmmm?"

"Were you and Sharky at the tournament this afternoon?"

"Yup."

"Were you anywhere near the sixteenth hole?"

"Why do you ask?"

"Hacker …"

I sat up. "Do you think *we* did that?" I tried to sound incredulous.

"Did you?"

"I am offended that you would think the father of your child could do such a thing," I said.

"You're the father of my child because we had passionate sex on Christmas Eve," she said. "That has nothing to do with you creating some kind of ruckus at the U.S. Open. Which sounds exactly like something you would do."

"How do you know?"

"That you created a ruckus? Because …"

"No, not that," I said. "How do you know it was Christmas Eve when we got pregnant?"

"*We*, kemosabe?" she said with a soft chuckle. "I don't see *your* belly growing out four or five inches. I don't see *you* gaining thirty pounds or having to pee every forty minutes."

"Point taken," I said.

"I can count, you know," she said, reaching out and taking my hand in hers. "The doctor told me how many weeks pregnant she thought I was, and I counted back."

"Maybe we should name it Santa," I said.

She laughed, softly. "Maybe," she said. "Be better than naming it Jesus." She pronounced it 'Hay-seuss.'

That made us both laugh. I reached out and snaked my arm around her shoulders and pulled her in tight. Her head nestled into the crook of my arm. Her hair smelled like lilacs and sunshine.

"What are we going to name … the baby?" I hated calling it "it." Mary Jane knew the baby's sex: she had seen several ultrasound images already. I didn't want to know. I wanted to be surprised, like most fathers down through the millenia.

"I don't know," she sighed. "We've got time to decide. Three months to go."

Three months. Then life as we knew it would change forever. My life. Her life. Victoria's life. We all knew it was coming, yet none of us had the slightest idea what that change would be like.

"My father's name was Daniel," I said. "I really don't remember much about him, but that's a pretty strong man's name. Daniel Hacker. Danny. Dan. Works for me."

"Mmmm," she said, sleepily.

"My mother's name was Vanessa. Maiden name O'Rourke. Not crazy about that name, but I wouldn't object. Of course, we could go with your Mom or Dad's names, too. Jim and Janet, right?"

"Mmmm."

The news was now telling us about a transit strike up in San Francisco. A group of homeless people were protesting because I guess they sleep in the subway and having a strike harshed their vibe, or something. And in California, marching and protesting is something everyone does.

"Actually," I said, "To answer your question, yeah, it was me that sent that golf cart down the path this afternoon. These two thugs were coming after Sharky and me. Sharky thinks they were sent by Meyer—he saw one of them in the lobby yesterday when we sent Mr. Chin in to find out about their real estate scam. I figure Meyer suspected we knew what was going on, and sent these two leg-breakers out to reason with us sweetly or something."

She didn't say anything.

"But I think Meyer tipped his hand," I continued. "Sending thugs out must have been exactly what he did to poor Charlie Sykes last December. They reasoned with *him* too…reasoned him right over the cliff. Which is why I felt it the better strategy to evade them today. Sharky concurred. Which means he took off like a scalded rabbit. You should have seen it. Anyway, I was just trying to slow them down. Buy us a little time to get away. I had no intention to leave them with broken bones or anything."

Mary Jane was still silent. I raised my head a bit and looked at her. She was fast asleep in the crook of my arm. Her chest rose and fell in the quiet rhythm of sleep. The hot moist puffs of her exhalations warmed the side of my chest. If she had been a kitten, she would be purring.

But she wasn't a kitten. She was my beloved wife. And she held within her a baby—*our* baby, who was growing and kicking and preparing, inexorably, to make his—or her—way into the world and kick that world into a completely different gear.

I fell asleep with the television still on and tried to conjure, in my dreams, the face of my child, so I could see who it was. If I could see its face, maybe I'd know what I needed to do to be a father. But instead, I dreamed of bad faceless men coming up the hill, trying to grab me.

CHAPTER 34

IT WAS AROUND noon on Sunday. Mary Jane, Victoria and I were one of the many thousands of spectators milling around near the wrought-iron clock next to the practice putting green at Pebble Beach. The air was as electric as it always is on the last day of a major golf tournament. The other three days are interesting, sometimes dramatic, often exciting. But Sunday is the day when all the marbles are on the table. Do or die. Metaphorically, of course.

I had arranged to meet up with Sharky and Agatha at the clock. I thought we'd all go somewhere and have lunch and then find a place to watch the final round unfold. The leaders were not scheduled to tee off until around three. That meant the folks watching on television back east would get to watch the tournament unfold in prime time.

The Vickster was loving all the crowds, the hubbub and excitement. Any kid would. Mary Jane was casting nervous glances around, no doubt trying to figure out where the nearest rest room was to take care of her once-every-half-hour need to whizz.

Sharky and Aggie arrived at almost the same time as Jack Harwood, once again dressed in his old-man disguise with the big-brimmed floppy hat and face-hiding sunglasses. Shark and I had been discussing where we should go to eat—he recommended the volunteer tent for its excellent buffet and shady cool calm—when Harwood walked up.

"Hey, Hacker," he said. "Say, we're about to have a board meeting upstairs. Maybe you'd like to come?"

I smiled and turned to Mary Jane.

"Honey," I said, "I'd like you to meet Jack Harwood."

Jack turned to her, whipped off his sunglasses and gave her one of his patented crooked grins, eyes and eyebrows dancing.

"Ms. Hacker," he said, leaning in to kiss her on the cheek. "It's a pleasure to finally meet you. Hacker has spoken highly of you. And this must be young Victoria ..." He smiled down at Vickie. She wasn't entirely sure who this man in the strange hat was, but she beamed back at him anyway.

Mary Jane was struck dumb. She looked at Harwood with glistening eyes that spoke of admiration and amazement and excitement all at once.

"I ... you...I'm..." she stammered.

"Yes, I know," he said, smiling. "Listen, I'd like to borrow your husband here for about an hour. After that, I'd like to invite all of you to join me in the owner's skybox on the eighteenth. It's quite a comfortable place to watch the golf. We can talk in peace there. Sound okay?"

Mary Jane could just smile. And nod.

Sharky volunteered to take everyone up for lunch at the tent and we agreed to rendezvous again in an hour.

Harwood repositioned his sunglasses and led me into the Lodge. In the lobby, he walked over to a little man dressed in a light gray business suit. The man had frizzy gray hair surrounding his head like a halo, a pair of horn-rimmed spectacles perched on the end of his nose and was holding a large leather satchel in one hand. They shook hands.

Harwood nodded to me. "Hacker? This is Maurice Cohen. He's been my lawyer for the last fifty years. Maury, this is Hacker. I told you about him."

The lawyer smiled at me. "Good afternoon," he said.

Harwood led us upstairs and into a long conference room that looked out onto the 18th green and the seawall beyond it. The morning fog had burned off already and the sun was shining gloriously on the golf course. It looked like several million people had gathered around the green and down the fairway to watch the early players finish their rounds.

Cohen took up the position at the head of the conference table, opened his valise and began pulling out stacks of papers and documents which he arranged neatly in front of him. The door opened and Will Becker walked in. He was dressed in slacks, a golf polo and a blazer.

"Hey, Will," Harwood said, and went over to shake his hand. "I think you know Hacker, here don't you?"

"Hiya, Boston," the old pro said, and sat down. He nodded at Maury Cohen, who was now sitting calmly at the head of the table, hands folded. "Where's the fuckwad twins?" he said.

As if on cue, the door opened again and in walked Harold Meyer and Jake Strauss. Strauss was wearing his USGA uniform of blue blazer, shirt and tie, gray slacks. Meyer was less formal: he wore black slacks and a lightweight blue silk sweater over a white golf shirt.

"What the hell is this?" Meyer rasped.

"Please come in and take a seat," Maury Cohen said. For an old man, his voice was clear and authoritative. He gestured with his hand for the two latest arrivals to take their seats. They did. The rest of us also sat down opposite.

An Open Case of Death

"This is a duly authorized emergency meeting of the board of directors of the Pebble Beach Company," Cohen said.

"Authorized by who?" Meyer said. "I didn't authorize anything of the kind. You can't just …"

"According to the by-laws of the corporation," Cohen said, picking up a sheet of paper from one of the stacks arrayed in front of him and holding it aloft, "An emergency meeting can be convened at any time by the votes of a majority of the board. Messrs Harwood and Becker have so voted."

"Well no one asked me about any vote," Meyer said, his face red with anger. "And I do not approve."

"Very well," Cohen said. He pulled a yellow legal tablet in front of him and began to scribble notes on it. "The minutes of the meeting will reflect that two directors have voted to convene this meeting, and one director…" He nodded at Meyer … "…has voted no. Since there are currently three directors of the corporation, the vote is two to one and the emergency meeting is thereby convened."

"What's the emergency?" Jack Strauss spoke up.

"Also in attendance at this meeting is Mr. Jacob Strauss, executive director of the U.S. Golf Association," Cohen continued, jotting notes as he spoke. "Mr. Strauss is an ex-officio adviser to the board, but has no voting authority under the by-laws. And we also have with us today one Mr. Hacker. How would you describe Hacker's role in this, Jack?"

"He's the official historian of the Pebble Beach Company," Harwood said. "Or at least he will be if you make us take a vote on it. He is here to memorialize the discussion we are having here today."

"I object!" Meyer said, slamming his hand on the table.

"Objection duly noted," Cohen said in his calm lawyerly voice, writing along on his tablet.

"Who the fuck are you?" Meyer said, looking at Cohen.

"The first order of business is to appoint a guardian administrator for the Pebble Beach Company," Cohen said. "Under the by-laws, such appointment is called for when a majority of the board believes such an action is required to prevent adverse fiscal or legal exposure for the company."

"What the hell is he talking about, Jake?" Meyer turned to Strauss, holding his hands out wide.

"I nominate Maurice J. Cohen to be the guardian administrator," Jack Harwood said.

"Second," Will Becker said.

"All in favor?"

"Aye," Harwood and Becker said in unison.

"Opposed?"

"I will sue the both of you for every last goddam cent," Meyer fumed. "I will take your ownership stake, I will take your houses, I will take your bank accounts. I will sue your children, your wives, your fucking dogs. I will …"

"The vote being two in favor and one opposed, the motion carries," Cohen said calmly. "As the legally appointed guardian, Mr. Meyer, it is my duty, and may I say my pleasure, to inform you that your services as a director of the board of the Pebble Beach Company are no longer required. This action is being taken because of information that the board has received concerning an apparently fraudulent business transaction or transactions that have been going on for some time, in the matter of the proposed development known as Huckleberry Hills condominiums."

"The fuck are you talking about?" Meyer blustered. "You can't fire me. I'll have your law license. I know the fucking governor of this state, you little kike bastard, and …"

"I might add that your behavior and statements here today are also a prima facie violations of company policies regarding personal comportment and tolerance which alone would justify your immediate removal from your position," Cohen said.

"Wait until I get my own attorneys," Meyer said. "They'll grind you into dust, you little piece of shit."

"The next order of business is the replacement of Baruch Brothers as official financial adviser to the Pebble Beach Company," Cohen said. "I will entertain a motion."

As before, Jack Harwood made the motion, Will Becker seconded and the two voted to fire Jake Strauss' former company. Meyer sat there silently and said nothing.

"Moving on, "Cohen said, "Jack, I believe you have another item to address?"

"Right," Harwood said. He picked up his phone, dialed and said "Send him in."

In less than a minute, there was a knock at the door.

"Come," Cohen said.

The door opened and Lt. Johnnie Levin strolled in. He was wearing a full dress policeman's uniform, not his usual detective's civilian garb. He had on the dark olive pants, tan uniform short-sleeved shirt with epaulets and patches on the side of his shoulders, the six-pointed gold badge over the heart, and an off-white Stetson hat that made him seem even taller than he was. He wore his gun on his left hip.

"I believe you have an updated report for the board of directors regarding the Huckleberry Hills matter, detective," Cohen said. "The floor is yours."

"Thank you," Levin said. He removed his Stetson, tucked it under his arm and stood next to Cohen at the head of the table.

"Thanks to Mr. Hacker and Mr. Harwood here, the Monterey County Sheriff's Department was made aware of certain business activities taking place by principals of the Pebble Beach Company," he said. "To wit, this information alleged long-term fraudulent sales activities regarding the condominium property known as Huckleberry Hills, and the illegal selling of EB-5 visas to foreign nationals in return for their investments in this fraudulent project. Mr. Harwood has provided us with a signed statement from a Mr. Chin Wan Ho."

I was watching Jake Strauss while Levin was talking. His face had gone white and his eyes began darting around the room, as if he were looking for a place to run and hide.

"When the Sheriff's Department was made aware of this activity," Levin continued, "We did what any investigative organization should do. We contacted our colleagues in law enforcement. To wit, we have spoken with the San Francisco office of the Federal Bureau of Investigation as well as officials from the Securities and Exchange Commission, the State Department and the Customs and Border Protection office to report the facts and allegations."

"Jesus fucking Christ," Meyer said.

"The FBI informed us that they had already been pursuing an investigation into this matter," Levin said, "And they anticipate bringing enforcement action upon the two individuals named in short order. That would be Mister Meyer and Mister Strauss."

Jake Strauss' shoulders slumped. He looked like he was about to cry.

"It was all Harold's idea," Strauss burst out. "He cooked this whole thing up. I had nothing to do with it. Nothing!"

"Oh, shut up you little queer," Meyer growled. "Just shut the hell up!"

"In addition," Levin continued, "We have been pursuing an open homicide investigation into the death of one Charles Sykes, Junior, since last December. There have been suspicions that Mr. Sykes' unfortunate death was not accidental, but was in fact, an act of deliberate murder.

An Open Case of Death

"Yesterday, our officers were investigating an apparent accident here at the golf tournament," Levin said. "Two of the persons injured in that accident were known felons. When our officers began talking to these two subjects, certain facts came to light that appears to link them to the murder of Charlie Sykes."

"What facts were these?" Cohen asked.

"Both suspects indicated that they had been ordered by Mr. Harold Meyer of San Francisco to, and I quote, 'put an end to Sykes once and for all.' Endquote."

"That's a fucking lie!" Meyer yelled. "You're gonna believe a couple of lowlifes like Quinn and Abruzzo?"

"Nobody from our department has identified the names of these two suspects," Levin continued with a slight smile. "So the fact that you apparently know them is additional proof of what they are telling us."

Meyer sank back in his chair.

"You murdered Charlie Sykes?" Strauss was looking at Meyer. "How could you do that? How?"

"Shut up, you fool," Meyer said.

Levin held up his hand. The room fell quiet again.

"There is one more matter which is still under investigation," he said. "And that is the matter of the death of your former colleague, J.J. Udall. At Mister Hacker's suggestion, we asked the University of California San Francisco Hospital to produce security tapes for the days Mr. Udall was in residence in the hospital before his sudden and tragic death. We now have those tapes."

I looked at Jake Strauss.

"They indicate that Mr. Jacob Strauss was the last visitor to Mr. Udall's room," Levin said. "He is shown entering the ICU at approximately 1:25 p.m. on the afternoon of November 15th. He was in Mr. Udall's room for twenty minutes. Mr. Udall died approximately two hours later."

Everyone was now looking at Jake Strauss.

"Mr. Strauss once served as a medical corpsman on the U.S.S. Ronald Reagan," Levin said. "He was trained in basic medical knowledge: how to give injections, how to perform an intravenous intubation, how to monitor and control breathing and medicinal applications."

Levin paused.

"We do not, at this time, have enough solid evidence to arrest Mr. Strauss and charge him with the premeditated homicide of Mr. Udall. However, he remains a person of interest, and our investigation will continue. I will be asking a judge on Monday morning to order the exhumation of Mr. Udall's remains so that our medical examiner can conduct further testing. Until then, the case will remain open."

"An open case of death," I said. "Perfect."

An Open Case of Death

Chapter 35

JACK HARWOOD WAS right about one thing: the skybox at the back of the 18th green was a great place to watch a golf tournament. Out front, there were three rows of padded folding stadium seats, shaded by a dark-blue awning, providing a great view of the last green and the approach shots coming in from the narrow green ribbon of fairway.

Inside the skybox was a comfortable air-conditioned space filled on one side with several groupings of sofas, love seats and upholstered chairs, all facing one of several 50-inch television screens showing all the action from around the golf course. The other side of the box held two long dining tables. At the back, there was a long steam-table buffet set up, manned by tall, white-toqued chefs who kept moving the stainless trays of food in and out. At the end of the table was a carving station where a round of beef the size of a basketball sat under the hot warming lights, glistening with juices as the chef wielded his carving knife to slice delicate little pieces off and slide them onto the plate of the diner passing through. There was a large round table groaning with desserts: slices of cakes and pies, round little tartes decorated with whipped cream, bowls of fresh fruit and plates of all kinds of cookies.

There was another station next to that which functioned as the bar. Bottles of spirits and fine wines were lined up like soldiers, and two huge coolers held an endless selection of cold beer and soft drinks.

"I think I've died and gone to heaven," Sharky sighed when he first walked in.

"Too bad you've already had lunch," Aggie said, laughing as she held his arm.

"Not to worry," Sharky said, "The boys still have the back nine to fight over. I'll be hungry again soon."

He was right. Freddie Hollister was holding on to a one-stroke lead as he played the eighth hole. Dustin Johnson was one back and a couple holes ahead. Rahm and Franklin were three back, but lurking.

Victoria had made best friends with the lady in charge of the dessert table, and was now happily downing a large sundae with whipped cream and cherries. She looked at me with chocolate sauce dribbles on her chin.

"Golf rocks, Hacker," she said.

As for Mary Jane, she was out in the stadium seats next to Jack Harwood, who had lost his hat-and-glasses disguise and turned himself back into the well-known and instantly recognizable star of the screen. They were chatting away happily. Mary Jane glanced once inside, found me and waved her hand in my direction. I believe that wave meant *I am in hog heaven, I am talking to a big movie star I've loved all my life. Stay away from me and let me have this moment.*

Sharky and Agatha came over, he bearing two ice-cold bottles of beer, and we settled into one of the comfy seating groups to watch some of the golf.

I told them what had happened at the board meeting.

"So nobody got arrested?" Sharky said when I finished. "I was kinda hoping they'd drag ole Harold off to the hoosegow. God knows he deserves that."

"Oh," I said, "I think his troubles are just getting started. Jake's too."

An Open Case of Death

I felt a little bad about Strauss. True, he was a little hard to take sometimes. And, he *had* participated in a screamingly illegal scheme to defraud both the people who gave him their money and the government which set up a program designed to help the inner cities. And there was a very good chance that he had killed J.J. Udall to protect himself and Harold Meyer from discovery. And that he had hired me to find the mysterious Michael Newell letter writer knowing full well what might happen once I found him.

After reviewing that list, I decided I didn't feel so badly that Strauss' ass was probably in six kinds of slings.

I went out to the seating area, while still keeping plenty of distance between me and the happy conversationalists, who were still talking up a storm over in the front row. Even if you hated golf, the views from the skybox were killer: you could see all the way back to the white sandy beach at Carmel, and all the way across to the rocks at Point Lobos, with all the ocean and waves and rocks in between. And if you loved golf, as I do, all the action on the 18th green was unfolding virtually at our feet.

I pulled out my phone and hit a number. It took a little while, a couple of requests, before Carmine Spoleto came on the line.

"Good evening," he said. "Are you still in Cali?"

"Yeah," I said. "Mary Jane is here. She's talking with one of her favorite movie stars about fifteen feet from me."

"Mr. Pacino?" he asked.

"Nope."

"Bobby DeNiro?"

"Nope."

"Ah, well, I suppose there are other stars," he said. "And how is Victoria?"

"She's into her second chocolate sundae," I said. "I think she's pretty much perfect."

"She is indeed, Mister Hacker," Carmine said to me. "She is indeed."

I told him he could send Mike Nelson home. "The problem that was keeping him away has been settled," I said. "He's good to come home. He might have to talk to the cops, but his life is no longer in danger."

"That is very good news," Carmine said. "I hope you were able to accomplish this without too much bloodshed. It is always better that way."

"No," I said, "No bloodshed. I let law enforcement handle it."

"I see," he said. There was silence. "*Bene. Va bene.* I am glad of that. Too many people have died in this world. It is better when that doesn't have to happen."

On the TV, I watched Freddie Hollister make a thirty-foot putt on the ninth green for birdie and a two-shot lead. The fans went crazy. Freddie's caddie gave him a chest bump. Freddie's face lit up as he grinned from ear to ear. He was still in that Zone, the place you can't get to—it comes to you. And when it does, the sky turns rosy, the noise is unheard, the inner voices are quiet, except for one unmistakeable message: *go.*

"What is next for you, Hacker?" my kinda-sorta father-in-law said, from three thousand miles away.

"Dunno," I said. "We fly home tomorrow. Get ready for the baby. Figure out what to do next."

"*Bene*,' he said. "I hope you will come and visit this old man when you can. And do not worry. Life will provide a path for you to follow. It always does."

"Right," I said and we hung up.

I got up and moved over, sitting down behind Mary Jane and Jack. She looked up at me and smiled. Her eyes were happy.

"This may be the best place you've ever taken me, Hacker," she said.

An Open Case of Death

"Better than Scotland?"

"Warmer than Scotland," she said. "Fewer Russians running around. Although I do miss those Mi5 commandos. They had nice, uh, uniforms."

I laughed.

"Listen," she said, reaching out and touching Jack Harwood, her new best friend forever, on the shoulder. "Jack and I have been talking. He gave me this ..."

She reached out and gave me a business card. It was one of Harwood's. But on the back, she had written down a name and a number.

"Who is Billy Pulte?" I asked.

"Head of sports broadcasting for IBS," Harwood said. "Good friend of mine. I called him last night and told him he should meet with you. Told him you could add a lot of color to their golf broadcasts. History. Anecdotes. Inside baseball stuff, but for golf, of course. You could be the little voice in the ear of their announcers. Feed 'em historic color. He liked the idea and wants to meet with you as soon as possible."

Mary Jane was grinning from ear to ear.

"You responsible for this?" I asked.

"I'm your wife," she said. "And the mother of your child. Who needs a daddy with a good job, doing something he loves."

"I'd have to be away from home a lot, on weekends," I said.

"Yeah," she said. "We can work that part out."

Harwood turned in his seat to look at me.

"Sonny boy," he said. "Don't fuck this up. You've just been given a chance to change things. Probably for the better. And your wife approves. In my book, that's called a win."

I thought about it. Out in front of us, Brandt Snedeker made a monster putt for an eagle three and the people ringed around the green screamed their approval. I took it as a sign.

"A win," I said. "I'll take it."

An Open Case of Death

Epilogue

It was a fine day in early October, cloudless skies, temperature around 70. I was out playing golf, of course, because what sentient human being would not on such a day?

I was at The Country Club in Brookline, that hallowed old course where young Francis Ouimet defeated the grizzled and heavily favored English giants Harry Vardon and Ted Ray to win the U.S. Open of 1913. I had been invited to accompany my new boss, William H. Pulte of IBS Sports, for a round. He had flown up from New York that morning, we signed my new contract over lunch in the clubhouse and we had made it to the 13th green, just below the yellow clubhouse, when one of the assistant pros came out driving a golf cart. Since most people walk and take caddies at TCC, I suspected something was up.

"Mister Hacker!" the kid yelled when he got near. "Your wife called…it's time!"

"Go!" Pulte said to me, pounding me on the back. "Go! And good luck!"

I left my clubs with the caddie and jumped in the assistant's cart. He took me to the parking lot, driving past complaining players and cutting across lawns God never intended to be driven on and, still in my golf shoes, I blasted away out of that sylvan oasis on the edge of the city and soon was bombing down Commonwealth Ave., honking and weaving my way through Boston traffic.

I screeched to a halt at the valet parking station at Mass General and flew up to the tenth floor. My heart, when it wasn't beating at a couple hundred miles an hour, was lodged firmly in my mouth. I couldn't possibly imagine what my blood pressure was at that moment, but I knew it was reaching the upper stages of lethality. I could hear the Star Trek engineer, Scotty, in my mind: *"She's gonna blow, Captain!"*

I dashed into the OB/GYN wing, my rubber golf spikes gripping the shiny floor for dear life. I had just enough oxygen left in my lungs to gasp out my name to the nurse at the round desk and she pointed down the hall and said a number.

When I rushed into the room, Mary Jane was lying in a bed, rails up and a pool of light surrounding her like a sunbeam from heaven. Her hair was a bit tangled and sweaty and she was wearing a hospital gown. She was holding in her arms a bundle of something wrapped in blankets and wearing a tiny little knitted cap on its head. A blue cap.

Mary Jane looked up at me, her eyes filled with tears of happiness.

"Hacker," she said. "Meet your son, Daniel James Hacker. I think we'll call him DJ."

DJ squirmed around a little and let out a sigh. It was a sound of utter contentment.

"I was one over par through twelve," I said. "At Brookline, for Pete's sake. I may never forgive him for that."

I bent down and kissed my wife. Then I kissed the head of my son. He smelled like baby: warm, new and hopeful.

"Oh," she said. "I think you will."

ABOUT THE AUTHOR

James Y. Bartlett is one of the most-published golf writers of his generation. His work has appeared in golf and lifestyle publications around the world for more than thirty years. He was a staff editor with *Golfweek* and *Luxury Golf* magazines, and edited *Caribbean Travel & Life* magazine for several years during his "golf hiatus" period.

Bartlett was the golf columnist for *Forbes FYI* magazine for the first fifteen years of that publication's history and wrote a similar column on the golf lifestyle for *Hemispheres*, the in-flight magazine of United Airlines for nearly twenty years under the pseudonym of "A.G. Pollard, Jr."

His first Hacker Golf Mystery, *Death is a Two-Stroke Penalty*, was published by St. Martin's Press in 1991. *Death from the Ladies Tee* followed soon thereafter, and Yeoman House Books proudly continued the series with *Death at the Member-Guest*, *Death in a Green Jacket*, and *Death from the Claret Jug*.

Bartlett is currently at work on the final title in his "Major Tournament Series," entitled *P.G.A. Spells Death*. Look for its publication in 2020!

Add these other Hacker Golf Mystery titles to your library!
Available in Trade Paperback and e-book versions

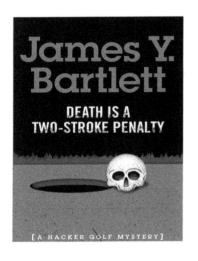

Golf reporter Pete Hacker is covering the PGA Tour event in Charleston, S.C., when an up-and-coming Tour star is found dead on the course. Or was he murdered? Hacker digs into the case, tracking a drug-dealing caddie, a bevy of golf groupies and a strange, Bible-thumping Tour chaplain before he finds the killer.

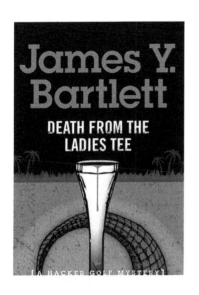

As a favor for an old friend, Hacker agrees to cover the LPGA event in Miami. There, he finds that one of the Tour's stars holds an unhealthy degree of control over the Tour and its players. When he begins to dig in, bodies turn up everywhere and his own life is threatened during the explosive final round! Who said girls always play nice?

When a friend invites Hacker to a long weekend of fun at a private country club outside Boston, he leaps at the chance. But a body turns up in the cart barn, and Hacker spends most of the tournament trying to figure out who had the motive and opportunity to do the evil deed. Even the Boston mob gets involved in this case!

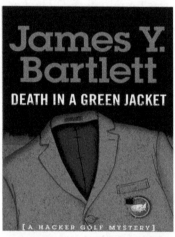

A body in a bunker at Augusta National sends Hacker off on a mad chase from Magnolia Drive to Aiken, SC to "the Terry" to find, and stay ahead of, a drug cartel assassin. Talk about a drama-filled back nine on Sunday ... this is a Masters unlike any other!

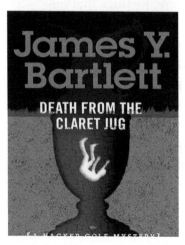

Hacker and Mary Jane are in Scotland for the Open at St. Andrews. But a dead golf official sets off a chain reaction, with Russians, aristocrats, Mi5, an alcoholic caddie, an anti-golf professor and even a flamboyant American developer creating a Royal & Ancient mystery for the ages!

Lightning Source UK Ltd.
Milton Keynes UK
UKHW020620181119
353752UK00011B/1268/P